Dick & Jimmy's Adventures At Glen Afton

A novel by Frederick Corbin

Like us on face book or
fbcorbin@gmail.com

Copyright 2007 by Frederick Corbin

All rights reserved. No portion of this book or its cover art may be reproduced, stored in a retrieval system, or transmitted in any form or by any means without the expressed written permission of the author.

Copyright registration: TXu1-354-497.

ISBN-10: 1489597743
ISBN-13: 9781489597748

DEDICATIONS

To my Mother, whose life was quietly given over to loving and caring of others.

To my Father, whom I saw shed tears only twice, once while grating horseradish in our Fairview kitchen in Altoona, and once at Glen Afton in somber reflection of something beautiful which was lost and now only experienced through fond memories.

ACKNOWLEDGMENTS

To Kay Shade, who believes in my work and informed me about a writing, publishing and marketing course taught by Bob Broadwater.

To Bob Broadwater and our charter-member class, who encouraged and helped me on this writing journey.

To Gwen Pattillo, whose initial editing helped me correct many obvious mistakes and who gave me several valuable pointers.

To Blair Fornwalt, whose cover art is an eye-catcher that perfectly illustrates one of the most unique scenes in the novel.

To the Altoona Writer's Guild whose members continue to encourage, not only me, but each other in our respective roads to better writing.

INTRODUCTION

How does one write about a time in which he didn't exist, a setting in which he didn't live, or an era in which he held no place?

And yet through the eyes and minds of others I have beheld Glen Afton. It was a simple, seven acre homestead with a large, green and white dormered cottage nestled in the forest along the isolated eastern shores of the Juniata River near Thompsontown, Pennsylvania. Because of the depression, it became a refuge where our extended family had to become a larger nuclear family, where the resources of each were shared by all.

As I look through the yellowed pictures in my Mother's black photo album and recant the tales I've heard, I begin to see them like pieces of a jigsaw puzzle scattered about in my mind. Here I find photos of river scenes, family portraits and images of the homestead and its grounds.

So many times I heard the tales of love and sharing as well as cowardice and evil, of new awakenings as well as bittersweet endings. How often these stories would bring a tear or sparkle to the teller's eye. So rich and vivid were these oft-told tales that I felt I had been a part of what they experienced.

These were the incentives, though not the main reason, why I now share the stories, myths, and legends that was Glen Afton.

CONTENTS

Chapter 1	Camping on the Juniata	1
Chapter 2	The Summer of 1941	9
Chapter 3	Serpents and Steamers	13
Chapter 4	Muck Out	21
Chapter 5	Pipeline	31
Chapter 6	Water, water, where art thou?	45
Chapter 7	Hobo Jungle	51
Chapter 8	Unwelcome Visitors	57
Chapter 9	Just Desserts	75
Chapter 10	Renegade Hobos	81
Chapter 11	Garden Intruder	89
Chapter 12	Taylors Arrive	91

Chapter 13	Dick and Hayla	105
Chapter 14	Cable Swing	113
Chapter 15	Taylors Depart	125
Chapter 16	Skipped Generations	131
Chapter 17	Dog Medicine	135
Chapter 18	Russell's Fudge	137
Chapter 19	Floods	141
Chapter 20	Renegades at Glen Afton	161
Chapter 21	Prison Time	171
Chapter 22	Jake returns	185
Chapter 23	Breaking Camp	197

Chapter 1
CAMPING ON THE JUNIATA

The explosion echoed throughout the Fairview neighborhood! Hot melted wax showered across our back yard, splattering my dad, my brother and me. Howls and yelps of pain soon turned into peals of laughter as the three of us began peeling blobs of wax off hairy arms and legs.

"Didn't I tell you to be careful with that concoction?" Mom scolded out the kitchen window from above. Our home was a modest three-story plank house originally covered with white wooden clapboards and later with red insulbrick siding which didn't resemble brick by any stretch of the imagination.

"We'll be more careful, Mom," my older brother Dick answered.

"Good Lord," she snapped as she returned to her chores. "Next time I wouldn't be surprised to look out there and see three human torches running around the way they're going about that job."

My mother, Catharine Coleman, aka Cass, was a tall, plain, hard-working woman of forty seven. Her prowess in the kitchen was only overshadowed by her ability to keep my dad, brother, sister Fay and me from all but destroying ourselves in the various predicaments we managed to get ourselves into from day to day.

It was late July in 1954 and the annual ritual of coating our old canvas umbrella tent with a mixture of hot paraffin wax and gasoline was the only way we knew how to keep it water tight. I had camped in that old tent with my dad and brother a few times at Trough Creek and the Colerain camp grounds on Spruce Creek, but this was the first time I was deemed old enough to go camping along the banks of the Juniata River where our family's cottage had once stood. At thirteen years of age, the thought of camping along a river the size of the Juniata brought images of new adventures.

1

But even more intriguing to me was to visit this special place that had generated such a great abundance of tales.

We packed our black 1936 Ford sedan with the tarred canvas roof that Friday evening according to dad's 'Camping on the Juniata' list. My father, Dave Coleman, was never one to leave anything to chance. He made grand and detailed lists for all such family excursions: weekends at the Diamond Valley hunting camp, fishing at Spruce Creek, and visits to grandma Houck's home in Petersburg.

"Looks like everything's here," he stated proudly as Dick and I proceeded to load the trunk, back seat, and car top carrier.

"We'll never have enough room for all this stuff," I said in frustration.

"Just stand back and watch the master at work, Fred," Dick replied with a wink. Fifteen years my senior, Dick was a great older brother, who had taught me much about sports and standing up for myself. I stood in awe as the packing was completed and nary a void was left! Every available space was occupied by some neatly stowed object. To this day I have never witnessed anyone who could rival my brother in packing fifty pounds of gear into a twenty-five pound container.

Next morning (to me, still the middle of the night) we arose at 2:00 AM, downed a quick breakfast, and were on our way by three. Alone in the back seat, where I was stored as the final piece of gear, my thoughts drifted again to those stories of that place called Glen Afton. I soon dozed off to the sound of the engine's hum and the voices of my dad and brother chatting about experiences of past trips and the promise of new adventures during this one.

An hour later I was awakened by the silence of the night; I realized we had stopped but I had no clue as to why. In my semi-awakened state the moon appeared to be playing hide and seek with the slow drifting clouds around it. The warm, still night air hung heavy with the pungent smell of damp earth and cow dung spread on the fields nearby. I sat up, wiping the sleep and sweat from my eyes and it was then I realized my dad and brother were no longer in the car! Frantically, I got out and began looking for them, but they were no where to be found.

Eventually I heard a sloshing noise in the stream nearby and cautiously walked to the bank and peered over its edge. That's where I beheld the two of them in a flurry of activity.

"Hold the net steady Dick," dad instructed.

His hip boots scuffed and dug into the stream's shallow bed as he worked his way down-stream toward Dick who was holding a bait net across the water. As the two came together the net was lifted, revealing its bounty of minnows, chubs, and soft-shelled crabs.

"That should be plenty," Dad said as they transferred their catch from the net to our rusted green bait bucket. The bait and gear were stored in their proper places and once again we were on our way.

The clouds had cleared from the night sky leaving the half-moon and twinkling stars free to illuminate the landscape around us. A few minutes later we exited route 22 and turned right onto a dirt road bordered on both sides with tall fields of corn. As we neared the farm house I could see lights in the windows and, having no experience with farm life, I assumed they were expecting us.

Farmer Beecham, a tall, thin, bearded man in worn bib overhauls, and dad greeted each other with glad handshakes and expressions of those who knew and enjoyed one another's company in former times. Pleasantries were exchanged and questions of families were asked and answered.

"You and yours are always welcome to camp down here as long we're on this land, Dave," the farmer assured.

"And we sure do appreciate that, John," dad replied.

His stout wife, a pleasant, aproned woman, invited us to stay for a bite of breakfast, but dad politely declined her offer, stating that we had better get about the business of setting up our camp.

"Enjoy your stay," John said as we bid farewell and piled back into the car

The dirt roads became rougher as we continued our journey through more of the farmer's corn fields and dad explained this was because these roads were only used by the farmer on his tractor to get from one field to another.

"Hang on, Fred," Dick said as we bounced across one rut after another. Soon we came to a stop beside a tall stand of oak and willow trees that bordered the river.

"You two carry the gear down by the water while I tend to the boat," dad instructed.

A steadily increasing glow from the east was beginning to chase the darkness from the sky as we carried the first load of camping supplies down the crooked earthen path to the river's edge. The air was dead still, intensifying the sounds we were making. Rounding a stand of bushes near an old gnarled oak, I beheld, for the first time, the Juniata river in all of its splendor.

I suspect being a Pisces, my love of water comes naturally and although I had seen other rivers at a distance while crossing them on highway bridges, I never fully appreciated their true magnificence until that morning. I stood in awe as I watched it silently course by in the gathering light of day. A thin mist played upon its glassy surface as I realized this beautiful aggregate, this flowing body of adventure was to be mine, all mine for the next eight days!

As we returned to the car for the next load, I noticed dad struggling with our boat. I had often seen this unseemly mound of canvas, staves, and boards but it escaped me as to how such a contraption could float, let alone carry human and camping cargo across a large body of water such as the Juniata! As my brother and I continued to unload the camping gear I watched in wonderment as our craft began to take shape.

"There!" dad exclaimed with an air of satisfaction as he carefully rolled it over, only to find several small tears in the fabric. My heart sank as the thought, *no boat, no camping* entered my mind, but this didn't discourage our ever-prepared father.

"I thought there might be a few holes in her after being stored for a while," he said confidently, "so I borrowed a little water-proof glue and cloth from the Pensy."

Father had been a Pennsylvania Railroader since the age of sixteen. He started out as a steam engine mechanic but as the mighty steamers began to be replaced with the more efficient, but less romantic diesels he bid into the carpenter's shop at Chestnut Avenue. There, he repaired and rebuilt the wooden supports and bodies on freight cars. As he perfected his trade, he worked on the more elaborate passenger cars where he would carve and shape the decorative wood trim for them including the president's personal touring car. I remembered him patiently drawing pictures for me of the steam locomotives and the lavishly decorated cars he had worked on during his career. How I wish I'd saved those drawings.

We launched our canvas vessel and watched for leaks. It now appeared to be water-tight so we carefully loaded the camping cargo on board and then Dick and I shoved off for the year's first voyage across the Juniata. Dad remained on shore with the rest of the gear as my six foot tall, portly, but powerful brother began to row us across the river to where we were to set up our camp.

One of the unique features about the site at Glen Afton is its limited access. One had to either boat across the Juniata or use the alternate route of walking three miles along the Pennsylvania Railroad's four main lines from the Thompsontown station and then down the fifty-yard spring path. Those who didn't own a car had to choose the later, more exhausting route.

As the rhythmic sound of the oars in their oarlocks filled the morning air I began scanning the semi-clear water for signs of life. At mid-stream my search for aquatic life turned to thoughts of disaster as I began to see canvas patches floating beside our boat! My attention quickly moved from the river to the bottom of the boat where water was pouring in through the once-patched holes! I looked at Dick and he at me, but no words were exchanged. Already aware of the problem, he had quickly turned our sinking craft around and began rowing back to shore.

"Find something to bail with," he shouted.

I rummaged through the camping supplies and found a small cook pot, but it couldn't keep up with the flow.

"Stuff something in the holes!" was his second command.

A pair of white cotton socks slowed the flow and enabled us to struggle back to shore.

"What's the trouble?" dad asked as we hit the bank.

"I'm afraid your patches didn't hold up," Dick replied.

Once again my heart sank. We unloaded our leaky craft, pulled it ashore and flipped it over. Dad examined the canvas and sized up the problem.

"Perhaps we were a bit hasty to get over there," he noted.

This time we gave the glue an ample chance to dry while we fished along the shoreline and after a bite of lunch we tried again.

"You stay here, Fred," dad instructed. "Dick will pick you up on the next run."

Upon Dick's return we positioned the second load on board and started across. I cast a wary eye on the surface of the water but no patches appeared and our canvas craft bore us safely throughout the rest of our stay. The birds began their unharmonized chorus as the sun climbed higher and hotter in the afternoon sky. Buzzing insects and bright orange monarchs filled the air as the Juniata quietly coursed along its way.

"You start helping dad set up camp," Dick said as we neared the stony shore. "I'll go back and get what's left."

As he pushed off I looked to the top of the bank where I saw dad walking among the oaks and maples that lined the edge of the property that once was Glen Afton.

I started up the bank, following the indented, zig-zag earthen path left by the old switch-back stairway. At the top of the bank I turned to view the river and it soon became clear as to why the original owner had chosen this spot to build his summer home. The sweeping view of the Juniata and the panorama of forests and mountains gave light to the selection of this pristine location.

The story has it that a widowed Pennsylvania Railroad executive built Glen Afton for himself and his chronically ill daughter. There she lived out her remaining years and, not being able to bear the memories of that place alone, he sold the home to our family.

One of the mysteries of it was how he managed to truck in all of the material used to build his fine home into such a remote location. The most logical answer was, being a railroad executive, he had a local freight drop it off at the spring path and let the contractor's men haul it down to its present location.

As I turned, I looked across the large flat area that was once the lawn grand-dad Coleman had so lovingly cared for. It was now a scrub-infested field overrun by weeds, brush and saplings. Near the right border of the property was the remnant of a sprawling purple lilac bush. As I ventured across to the left I came to a wild, rambling rose bush still clinging to the last of its decrepit trellis. These vestiges along with the concrete-filled terra-cotta pipes that were used for the cottage's foundation were the only signs that gave hint to earlier habitation.

I stood there for a moment…trying to visualize the scenes that I had been told about so often in the past. A soft breeze from the river caressed me as my mind wandered along with it across the weed-choked, unkempt lawn. My eyes stopped where father was standing. He was facing away from me and as I approached him I noticed he was holding a strange looking object. As I came closer I saw a distant look on his face and the trace of a tear in his eye.

"What's that, Dad?" I asked.

Realizing my presence he immediately turned away, wiping his eyes.

"Oh, nothing," he replied, appearing somewhat embarrassed. "Just an old bauble." He hesitated for a moment.

"We'd better start setting up our camp," he said as he dropped the object and headed toward the river.

As he walked away I realized this was the first time I had ever seen my father shed tears. I stooped down and carefully picked up the object that had welled up such emotion in my usually stoic father. I didn't know then what the object was, but later realized I was holding the mainspring and gear box of their old Victrola record player. I wondered what images of the past, what sounds or memories had been conjured by this old relic. Since my father was not one to readily express emotions I tried to imagine what events he had experienced at this place to elicit this show of sentiment.

I moved to the edge of the river bank with the towering trees along its border as father descended the old stair impressions. I watched as my brother rowed the last of our camping supplies across the river. It was then I remembered that Dick was the same age as me when he last came to this place.

Once again, in the summer of 1954, my mind began to recall the tales that were told of Glen Afton, this place where I played no part.

Chapter 2
THE SUMMER OF 1941

Those already at Glen Afton had thoughtfully left the large john boat tied to the opposite shore, knowing the Coleman family was soon to arrive. The large wooden Hoffman boat easily held Dave, his wife Cass, their fifteen year-old daughter Fay, son Dick of thirteen years and his friend Jimmy.

This was twelve-year old Jimmy Varner's first trip to Glen Afton and he marveled at what he was seeing. Jimmy's parents dearly loved their oldest son, but it was a blessing to them for the Coleman's to take him that summer. They had six other mouths to feed and precious little money to do it with since the depression had stripped Tom Varner of his job at the brick yards at Claysburg.

Dave easily rowed the craft across the clear, smooth expanse to the far shore and then up river through the calm shoreline waters. At no other point was the one hundred mile-long Juniata so broad and serene. A stony outcropping in the river a hundred yards downstream, known as the rocks, partially dammed the river, pushing its waters a mile upstream, creating what is known as Yoder's Loch.

As they moved along the shore, the dense woods and scrub-lined banks soon gave way to a wide expanse of cleared, landscaped terrain. A narrow wooden dock extended out into the river with a small swimming platform at its end forming it into the shape of a tee. Familiar forms and faces of aunts, uncles and cousins, most clad in bathing suits and smiles, shouted greetings at the new arrivals. A few brave souls dove off the dock and swam toward the approaching vessel.

"It looks like Hat and Bessie finally convinced your dad to replace those steep, worn-out stairs," Cass noted, skinning an eye toward the shore.

Dave turned to see his ambitious father busily putting the final touches on the new switch-back stairs leading from the dock up the steep bank to the lawn above. The sound of his hammer echoed up and down the river.

"Never thought I'd see the day Hat and Bessie would win that one," he muttered under his breath.

"What?" Cass asked with a smile.

"Nothing," he sheepishly replied. "Dad does have a lot of time on his hands now that he's retired and those old stairs were in bad shape."

The new switch-back stairs Dave's father was finishing led to a large, well manicured lawn which lay ten feet above the river. In the center of the lawn was nestled a handsomely constructed two-story frame cottage. The full-length porch facing the spring trail toward the railroad was matched by a smaller, screened-in rear porch off the kitchen which granted a most wonderful view of the river.

Directly below the rear porch roof hung a dark-stained oak board with deep-carved letters painted white. It proudly displayed the name of this lovely refuge to all who traveled the river.

Noticing the sign, Jimmy slowly stood up in the boat and jokingly proclaimed, "What a great name for a cottage, Green Afternoon!"

Hug and kisses were exchanged and all but Russell, Dave's younger brother, helped the new arrivals lug their belongings up the almost completed stairway. It was early summer and the appearance of Glen Afton made it obvious that Dave's father had been busy since the early spring thaw.

"You folks got here sooner than we expected," GW claimed.

Named by his fiercely patriotic immigrant mother, George Washington Coleman was in his late sixties and the old gentleman was one of the first to benefit from the Pennsylvania Railroad's retirement program. GW, as he was known by his closest associates, started with the Pensy as a track walker. Later he worked in the supply buildings at the east end of Altoona, but soon his keen mind and natural abilities helped him advance to his final position as assistant yard master at Juniata.

"I wonder if Katie is here, Mom?" Fay asked as they crossed the dock. Katie Hahn, Fay's best friend had frequently visited her grandfather's cottage which lay a quarter mile upstream from Glen Afton.

Fay's mother smiled and pointed toward the shore. There, high up on the river bank, skipping along the trail between the cottages came the skinny, long-legged red-haired girl herself.

"Katie!"

"Fay!"

The happily shouted names overlapped as Katie quickly traversed the remaining path and the equally long-legged Fay bounded up the stairs toward her friend. Happy shrieks and squeals filled the air as the two embraced and spun each other around. Off they went, arm in arm over the path to the Stackhouse cottage talking, laughing and occasionally swinging and twirling together in that special dance they conjured last summer that only girls of 15 could do.

Dick and Jimmy watched the two rather objectively.

"You know," Jimmy noted, "if you put all eight legs and arms on one of their bodies you'd have the perfect spider."

"About the only thing girls would be good for," Dick agreed.

The two boys grinned at this new revelation and with chorused voices shouted, "Spider woman!"

The girls, quite content with each others company, ignored the boy's attempt at sarcastic humor.

GW took great pride in his position as caretaker of Glen Afton. The spacious yard, weed-free and void of any bare spots, was immaculate and his garden would have been a surveyor's delight. All the plants were in neat soldier's rows where none would be tolerated out of line. The meager excess from his pension allowed him to purchase an occasional shrub or flat of young flowers which he would use to border everything from the edges of the river bank to the path leading to the old railroad spring. Even the uniquely designed outhouse was surrounded by fragrant perennials and annuals and smelled mostly of lilacs, honeysuckles and roses... mostly.

Freckles, a beagle, and Brownie, a golden retriever & collie mix, greeted one and all with warm licks and cold noses. GW's old hunting dogs were the permanent mascots at Glen Afton.

"Danny and Kit arrive yet?" Dave asked.

"No, but we expect them soon," his father replied.

"They could come any time between now and the end of summer, knowing those two," Dave remarked.

Most men working for the railroad had survived the depression years, but those without seniority, like Dave and his brother-in-law, Danny, eventually lost their positions.

"Told you boys another layoff was coming," his dad reminded him. "Even a power like the Pensy has to bow to the misfortunes of the times."

"They say how long you'd be off?" he inquired.

"Nope," Dave replied, "but other folks in our situation are a lot worse off than us. Many of them don't have a place like this for refuge."

He looked around and gave out a sigh.

"I never thought our summer retreat would become…well, more than a summer retreat."

His father shook his head in agreement as the two walked toward the cottage.

Chapter 3
SERPENTS AND STEAMERS

"It looks like this is where the work is," Cass remarked as she entered the kitchen.

Aunt Bessie and Aunt Hat (Harriet) were busy preparing lunch for the hungry clan. GW's two older sisters were as different as day and night. Hat was the younger, taller and heavier one. She was a willing worker, to a minor degree, but was constantly going on about her 'delicate condition'. Bessie, the older, smaller sister was the feisty one and in spite of her five foot, hundred pound frame, could hold her own with anyone in a war of words.

"Well, don't just stand there," Bessie snapped. "Grab a knife and start peeling those carrots."

"It's good to see you too, Bess," Cass returned as she joined in preparing the meal.

Freshly baked hens from Bessie's chicken coop and a variety of fresh produce from GW's garden would be the late afternoon fare.

"How have you been, Olive?" Cass inquired.

"Very well, in spite of being unemployed for the summer," she returned.

Olive Lee was Dave's youngest sister. Her dark brown eyes set in an oval face along with her wavy brown hair, lovely smile and slender silhouette had often caught the eye of many would-be suitors.

But to Cass, home is where the heart is...along with brooms, mops, pails and various cleaning solutions. Her incessant desire for 'neat and clean' at times drove the other women to distraction. 'No play or relaxing until all was spic and span throughout the cottage,' was Cass's motto. Her obsession clearly paralleled her father-in-law's desire to maintain the surrounding property in pristine condition. To some it appeared that the two were in some strange kind of competition, each trying to out do the other in their quest for perfection.

"Russ, could you fetch a couple pails of water for us to clean these vegetables?" Cass asked.

"I think dad wants me to go down to the store and fetch more lumber for his stairs," he replied.

"Liar," Aunt Bessie whispered to Cass. Bessie's one word oratories could clear up much confusion as to what others truly had on their minds.

"Come on, Russ," she urged, "a little exertion on your part would do you some good."

Russell, Dave's younger brother, had no end of handsome or lazy and it was the latter characteristic that Cass was about to dwell upon.

"And I don't mean river water," she added, "get it from the spring."

"I'll see if maybe Fay or someone else will…."

"Never mind, Russell Billings Coleman, I'll get it myself," was Cass's brusque reply.

"We'll fetch it for you, mom." Dick said, much to Russ's relief.

"Thank you, Dick," his mother replied as she cast a dissatisfied look in Russell's direction.

"Come on, Jimmy," he said, "this will be fun."

The pair headed for the garden shed beside the cottage. The yoke Dick's father made in the railroad carpentry shop was ideal for carrying two pails of water from the old railroad spring.

"I'll carry the yoke and you get the buckets," Jimmy said.

The winding path behind the cottage led to the Pennsylvania Railroad's four main east-west lines. As the two moved up the path Jimmy's foot became entangled in a twisted old root and down he went.

"Damn!" he shouted as he picked himself up.

Dick laughed.

"Wouldn't be so funny if it'd been you!" Jimmy shot back.

"I'm not laughing at you, dummy," Dick assured. "That old root's tripped just about everybody at one time or another."

"Then why doesn't somebody get an axe and chop it out?" Jimmy questioned.

"Some threatened to, but once you know its there you get used to going around it," Dick explained.

A warm breeze mussed their hair as the two emerged from the path into the open expanse of the four main lines. Frequent polishing of the wheels on passing trains made the four rail lines gleam like silver in the summer sun. These solid ribbons of steel faithfully carried their charges East to Millerstown, Harrisburg and Philadelphia and West to Thompsontown, Altoona and around the Horseshoe Curve to Johnstown and Pittsburgh.

As the boys crossed the tracks the pungent smell of creosote from the freshly treated ties filled their nostrils. The shrill blast of a steam whistle cut through the afternoon air warning the boys of approaching danger. The massive M-1 east bound engine was pulling over one hundred hopper cars filled with more than ten thousand tons of western Pennsylvania's bituminous coal.

The boys could feel the ground tremble beneath their feet as the ponderous freight neared. Steam flew from every orifice as the powerful engine passed them. It's side arms and connecting rods whirled and churned to the rhythmic sound of the belching smoke-stack. Steel rails and strong oak ties rose and sank against the shale ballast with the passing of each set of wheels. The engine's thunderous chug-chugging soon gave way to the metrical click-clack, click-clack of the hopper car's wheels as they passed over each rail joint. As the pair watched this spectacle of power and speed, Dick's grandfather's words came to mind, *you can't beat the railroad for heavy haulin*. The two crossed the tracks behind the bright red caboose and continued their trek beside the mainlines.

"How far is this spring?" Jimmy asked.

"Not far," Dick replied.

Neither of them noticed the large diamond-back that had come out to warm itself on a flat rock beside the rails. The serpent tensed as it became aware of the approaching boys. The diamond-back coiled itself and rattled its beaded tail as the intruders came closer, but its warnings were drowned out by the sound of the rumbling freight.

As the boys came closer the rattler drew its head back in preparation to strike. Jimmy saw the coiled reptile first, but his leg-lifting reflex to turn and run was too late! Sharp fangs sank deep into the lower side of his sneaker. He screamed and fell against his unwary friend sending yoke, buckets and terrified boys to the ground.

Immediately Jimmy began crab-walking backwards, dragging the hapless snake with him.

"Get him off, Get him off!" he howled.

Dick tried to gather his senses and figure out what to do. The now hysterical Jimmy continued to try to shake the serpent loose to no avail. Writhing and coiling, the huge rattler tried as hard as Jimmy to get free.

"Get my shoe off!" he begged. "Get it off!"

"Hold still!" Dick shouted.

Jimmy froze as he lay on his back, looking at Dick with pleading eyes. Dick began easing down Jimmy's side on his hands and knees toward the wary reptile, but as he reached for Jimmy's sneaker the diamond-back tensed and hissed.

"Good Lord!" he exclaimed as he quickly retreated.

He can't strike me, Dick mentally assured himself. *His fangs are stuck tight...he can't get loose.*

He cautiously returned and quickly untied Jimmy's sneaker just inches from that menacing, gaping mouth! Once again the rattler hissed and writhed as Dick loosened Jimmy's shoe. At last Jimmy was able to pull free and the two quickly moved away as they watched to see what the entrapped serpent would do.

"Did he get you?" Dick asked.

"No, I don't think so," Jimmy replied nervously, checking his foot.

Slowly the large snake backed down off the railroad embankment and into the brush below, dragging Jimmy's sneaker with him. The boys cautiously followed the serpent.

"What's he doing?" Jimmy questioned.

The rattler blindly backed between two small trees and, after a flurry of twisting and pulling, the reptile's fangs finally came loose. The liberated snake slithered through the brush and down into the drainage ditch beside the railroad. The boys quickly followed and retrieved Jimmy's shoe.

"It's soaked!" Jimmy exclaimed. "Look, the inside is soaked with his poison."

"Don't put it on," Dick cautioned. "We'll wash it out at the spring."

After gathering up the yoke and buckets they were once again on their way and soon arrived at their destination.

The cool mountain spring was once a source of water used to fill the old wooden water tower which quenched the thirst of the Pensy steamers. Ten years earlier it was torn down and replaced by a more modern steel tower a mile west of Millerstown. The only remaining structure left was the four by twenty foot concrete pond running three feet deep. It was used as a settling pool to clean the water before it was pumped into the original tower. The water was always cool and clear and now slaked the thirst of the two shaken boys.

The dark, slowly moving objects in the water caught Jimmy's eye.

"What the…!" he shouted as he jumped back.

"Fish!" he exclaimed. "How in the world did they get in there?"

"Gramps catches them and puts them in here," Dick explained.

"What for?" he asked.

"It helps clean the muddy river taste out of them," Dick continued. "Pretty smart, huh?"

"Yea, your gramps is a lot smarter than he looks," Jimmy remarked.

"Now what's that supposed to mean?" Dick snapped.

"Well, he's kind of old and I never figured old folks never knew that much," Jimmy countered. "I figured they'd forgot most of what they knew or maybe…"

"Yeah, yeah," Dick replied with an air of indifference. "Here, help me feed them."

He handed Jimmy half of the block of homemade fish food his grandfather had given him before they left.

"Do we just toss the whole thing in?" Jimmy asked.

" No, dummy, you break it into small pieces like this," Dick explained as he looked at his friend out of the corner of his eye and shook his head.

The hungry fish devoured the food as soon as it hit the water.

"Man," Jimmy exclaimed, "they sure like this stuff."

"Let's get these buckets filled and head back," Dick replied.

"I'll carry them first," Jimmy offered.

"Be my guest, little buddy," Dick obliged.

They took a final drink and after washing out Jimmy's sneaker, they started back. The spot where the snake attack had taken place was now clear, much to the boy's relief.

"Wonder where he's hiding?" Jimmy questioned as he scanned the ground around them.

"Probably hunting mice in that rocky area, " Dick replied,

The two waved at the crew as another freight rumbled down the mainline. They were still chatting about the snake encounter as they started across the tracks behind the slow-moving train.

A blast from the express train's whistle startled the boys, causing them to fall back on the tracks behind them! Water sloshed from the buckets as knees and elbows cracked down hard against the rails and ties. Churning rods and side arms on the engine's huge drive wheels whirled dangerously close to the terrified boys and a blast of air from the speeding express put the boy's hearts in their throats!

Once again, Dick's wise old grandfather's words flashed through his mind, *Never cross tracks behind a train without looking for that hidden killer on the next line.* The two looked at each other and, without a word, gathered up their gear and headed back to the spring.

"That was close!" Jimmy remarked.

"For once I'll have to agree with you, old buddy," Dick returned.

As the boys loaded the yoke on Dick's shoulders, they noticed three men walking up the tracks toward them from Millerstown. Their clothes were thread-bare and their unkempt appearance and menacing looks gave the boys reason to cross the tracks and head toward the cottage with utmost haste. The men stopped and looked toward the boys. The larger one turned to his companions and said something that made the three of them laugh.

"Who in the world are those guys?" Jimmy questioned.

"I believe they're hobos," Dick replied. "Dad says there's a hobo jungle in the mountains near Thompsontown and that we should stay clear of it."

The two watched the rough looking men as they stopped at the spring to drink.

"You wouldn't have to tell me twice after seeing those three," Jimmy replied.

"Amen," Dick agreed.

The two continued back to the cottage, this time more alert for serpents and steamers. The boys didn't mention the near-miss with the express train, but greatly detailed the rattle snake incident using Jimmy's fang-marked sneaker as evidence of their adventure. All were enthralled as Dick and Jimmy told the tale of the attack.

"This hot, dry weather brings 'em out," GW explained. "We'd better be a little more cautious as to where we put our feet around here for a while."

"Don't rattlers buzz before they strike?" Fay questioned.

"True," her dad agreed. "You boys hear anything?"

"No," Dick replied, "nothing but a coal train that was going by when it struck."

"Grandpa," Dick continued, "didn't you and dad talk about putting in a pipeline to the spring?"

Dave and his father looked at each other.

"Yeah," GW answered, "but that's about all it was, just talk."

"It would be a great labor saver," Russell added.

"Why couldn't we do it now," Dick continued. "We have plenty of folks here to help and all we need is some pipe."

"Some pipe?" his father said with a laugh, "It's about two, maybe three hundred yards from here to that spring."

"But maybe we could get some used pipe somewhere," Dick insisted.

"Whoa, boys," GW cut in. "It's gettin kind of late to discuss a project of that size. Let's sleep on it tonight and talk about it tomorrow."

All agreed.

As Dick climbed the stairs, he smiled to himself, knowing he had rekindled a spark in the old gentleman's mind for the waterline project.

Chapter 4
MUCK OUT

All slept well that night. The rigors of travel and greeting family members not seen for over a year had taken its toll on those at Glen Afton. Even the mournful wail of the night trains failed to disturb the weary family.

Next morning Dick and Jimmy were awakened to the smell of fresh coffee and bacon and the sound of morning voices down in the kitchen. The bright sunlight streaming through the bedroom window gave hint that morning was well underway.

"Something sure smells good," Jimmy said as he rose from the sagging old feather bed he and Dick were sharing.

"We'd better get down there before the others eat it all," Dick said in earnest.

The boys began to dress. Tee shirts, faded jeans, and black high-top sneakers would be the fashion statement for the day, as in all other days. Dick poured out a measure of water from the flowered crockery pitcher into the blue-white porcelain basin and washed his hands and face. Dick dried off as Jimmy began washing himself.

"What's that soup kettle doing up here?" he asked, pointing to the white porcelain bucket with a matching lid at the end of the bed.

Dick laughed.

"That's not a soup kettle," he replied. "It's a thunder mug."

"A what?"

"A chamber pot, a slop jar," Dick explained.

"What's it used for?" he asked.

"Now think," Dick urged.

Jimmy thought.

"You're kidding!" he finally blurted out.

"Now just think," Dick said. "do you want to walk outside at night to that creepy old outhouse and get bitten by another snake just to go to the toilet?"

"Well, no, but…"

"Well, that's what it's used for."

"That's awful."

"It's just pee for crying out loud," Dick assured him. "Someone would have to be mighty crude to crap in it."

"Do the women have one in their room too?"

"Sure," Dick replied.

"That must have been what I heard last night before I went to sleep," he noted.

"If you listen a little closer next time, you'll know why they call them thunder mugs," Dick added

The boys looked at each other and burst out laughing.

"Who's going to haul it down?" Jimmy inquired.

"I guess you will," "Dick teased, "since you're the youngest one here."

"Oh no!" Jimmy squealed. "It's your cottage and besides I didn't even use it."

"What a sis," Dick remarked as the two bounded down the stairs and into the kitchen.

Aunt Bessie was busy cooking bacon and scrambling eggs over the wood-burning stove in her prized cast iron skillet that weighed almost as much as she did. Cass and Olive Lee were busy setting the table as Fay got out the condiments.

"When's breakfast gonna be ready?" Dick asked. "Were starving."

"Sit yourselves down," his mother answered. "It's almost ready."

"Fay, get a jar of grape jelly out of the bottom cupboard and if it has some mold on it, just scrape it off." Cass instructed. "Olive, call in the men."

The sight and smell of the bacon, eggs and home fries had the boys salivating.

GW and Dave came in and washed the garden dirt from their hands.

"Looks like we're going to have a bumper crop this year, Bessie," GW proudly announced.

"That's if the bugs and varmints don't get 'em first," Bessie added.

"That chicken wire fence and an occasional dose of dried rabbit's blood around the borders should keep them out," he assured.

Over the years GW had learned enough about gardening to teach a botanical course at most universities. His hothouse, which was attached to the southern side of the tool shed, caught enough sun in the early spring to give his plants a head start on his neighbor, Clare Stackhouse's garden. This always pleased GW's competitive spirit.

Bessie turned to Russell.

"Don't forget to plant them marigolds around the outside of the garden fence like I asked you," she instructed. "Critters don't take much to their smell."

"Yeah, okay," he replied.

"Save some for the rest of us, boys," Bessie cautioned as the pair quickly gobbled down their share of the offering.

"What do you two have planed for this morning?" Dick's father asked.

"I guess we'll take a dip down at the dock for starters," Dick replied.

"How about fetchin' some spring water after while," Bessie suggested. "We're gettin low."

"Okay," they replied as the two headed up stairs to change into their swim trunks, which consisted of cut-off jeans.

The mid-morning sun peeked in and out of the white fluffy clouds creating great shadows that raced across the lawn. As the boys descended the newly constructed stairs, Jimmy noticed some impressions in the earth going straight down to the river bank.

"Is this where the old stairs were?" he asked

"Yeah," Dick replied. "They were in bad shape. Aunt Bessie said they were too steep for the older folks so gramps came up with this switch-back design."

Jimmy looked admiringly at the old fellow's work.

"You know, the more I learn about your Grandpa, the smarter he gets."

"I know," Dick replied. "Gramps and Dad are always coming up with neat ideas to try out around here."

Indeed, Dick's father and granddad seemed to have an unspoken agreement. They always built and repaired every item at Glen Afton in a unique and untraditional way. To them, this was a special place and ordinary construction methods just wouldn't do. As much as possible their love for this little patch of Eden would be reflected in the way they designed and fashioned just about everything.

Startled by the boy's sudden presence on the dock, the large mud turtle scurried from his sunning spot to a deeper, safer abode leaving a cloudy mud trail in the clear shoreline water .

"Look," Dick said as he pointed toward the shore down river. There in the shallows, a large blue heron was quietly fishing for her breakfast. She gave hint of a more tropical climate as she gracefully moved through the water on her long, rear-jointed legs.

"I didn't know that kind of bird came around here," Jimmy exclaimed.

"They come here in the summer to nest and have their young," Dick explained.

Just then the large bird squatted down, spread its long wings and with a thrust of her powerful legs, took flight. The first few flaps touched the tips of her blue-grey wings in the water as she flew out toward mid-stream. Her gracefully curved neck folded back between her shoulders and soon she cut an arc out over the water and then across the dock where the boys stood transfixed. Her flight was as silent as the morning. Their eyes followed the heron until she was out of sight.

"That's something you don't see every day," Jimmy exclaimed.

Dick looked at him with a devilish grin.

"Let's see just how well you can fly, Jimmy boy!"

He grabbed him around the waist, lifting him skyward.

"Fly into the river that is!"

"Oh no! If I'm goin in, you're goin too!" Jimmy shot back as he held on to Dick's head. The two wrestled around and soon fell together into the cool depths of the Juniata. It wasn't long before others joined the playful pair. Sister Fay and Katie and Andy Hahn splashed in. The Hahn twins sported bright red hair and freckles, giving rise to their nicknames, 'Raggedy Ann and Andy.'

GW, Dave and Russell, joined the others along with their sister, Olive Lee. Cass and Bessie came to watch while big Aunt Hat brought her stool and joined the other swimmers. She sat in the shallows allowing that the water should not come above her chest.

"The pressure on a heart of my condition just might do me in," she admonished.

The happy assemblage dove, splashed, teased and swam as if hard times and the depression were of another time and place. A pair of mating dragonflies landed on Dick's shoulder. Their shimmering wings, like fine gauze, gleamed of bright blue-green in the sunlight.

Soon another winged creature joined the bathers. The large pesky blowfly seemed to take pleasure in seeing the frantic swimmers duck beneath the water to ward off an unwanted bite. The intruder continued its little foray until Russell's quick, stinging slap to Dick's back turned the winged nuisance into fish food.

"That's enough for me," Dick said as he hopped out and began drying off.

"Let's find something else to do, Jimmy."

Jimmy agreed and the two headed for the stairs. The afternoon sun created dappled patterns of light on the lawn as it streamed through the majestic oaks.

"Don't forget, we promised your Aunt Bessie we would fetch her some more spring water," Jimmy noted, although his mind was set on the exploration of new territory rather than doing chores.

"Yeah," Dick agreed as they went upstairs to dress. "Now's as good a time as any to get that chore done."

As the they changed their clothes something caught Jimmy's eye outside the bedroom window. He stopped dressing and went over for a closer look, cocking his head to one side as a dog does when it's confused.

"What's that funny looking board sticking out the sides of the outhouse?" he asked.

"That's another one of gramps' inventions," Dick explained. "He calls it his adjustable sliding toilet seat."

"How does it work?" Jimmy questioned.

"Let's go down and I'll show you."

Once again Jimmy was about to see that nothing was ever designed or built at Glen Afton in a trivial or common-place fashion. Even the direction the outhouse faced and the way the door swung was important to GW.

"The outhouse must face east in order to let the morning sun beat in on you," he explained. "Now, if the door swings out and is partially open to let the sun in and a breeze blows it wide open, it could expose you and you don't want to have to stand up to pull it shut. But if it's built to swing in, you can have it partially opened and if someone does come along you can give it a shove while sitting down and take care of the problem."

As the boys walked the path Dick continued to explain.

"The women complained that there wasn't enough hole sizes to fit everyone, so Gramps came up with the idea of an adjustable seat board."

As they entered the outhouse, he continued.

"Now, if you pull this wooden peg out and put it in this hole, you can use it as a handle to move the seat."

"Awsome!" Jimmy exclaimed. "Let me try it."

He slid the seat board back and forth, trying each of the holes for a proper fit.

"This is the one I'll use," he said as he wiggled onto hole number three.

"It moves pretty easy, doesn't it?" he noted.

"Dad poured hot wax on the guide boards to make it slide easier," Dick explained.

"Yeah, but how about this," Jimmy observed. "Let's say you're sitting here, nice and comfy, doin your business and some ornery cuss outside decides to give the seat a shove."

"That's why you put the peg back in this rear hole," Dick explained. "It locks the seat board in place and keeps it from being moved."

"God, your gramps thinks of everything," he said shaking his head.

Fascinated by the structure, Jimmy returned outside to continue his investigation.

"Hey Dick, come here," he called from behind the outhouse. "Is this little door used for what I think?"

"Yep," Dick assured. "That's where they clean it out when it gets full."

"How can you tell when it's full?" he asked.

"You look down through the hole, dummy!" Dick replied with a sharp slap to the back of Jimmy's head.

"Oh, yeah," he returned. "Or when the sides start to bulge out."

They snickered at the thought.

"Or," Dick continued," when you have to stand on the seat to go!"

The two roared with laughter.

"Hey, look," Jimmy observed. "See how these knots here are kinda loose."

"Yeah, so?"

"So," Jimmy replied as he removed one with a prying motion of his pen knife, "if we remove a couple we can…"

"Yeah!" Dick said as they looked at each other with devilish grins. Dick pulled out his knife and the two began removing the loose knots. The fledgling peeping toms now laid in wait for there first eye-full.

"Here comes Olive Lee," Jimmy said excitedly.

"Shh," Dick warned, "she'll hear us."

Half way down the path the lovely lass stopped and began picking some flowers.

"Darn it," Jimmy whispered, "she's not coming in."

Soon afterward Fay and Katie came skipping down toward them, but then they veered off toward the spring path.

"Just as well," Jimmy remarked. "Nothing to see on those two skinny butts."

The two laughed quietly to themselves as they continued to wait.

"Here comes someone," Dick said in a hushed voice.

Now big Aunt Hat wasn't exactly what the boys had in mind, but as novice peeping toms, they had to start somewhere. The outhouse door creaked open and closed. The boy's eyes were transfixed at the knotholes as she moved the adjustable seat board to its largest selection and then secured the locking peg in its hole. The seat board creaked under her weight as she positioned her abundant behind on the seat board. The boys giggled to themselves at what they were beholding. Without hesitation, the old gal loudly flatulated prior to relieving her bladder. With hands over their mouths the boys could barely stifle their laughter!

Aunt Hat finished her business and started back up the path. Soon after, the two roared with laughter at the forbidden, but amusing sight they had just beheld.

Eventually they contained themselves and continued to wait for their next eyeful.

Once again, another unwary victim approached and this time Olive Lee didn't appear to have flower-picking on her mind.

"She's coming in," Jimmy whispered. Again their eyes were glued to the knotholes. Olive Lee pulled the lock pin on the seat and moved it to a smaller position. The two looked at each other and their facial expressions agreed…a much better view this time!

Their eyes snapped back to the knotholes in eager anticipation. Olive Lee was a lovely sight indeed, but the only cheeks the two saw were those of her beautiful face.

"Looking for something, boys?" she cooed.

That was their first shock! The second was far more unpleasant and physical.

Hair was pulled as both of them went tumbling backwards on their rumps!

"So!" Aunt Bessie growled. "You want to see some rear-ends, eh?"

"We'll see whose rear-ends pay for this!" Hat roared, her voice filled with rage and indignation. With the boy's hair firmly in hand, Hat and Bessie dragged the two wrong-doers to the cottage while the giggling Olive Lee followed.

"Don't tell dad," Dick pleaded. "Please don't tell my dad."

Fortunately for the pair, Dick's father wasn't there when they entered the cottage. Unfortunately, Dick's grandfather was and he was assigned the role of acting judge and jury by the two women. After hearing prosecuting attorney Harriet's version of the crime GW turned to the accused.

"You two have anything to say for yourselves?" he asked in his most serious voice.

"We'll never do it again, Grandpa, never," Dick said anxiously.

Jimmy nodded in fearful agreement.

GW looked at one offender and then the other. He appeared to be enjoying his position of authority and perhaps this incident brought back memories of his first taste of sin as a young lad. He smiled inwardly.

"I believe you two deserve a good thrashing," he sternly announced.

The boys cringed.

"However, since I'm not your father, Jimmy, that wouldn't be right," he added.

The ladies appeared to be disappointed with this decision. Rubbing his chin, the old man began to weigh the possibilities of a proper punishment to fit the crime when Bessie whispered something to Hat and a devilish grin spread across her face as she nodded in agreement.

"You know, George," Hat began, "the outhouse is beginning to get mighty full."

"And pretty smelly," Bessie added. "Why even the lime doesn't hold down the odor anymore."

"That's true," GW agreed, noticing the smiles on Hat and Bessie's faces.

"Well, boys, since you're going to have to patch those knotholes anyhow, you might as well muck out while you're back there."

"Muck out," Jimmy said. "What's that?"

Dick let out a groan.

"Come along you two," GW ordered.

The old gentleman took the culprits out to the tool shed.

"Grab those shovels, Dick," he instructed. "Jimmy, you get the wheelbarrow."

He led the two boys fifty feet into the woods behind the outhouse to a small clearing.

"Dig a hole right here," he commanded. "The soil is soft so it shouldn't be too hard to do"

The pair dutifully obeyed and after reaching GW's required depth, he led the two wrong-doers to the back of the outhouse. The rear door was unlatched and propped open, revealing its disgusting contents. Dick and Jimmy looked at each other in disbelief.

"Don't we usually do this in the winter when the smell's not so bad?" Dick whimpered, with a slim hope of a reprieve.

"Wouldn't be much of a punishment then, now would it?" his grandfather replied with a wink.

"When you're done, take the shovels and barrow down to the river and wash them good," he instructed as he turned and left the boys to their unpleasant task.

"Oh, and don't take too long, boys," he urged. "Never can tell when someone might have to use it."

The two stood there for a while, contemplating their nauseating task.

"We might as well get started," Dick grumbled as he disappeared into the outhouse and returned with two wads of toilet paper, handing one to Jim.

"What's this for?" Jimmy asked.

"In case you splash some of it on you, dummy."

"No way!" he blurted.

"It won't kill you, you big sis," Dick said, shaking his head.

"I'm not so sure of that," he added, looking at the heaping brown mass.

They began to shovel out the contents into the rusty wheelbarrow.

"This is gross," Jimmy muttered in disgust." It wouldn't be bad if it didn't smell so awful."

Dick stopped shoveling and thought for a moment.

"You know, Olive Lee had a hand in getting us into this mess," he noted with a gleam in his eye. "Maybe she can help us out."

"How?" Jimmy questioned.

"Never mind," Dick added, "I'll be right back."

Dick sneaked up to the cottage and soon returned with a fancy bottle in his hand.

"What in the world is that?" Jimmy asked.

"It's some of Olive Lee's perfume," Dick explained.

"They call it toilet water and this is a toilet, so…"

"All right!" Jimmy said with a smile.

Dick dispensed a generous portion of the bottle's contents over the waste and the two culprits continued their task with a more pleasant air about them.

As for Olive Lee, she could never quite understand the disappearance of almost all of her precious toilet water.

Chapter 5

PIPELINE

Most folks usually do things for more than one reason and it was a combination of Russell's ingenuity and laziness that led him to agree with the saying, Necessity is the mother of invention. After breakfast the next morning he approached the other men in hopes of rekindling the discussion about the pipeline.

"You know, Dave," he began, "maybe we ought to give some serious thought about Dick's idea of a pipeline to the spring. It would save us a lot of time and trouble in fetchin water."

Dave shook his head in disagreement. "Russell, do you have any idea how much pipe we would need and how much it would cost?"

"And besides," he added, "how would we get it under the railroad tracks?"

Dave was the conservative one of the clan, but he wasn't above considering a practical, labor-saving project.

Dick's eyes lit up.

"Jimmy, do you remember that old stone culvert we saw when we went for water the other day?" he said.

"How could I forget it, after that rattlesnake tried to…"

"Maybe we could use it to go under the railroad," Dick added.

"I don't know," his grandfather returned. "The cost of pipe alone…."

"You're always telling us about the great deals you made on surplus from the railroad, Dad," Russ noted, "and maybe you could get in touch with some of your old cronies who are still working there."

GW rubbed his chin.

"Well, if you fellas are so intent on doing this project, I suppose I could give it a try," he replied.

"You're not seriously considering this fiasco, are you?" Dave asked.

"Hold on, Dave, maybe we ought to give it a little more thought," the old boy suggested. "I know it would be a challenge, but we haven't backed away from any other challenges down here."

GW sat back in his rocker and thought for a moment.

"I heard Sam Peterson is still in charge of material handling at the Juniata shops and I believe if anyone would know about scrap pipe it would be him. Come to think about it, he still owes me a favor or two."

"Just think," Dick said excitedly, "then the women would have all the water they wanted to clean and scrub everything all the time."

"Yeah," his dad replied with a touch of sarcasm, "I'll bet that idea will thrill them."

Russell continued his argument.

"We could build a spring house out back to help keep things like milk and meat from spoiling so fast," he added.

GW lit a freshly rolled cigarette and ran his hand through his hair.

"Now, look here," he began, in a more serious tone, "if we decide to take on this project, everyone's gonna have to put forth a good effort to get it done."

He looked intently at his youngest son.

"No problem here," Russell assured his father with his usual initial enthusiasm.

"Okay, it's settled," GW stated. "Tomorrow I'll catch the 9:00 A.M. at Millerstown and see if I can round up any pipe at the Altoona yards."

Early next morning the sun rose bright in a cloudless sky, but a light breeze chilled GW on his walk beside the tracks to Millerstown. A white-tailed doe and her two spotted fawns hurried across the tracks toward the river for their morning drink.

S-irons needed in a lot of these old ties...ballast low on the north side of the east passenger line...west freight line needs danced back into place around this curve, he thought to himself as he continued toward town. As a trackwalker many years ago, it came second nature for GW to critique what his sharp eyes as needed maintenance on 'his' railroad.

A double row of staggered, evenly spaced holes in the path gave hint that his neighbor, Clare Stackhouse had made his way to Millerstown earlier that morning. Clare lived almost hermit-like in the only other cottage on the railroad side of the river and he was as independent as a person could be in his physical condition. His legs, crippled by a childhood bout with Polio, didn't stop this strong-willed character.

He used his crutches as skillfully as a mountain climber uses ropes and in spite of his sixty-seven years there was little he couldn't do for himself.

Clayton Hahn, his widowed son-in-law, tried in vain to get him to move to his Harrisburg home, but Clay could do little more than visit Clare in the summer with his kids, Katie and Andy and make sure the stubborn old fellow was well stocked with wood and supplies for the upcoming winter.

"What're you doin up so early?" Clare greeted as GW entered the tiny general store next to the station. "An old man like you should sleep in…get his rest."

"An old man like me has important business to tend to unlike some others who sit around wastin time gabbin and keepin poor Jess from his work," GW shot back.

"That's right," Stacky returned in mocked annoyance. "and just what is this important business you're tending to?"

"The boys and I decided to run that pipeline to the spring," he said in a more serious tone.

"Pipeline, huh?" Stacky replied with a chuckle. "You've been talkin that pipeline in for the last ten years and now you're finally gonna try and do it?"

"Not try," he answered, "we're gonna do it."

Stacky scratched his head through his porkpie hat.

"Where you fixin to get that much pipe?"

"That's why I'm here," he replied, "to go to Altoona and see what the railroad has in their scrap yard."

"Let me know if you need any help," Clare said. "Clay and Andy ain't been too busy around my place and they would most likely be glad to help."

"And what about you?" GW asked.

"Don't you fret none," he said smugly, "I'll be there. Heaven knows, you're gonna need someone who can supervise that project."

The 9:00A.M. was right on time.

As GW boarded, Clare called out, "Don't forget, you'll need fittings and some pipe, dope."

GW glossed over Clare's attempt at sarcastic humor.

"I know what I'll be needin, old man," he assured as the train pulled out. "Just you be there when you're needed."

Clare waved him off and headed back in to the store.

GW entered the kitchen at Glen Afton late the next day.

"How did you make out?" Dave questioned

"So far, so good," he began. "I caught old Sammy in a good mood. He and Doris finally bought that old Blake home in Hollidaysburg they had their eye on for so long. Seems Mrs. Blake moved in with her son and his family in Altoona, down Whenwood way I believe. Sam said the old girl couldn't keep house any longer and…"

"The pipe, dad," Russell cut in, "what about the pipe?"

"I'm gettin to that," he snapped. "Well, it seems the Blake home has this carriage house out back. After they bought the place Sam began to look it over, and as luck would have it, among all the junk he came across this old pipe on the second floor… twenty foot lengths…dozens of them."

"You think they'll be enough to do the job?" Dave asked.

"I counted over 50 lengths," his father noted," and I believe it's less than that to the spring."

"How much is he askin for it?" Russ inquired.

"Only ten dollars and he said he was glad to get rid of it," GW returned.

Dick and Jimmy looked at each other with more than a little enthusiasm.

"What about fittings and a valve and a pipe threader?" Dave asked. "We'll have to cut some of those lengths to fit."

"That's the kicker," his father said with a grin. "There was a burlap bag up there with the pipe and it's full of fittings and a couple of valves and Sammy says he can borrow a threader from a plumber friend of his if we promise to get it back to him when we're finished with it."

"What about gettin the pipe here?" Dave asked.

"That's why I stayed over last night," he replied. "Glad I did, too. Doris cooked up a couple of their hens and they tasted mighty good! Anyhow, this mornin Sam and I loaded up the pipe on his truck and hauled it to the loading docks at Fourth Street. Sam says he'll have it on the 7:15 A.M. run tomorrow."

"How much will that cost?" Russ inquired.

"Another ten bucks plus a little for the train crew."

"When will it get here?" Dick asked with a hint of youthful impatience.

"Sam said their scheduled arrival at Millerstown is 10:30 A.M. but he would tell the engineer to stop when he sees us flagging him down."

"Are they allowed to do that?" Dick inquired.

"No," his grandfather replied, "but it's a local freight and Sam said their schedule ain't that tight."

"All right!" Dick exclaimed in anticipation of another adventure.

The next morning was cool for late June and the gray sky threatened the five with liquid sunshine as they waited beside the tracks for the local freight.

Soon the little H-4 steamer came puffing and bustling down the tracks with it's ten gondolas, twelve boxcars and bright red caboose. It whistled and slowed as it neared the waving group of men.

"Make it quick, boys," the fireman shouted as the engine passed and came to a screeching stop. "Your pipe's in the third gondola."

Dave and Russ climbed aboard and began tossing the pipe to the ground.

"Careful, Russ," Dave warned, "don't let the ends dig in the dirt; make 'em land flat."

Meanwhile Dick climbed in and handed the burlap bag of fittings to Jimmy while GW went to the engine cab to get the pipe threader from the train crew.

"We sure do appreciate this, boys," he said as he handed the trainmen a couple of coins.

Soon the little train was on its way as the men began to inspect their bounty.

"Looks like a lot of work lyin there," Russell noted.

"Yes, but just think how great it will be to have clear, cool spring water down at the cottage," Dick reminded his uncle.

Soon the picks, hoes, and shovels were busily digging the necessary trench in the hard packed earth beside the mainline. After a while GW looked up and saw Clayton Hahn and Clare Stackhouse approaching.

"Good afternoon, gentlemen," he greeted them. "Mighty glad you could make it."

"Looks like you're makin pretty good time," Clare observed pointing with one of his crutches. "Surprising though, seein who's doin the supervising."

"And I suppose you'll help us pick up the pace, knowing your expertise at laying pipe," GW shot back.

"Can't be any worse than what you've been doin," Clare returned.

Not long after, Clay's boy, Andy came along, pushing an old cement lawn roller.

"I thought this roller might help pack the dirt down on the pipe," Clare explained.

"Probably the only good thought you'll have all day," GW scoffed.

"We'd better stop jawin and start diggin or we'll never get this job done," Clay noted.

Soon the eight were back into it. Dave and Clay opened the ditch with pick and shovel while GW and Dick screwed the pipe together and laid it in the ditch. Russell and Jimmy back-filled the ditch while Andy packed the earth down with the roller.

Clare went ahead of the work party and marked out the best route for the trench with his crutches as he continued to critique GW's work.

"Go easy with that pipe, dope," he reminded GW. "It's going to have to last for the whole job."

"I know that," GW snapped. "This isn't my first big job you know."

Clare shook his head. "One has to wonder, George, one has to wonder."

All went well for the pipe crew as they continued their work and soon they approached the little stone culvert that was to carry the pipe under the railroad. A welcome breeze cooled the hot, sweaty men as a turning elbow was screwed on to the pipe directing the line toward the culvert.

"How do we go about this culvert thing?" Dick inquired as the men took a well deserved break.

"Simple," his grandfather replied, "we screw a cap on a length of pipe to keep the dirt out and shove it in the culvert and then we screw another length onto the first one and keep on shoving them in until it comes out the other end."

"Not so simple," Dave said as he peered into the opening. "I can't see any light from the other end; it's either clogged up or there's a bend somewhere inside.

"Maybe if all you able-bodied fellas shoved it in together it would snake through on its own," Clare offered.

Dave looked at his dad.

"I guess it's worth a try," he said. "but I'll bet someone's gonna have to go in there and guide it."

The pipe slid in easily for the first forty feet, but then it stopped dead. No amount of twisting, turning, or shoving would coax it another inch. Again they rested as they pondered the problem.

"Now what?" Russell muttered.

"It's obvious," his father replied. "Like Dave said, someone's going to have to go in and guide it through that mess."

GW volunteered his son, Russ on the grounds it was his idea in the first place.

"No way!" he replied. "It's a still a great idea, but not that important for me to risk going in there."

"I'll go in," Dick said enthusiastically.

"No, Dick," his father said as he looked into the small, dark tunnel. "I'll do it."

"Looks at little tight for you, Dave," Clay noted.

Dave laid down and attempted to enter the tiny structure.

"I'm afraid your right, Clay," he said.

"Well, son, I guess you're going to be the one to do it after all," he said, looking at Dick.

"No problem," Dick returned, now filled with a renewed adventurous spirit.

"You'll need a light and maybe a pair of my canvas gloves," his father suggested.

"Well then, I guess I should go dress for the occasion," Dick added as he headed for the cottage.

He soon returned wearing a pair of old high-top boots, worn coveralls, and a striped railroader's hat. A carbide lamp for illumination and a brass cow bell to scare out any critters that might be lurking inside rounded out his choice of equipment.

One more time the men tried to force the stubborn pipe through and again their efforts were met with failure.

GW, Clay and the two other boys prepared to feed the pipe in as Russ and Clare positioned themselves at the other end of the culvert to keep watch and help when needed.

"Here we go," Dick declared as he sparked the carbide lamp and adjusted its flame to blue-white.

"See you at the other end," he said with an air of confidence.

Upon entering the old stone structure he realized it was narrower than it originally looked.

"Think you can make it, Dick?" Clay questioned.

"Yeah," he replied over his shoulder. "I'll just have to take my time."

He carefully checked the condition of the stone structure. It appeared solid enough and the ground at the entrance was fairly dry. Further in he began to sense a feeling of claustrophobia, but his objective mind swept it away as he began to concentrate on the mission at hand…fresh spring water at Glen Afton.

The dry ground at the entrance of the culvert soon gave way to wet, musty earth as he continued deeper into the dark hole. As his eyes adjusted to the flickering light of the carbide lamp he carefully examined the shaft for signs of hostile objects or movement of any kind. The noises from the outside were lost now. The scraping sounds of his movement against the sides and bottom of the culvert and his labored breathing were all he could hear. The carbide lamp's flame cast an eerie light down the small shaft, creating wavering shadows of false movement.

Soon he found there was no longer enough room for him to move on his hands and knees and now he was forced to crawl on his belly. The ceiling was only a foot above his head and the walls were just wide enough for him to elbow his way through this musty little hole. He mopped the sweat and cobwebs off his face with his free hand.

As he moved forward, the light revealed a stretch of stagnant water up ahead. The surface of the black water was dead-still. He called out and rang his bell. The noise it made was harsh in the otherwise quiet little tunnel, but nothing moved…all remained eerily quiet.

With a sigh of relief, he entered the murky pond as it gradually sloped to a depth of eight inches. The cool, foul smelling water felt good on his hot, sweat-soaked body. Ever watchful he slid forward, but the only movement in the water were the ripples he was creating. It was noticeably cooler in the mid-section of the tunnel, but the air stank of mildew and rotting wood as Dick continued on, focusing himself on his mission.

The light, now shining beyond the stretch of water, revealed the problem: debris, apparently washed in during previous storms had created a blockage where the culvert made its bend. It didn't appear to be enough to block his progress but he could see how the end of the pipe was digging into this pile of rubble. He approached the obstruction carefully, making his presence known by the use of voice, bell, and flashing light.

"Move out…coming through," he shouted

He did this to reassure everyone, including himself, that all was well…so far.

"You ready for more pipe, Dick?" Clay shouted.

"Not yet," he replied. "Wait till I clear out some of this junk."

As he began moving the dirt and wood out of the pipe's path, a large water spider startled him as it crawled out and scampered toward the far end of the culvert. Dick took a deep breath of stale air and blew it out, puffing his cheeks.

I hope that's the only critter in here besides myself, he thought.

"Okay, push it in," he shouted over his shoulder as he removed the last of the clutter from the pipe's path.

The pipe slid forward as he guided it among the rubble and around the bend. His carbide lamp began to grow dim. He gave it a bump with his hand and then gently shook it and it sputtered, but soon began to brighten. As Dick and the pipe rounded the bend he could see daylight at the far end of the little enclosure. He smiled. So far so good, he thought to himself. Victory seemed assured, but then he began to hear and feel a slight rumbling and as the noise became louder, the tunnel began to quake!

"Hang on, Dick," Russell shouted. "Here comes a freight."

His Uncle's words were soon drowned out by the increasing rumble of the coal train as it passed over him. The shaking grew worse and the noise became unbelievable as the whole culvert seemed to twist and writhe under its immense load.

Something touched his right leg!

He instantly recoiled and flashed the light. Loose stones had fallen against him from the tunnel's roof. He felt relieved that's all it was, but he didn't feel comforted by the fact that hundreds of tons of ground-shaking freight continued to rumble a few feet above him. Feelings of confinement returned to haunt him, but he composed himself and, as the train finally passed, he continued on his way through the foul-smelling mud and water.

"Send in more pipe," he shouted.

The progress began to go smoother as the pipe slid forward and the water in the little tunnel began to shallow out. The light at the end of the tunnel was becoming brighter as it revealed what appeared to be more rubble up ahead. As he approached this final obstacle, he thought he noticed movement in the debris.

He hesitated.

Probably just that damn water spider, he assured himself. He continued ahead toward the end of the shaft…but then stopped. Again, there appeared to be movement in the debris. He now realized what he was seeing was no water spider. Holding the lamp up and squinting, he saw what he feared most about coming into this tiny culvert. It was definitely a snake!

The earlier feelings of claustrophobia began to close in on him again. His eyes widened as he watched the reptile uncoil and begin to move toward the far end of the tunnel, but too soon he breathed a sigh of relief. The light at the end of the tunnel became partially blocked by Russell's form.

"You okay in there, Dick?" he shouted.

Dick could see the large reptile turn at the sound and sight of Russell and begin to slither back toward him! His sweating became more profuse. The panicked vision that flashed through his mind was of him screaming, standing up and crashing through the roof of his confinement! Clawing through the dirt, he reached out into the welcome warmth of sunlight and began grabbing anything…ties, rails, ballast, anything to free himself from this perilous place where he felt so trapped.

Okay, get a grip, Coleman…get a hold of yourself…deep breaths.

All right, all right, what can happen? he thought to himself. *I could scare it with the light and bell and it might crawl out the other end. That would be a good thing or it might just stay there...not so good! But then maybe I could back out the way I came in, but though all that debris? It was worth a try.*

He began crawling backwards, but upon hitting the original pile of clutter, it backed up and jammed the little tunnel.

Now what? he pondered nervously. *Maybe now it could have started to crawl out the other end, or it could continue coming this way. Not good at all! But then it could just be a black snake or a water snake, but water snakes are known to be aggressive and could bite like hell.*

Dick's mind began to race!

But then (he swallowed hard) *it could be that rattler Jimmy and I encountered earlier last week...definitely not good!*

"Hey, Dick," Russell's voice boomed in, "you fall asleep in there?"

Damn it, he thought to himself.

"There's a snake in here," he shouted nervously, "so be quiet."

"What kind?" he questioned.

"Damn it, Russ," Dick yelled back, "shut up or you'll scare him right into me!"

He could hear excited voices at both ends of the culvert and the faint sounds of footsteps overhead, but they could be of no help to him now. There was nothing but twenty feet of emptiness between him and the serpent. He focused his attention on the snake and again it was moving...in his direction!

Oh, God, he prayerfully thought, *let me be able to scare it out!*

He began to flash the light and clang the bell as loud as he could.

"Get out of here," he shouted. "Get the hell out of here!"

The reptile stopped...only ten feet away. Now the light revealed what Dick had dreaded the most...diamond-back!

Oh, God! he thought. *And me on my belly just like him!*

No more a snake to strike at his heal; no gun or club to ward him off or to kill. No where to run. Now, just face to face. Dick felt himself grow numb. The voices outside seemed even more distant and the light at the end of the tunnel seemed miles away. The moment he stopped ringing and yelling the rattler continued to slither even closer, perhaps confused by the hissing of the carbide lamp. At this point ringing and yelling seemed pointless. Like him, the reptile seemed to be driven on by its own sense of mission.

It was coming in on his right side so Dick slowly slid over to the left.

All right, free arm over your head and don't move a muscle, he thought.

All was quiet...and then he could hear it crawling. It was beside him now and he could feel it slide pass his extended right arm that held the lamp. It touched his side and then crawled over his legs to the left side of the culvert.

That's it, you scaly bastard, he thought, *just keep moving.*

"Dad went for the shotgun and another light," Russell yelled in. "You want one of us to come in?"

The rattler stopped. Dick could feel it lying across the back of his knees.

No...movement, he thought. *Remain...calm.*

The sweat from his brow ran into his eyes, blurring his vision. The urge to move was unnerving, but he managed to composed himself enough to remain still. After a while, his mind began to race.

Maybe it just feels like he's on me, he rationalized. *Maybe he did move on.*

Ever so slowly he turned his head to the right and eased the lamp around. There, next to his outstretched arm he saw the tail and the rattles!

Oh, no! he thought, now paralyzed with fear! The snake's body suddenly tensed and its tail quivered slightly, giving off that dreaded buzzing sound!

Don't move a muscle! he thought to himself. *It won't strike you if you don't move.*

Again, he composed himself and even in this most bizarre of situations he began to sense a slight feeling of being in control.

Okay, you slithering bag of garbage, he mused, *If it's a waiting game you want, you've got it!*

The minutes passed like hours as both boy and serpent remained dead still. Again Dick's mind began to churn.

You'd better make up your mind to start moving, he thought, *I've got family out there and they'll be coming in here after your scaly carcass.*

You ain't got nothin or nobody to help you, he reasoned. *You're all alone!*

It was like the diamond-back could read his mind.

Dick's heart jumped as the snake began to move.

Thank you, Lord! he said in a mental prayer. *Just don't let him stop!*

He listened as the large reptile continued on its way, but he remained motionless until the snake's crawling was no longer audible. Again, he slowly turned his head and lamp in the direction of the retreating reptile. It was fifteen feet away and going in the right and proper direction. Dick watched as the snake slithered toward the far end of the culvert as he breathed a muffled sigh of relief.

Again Russell's form filled the end of the culvert.

"You okay in there?" he questioned

"Yeah" he replied. "I'm good to go."

"He says he's okay." Russ told the others.

Dick began to crawl toward the end of the culvert.

All of a sudden his heart jumped as something cold and round moved under his right leg! He breathed a sigh of relief as the water pipe slid harmlessly beside him and toward the culvert's opening, but realizing the pipe had to move past his adversary he flashed his light in the snake's direction.

"Damn!" he shouted as the moving pipe caused the diamond-back to turn again. Dick spared no time or energy. Crawling frantically, he bolted for the entrance.

The fresh air at the opening never smelled so sweet and the sunlight never felt so warm and welcome to him as he emerged from the culvert.

"Dick's out!" Russell shouted to the others across the tracks. "He made it through."

All came running.

"You all right?"

"What happened?"

"What kind was he?"

"Did he get you?"

"I thought I told you guys to be quiet at this end," Dick said. "You scared him right into me."

The men looked at each other as Dick paused for a moment and took a deep breath.

"No, he didn't get me" he said in a low voice.

"What kind was he, Dick?" his Father asked again.

"Rattler," he replied.

"No way!" Jimmy exclaimed.

"Where is he now?" Russell asked.

Dick took a long, hard look at his uncle.

"You mean he's still in there?" Russ exclaimed. "That means you had to…"

"Yes," Dick continued, "we met, passed, and then went our separate ways."

The others expressed amazement at what had just taken place.

"Was he still headed toward the other end?" Clay asked.

"No, but with all the noise at this end, I'll bet he's going that way now," Dick said as he stooped over and peered into the dark culvert.

"Let's see if he made it out," Jimmy said as he started across the tracks.

The others followed and all watched the culvert entrance in silent expectation. Even the locusts and grasshoppers stopped their buzzing in seeming anticipation that something was about to happen.

Slowly, the diamond-back emerged, showing its full length of eight feet.

"I'll be damned," Clay said under his breath.

"Dick," Jimmy exclaimed, "he looks like the one that tried to bite me!"

GW took careful aim and the afternoon silence was split by the blast of his shotgun.

"That's one more story we'll have to tell," he said, putting his hand on his grandson's shoulder.

"Yeah, but let's not tell it yet," Dave replied. "You know how Cass and the others feel about snakes and such."

"I can't imagine how you kept your wits about you while that guy passed you in there," Clay said, shaking his head.

"Neither can I," Dick replied as they watched the dying reptile writhe and twist in the weeds that surrounded the entrance of the culvert.

"This ain't gettin the pipeline done, is it?" Clare said in an attempt to ease the tension.

"No it's not," Dave agreed in a voice more determined than ever to complete the task at hand.

"How close is the pipe to this end, Dick?" his father asked.

"About fifteen feet," he replied.

"You going back in there?" Russell asked.

"I don't think that will be necessary," Dave said. "The pipe will probably come through now that it's around the bend."

"You want to finish up that rattler, Clare?" GW asked.

"Consider it done," he said with a grin. "I'll have us a nice hide and a meal to boot."

"Are we going to eat that thing?" Jimmy asked with a sour look on his face.

"You like chicken breast, Jim?" GW asked.

"Well, yeah, but…."

"Well, that's just what one of those critters tastes like when Clare cooks it up," he assured the doubtful lad.

Jimmy and Dick looked at each other in disbelief.

"Never know what you're gonna like until you've tried it," Dave replied.

That evening, those brave enough dined on rattlesnake meat while all present admired the large eastern diamond back skin that Clare had stretched on his curing board.

At that time nothing was said about Dick's encounter with it in the culvert.

"Well, I think I've had enough excitement for one day," Dave claimed as he wiped his mouth and got up from the table. "We can pick up where we left off tomorrow morning."

All agreed as Clare mounted his crutches and headed for the door.

"Would seven be too early for you old timer?" GW teased.

"It's fine with me," Clare returned. "but if you want to sleep in a while, I think the rest of us could get along fine without you till, say around noon."

"Fat chance of that happening," GW returned.

The Colemans watched from the rear porch as Clare and his family headed for the river trail. The mourning doves and river frogs had begun their evening serenade as the lengthening shadows crept across the grounds of Glen Afton. Tired minds and muscles welcomed the night's call for much needed rest as the two families settled into their beds for the night.

Chapter 6
WATER, WATER, WHERE ART THOU?

Early next morning the men returned to the job of obtaining water for the cottage. Talk of the snake encounter the day before continued as they walked the path toward the railroad.

"Dry weather brings 'em out," GW noted. "Can't be too careful."

"Makes you realize what can be under your feet at any time, doesn't it?" Jimmy replied, half joking and fully attentive to where his feet were treading.

Presently Clare, Clayton and Andy came on the scene with morning greetings and soon all were back at their respective jobs of digging, laying pipe, backfilling and critiquing each others work. Now that the major portion of the job was done, everyone seemed more anxious than ever to complete the task.

"Look alive now, men," GW instructed. "Here comes the 9:15 passenger and the folks on board might think we're a Pensy crew, so let's give them a good show."

"Good show is right!" Clare said sarcastically. "If we really wanted to act like a Pensy crew we would be standin' here leanin' on our shovels jawin' the day away."

GW bristled. "Why, I'd put any one of my Pensy crews up against anyone of those construction gangs you used to ride herd on, Stackhouse."

"Sure," he shot back, "and if my gangs did any less than your railroad riff-raff they'd be tearing this pipe out instead of putting it in!"

The 9:15 roared past as the two old timers persisted in their banter while the others chuckled and continued with the work at hand. Soon the hard-packed ground beside the railroad gave way to the dark, rich soil of the forest as the small group of workers continued their trek down the spring path toward their goal. Chipmunks and gray squirrels in the surrounding oaks and maples briefly stopped their chattering and scampering as they watched this strange company digging and bustling through their domain. Higher still, in the majestic trees, cardinals, blue jays, and mocking birds seemed to be encouraging the crew's progress with their cheery tweets and melodious songs.

"Would it be asking too much if we put a tee in the line somewhere along here?" Clare asked. "One of these days we might run a line over to my place."

"Yes, it would be asking too much, old man," GW teased, "but I suppose we could stop all progress and do you the favor."

"Thanks, George," Clare returned. "You're all heart."

As the men continued working, each crew became more at ease with the job they were doing.

"Easier diggin' eh, boys," Clare noted.

"Yeah, but there's a lot more roots to put up with," Russ added as he swung his pick at the gnarled mass of surface roots.

"Hold up, Russell," Clare said, as he looked over the situation. "Why don't you loosen the dirt below the roots and slide the pipe under them rather than trying to cut them all out?"

His suggestion worked and soon their progress continued to improve. Clare had learned long ago that by taking a little time and looking a job over, rather than continuing to struggle, could result in an easier method of accomplishing a task. Clare's mental prowess more than made up for his physical limitations.

The cool of the forest shadows and a light breeze allowed the men to work more efficiently and soon they had developed a machine-like rhythm as the project neared completion. Hearts and spirits were lifted as the crew broke out of the forest and onto the lawn at Glen Afton.

"All right!" Dick shouted.

The men took a well-deserved break while Russell lit up his pipe.

"Only problem now is where do we go from here," he noted as he puffed his pipe to life.

"Most logical place would be down beside the garden," GW asserted. "That way we wouldn't be tearing up much of the lawn and I could water my garden with ease."

"What about the springhouse?" Dave questioned. "Wouldn't it be better to have it close to the cottage?"

"No," his father insisted, standing his ground. "I want it next to the garden like we talked about."

"I don't remember discussing where we were going to put the springhouse." Russell noted.

"Never mind, Russell," his father returned, "I've made up my mind; it goes beside the garden."

Dave looked up toward the cottage.

"Here come the women," he said, with an inward smile. "Maybe they can help us decide."

"Come on, Dave," his father insisted, a little perturbed. "We can figure this out ourselves."

"Lunch is about ready," Bessie called as they neared the workers.

"My!" Cass exclaimed. "You have it down this far already? That's great."

"What do you think, Cass," Dave began, "Where should we put the springhouse?"

His father glared at him.

"Well," she said, looking around at the possibilities, "since it's going to be used to store our perishables, I think it should be close to the cottage, like over near that patch of peonies."

"Oh no," GW cut in. "We're not digging around my Peonies. Besides, I don't think I should have to walk clear across the yard to water my garden every day, especially with my arthritis flaring up like it does."

With her arms crossed and rocking her shoulders back and forth, Cass looked the situation over and then at her father-in-law.

"All right, then, why don't we put it somewhere in between," she suggested. "That way no one would have to exert themselves very much to get their water."

Again, Dave smiled to himself, knowing quite well where all this was going.

"And don't forget about Bessie's bad hip," she continued.

"But Cass," the old persuader implored, "it would stick out like a sore thumb in the middle of the lawn."

"No one uses this end of the lawn anyhow," she challenged, "and I'm sure you could find just the right plants and flowers to make it look really nice, what with your knack for growing things."

"Ah, Cass," GW whined in frustration, "I have a lot more water to carry than you girls and my back ain't what it used to be."

"All right, then, how about using a hose?" she offered. "That way you would have all the water you need and you wouldn't have to haul it at all."

"Yeah, but then I'd have to lug out the hose every time I wanted to …."

"Oh, all right, Mr. Coleman," she snapped, throwing her arms up in frustration, "put the damned thing anywhere you like!"

They watched as Cass stormed back to the cottage.

GW turned to Dave and the others…all present remained silent.

It took the men only two weeks to complete the springhouse and the adjoining water trough beside the patch of peonies. During that time GW busied himself with the challenge of making the 'whole mess' look presentable in the middle of the side lawn.

It was clear that plenty of thought was given to the design of the new water system. A tee in the pipe split the water's flow in two directions. One went directly into the springhouse where a small, shallow pool would cool the food contained therein. The other fed a pipe which rose vertically out of the ground beside the springhouse and goose-necked over a metal trough made out of half an old water tank cut lengthwise. This trough was set three feet above the ground in order to facilitate the dipping of buckets without the strain of bending over. Both the springhouse and trough emptied into a common tar-coated, locust-wood drain which ran underground to the edge of the riverbank. Here it would discharge its contents into the Juniata River…if all were to go as planned.

Finally everyone was ready for the first surge of fresh spring water.

"Dick, you and Jimmy run up to the spring and open the valve," his father instructed.

"All right!" the two shouted as they ran toward the spring trail.

"Be sure you hear water flowing in the pipe before you come back," GW shouted as the boys disappeared into the forest.

The pair ran the distance to the spring pond in record time.

"Ready, Jimmy-boy?"

"Ready, big guy," he returned.

Dick turned the valve and both quietly listened for the sound of flowing water.

"It's moving!" Jimmy exclaimed.

"Let's see if we can beat it back to the cottage," Dick challenged.

The two were off, covering the distance back in even less time.

"Is it here yet?" Jimmy shouted as they entered the yard.

"No, not yet," Russell replied.

All gathered around the water trough, listening in quiet expectation…nothing.

"You sure you turned the handle all the way on?" Dave questioned.

"Yes, Dad," Dick replied.

"We even heard the water gurgling in the pipe," Jimmy confirmed.

"Dave, can you feel any air coming out?" Clare asked.

He wet his fingers and held them under the pipe…nothing.

Disappointment began to set in.

"You sure you checked every length of pipe for dirt, Russ?" GW inquired.

"Yes we did," was his curt reply. "We checked them all."

"I don't know," Clay remarked, "the way you and Dave were chucking them off the train."

"Oh sure, Clay!" Russ shot back, "and I don't suppose you guys in the ditch could have shoved an end into the dirt while you were putting it together."

"Now, boys," Clare broke in, "this bickering ain't gonna get us anywhere."

"Maybe if we banged on the pipe it would shake something loose," Dick suggested. They banged and hammered, but much to their dismay, the water from the spring would not appear and soon everyone was either arguing as to whose fault it was or suggesting how to make the elusive liquid flow.

"Listen!" Cass shouted from the springhouse. She turned to the others with her special smile and beckoned them to come. The men and boys almost fell over one another getting to the springhouse.

At first they heard a faint trickling noise and then, as their eyes adjusted to the darkness of the little stone and wood structure, they beheld a murky, black-brown liquid oozing across the bottom of the stone and clay pool. Soon the ooze became a steady flow of muddy water as all watched in silence.

"Look…look here!" Jimmy shouted.

The group turned to see the same ooze coming out of the goose-neck pipe and into the water trough.

"Yes!" Dick yelled as he jumped and drove his fists into the air. All joined in the jubilation as the flow of liquid continued to increase at both openings.

Before long the newly installed pipeline was flowing strong and soon, fresh clear spring water was quenching thirsts and cooling the springhouse and tempers alike.

Jimmy ran to the edge of the river bank.

"Even the drain's working!" he shouted as he watched the muddy water carve a trail down to the Juniata.

For the next few days all those at Glen Afton reveled at the blessing of cool running water. Clare renewed his commitment to bring the same to his home…it was never to happen.

True, the new pipeline was a great convenience, but something was lost at Glen Afton that summer. The daily chore of fetching water was a simple adventure that all shared in turn and during those trips something was seen or heard or another person was encountered at the spring to share a greeting and perhaps a story. This small, but pleasurable task was now part of the past, but the experiences of it would continue on in the memories of those who had lived them.

Chapter 7
HOBO JUNGLE

The depression of the thirties created a new caste of men... desperate men who weren't afraid of the challenge and hardship of the open road. Their quest for something better, for something different in their lives led them on the adventure of the American hobo.

(1954)

As the campfire crackled and hissed I noticed dad appeared to be lost in thought as he gazed into the flames. The sun had gone down and the cool damp of the night wrapped itself around our little tent camp which made the warmth of the fire feel especially good.

Dick packed his pipe and lit up as a large grey moth miller circled the fire.

"You're going to have to sharpen our machete, Dad," Dick noted. "I cleared the trail to the spring, but that blade is dull as a butter knife."

"I'll check it tomorrow," dad replied. "Anything new or interesting up that way?"

The moth spiraled down and landed in Dick's coffee, fluttering around on top. He picked it up by its wings, gently shook it off in his coffee and gave it a pitch into the weeds.

"I noticed you can still see some of the hobo markings on that old oak by the path near the railroad," he replied.

"I'll be darned," dad replied. "It doesn't seem so long ago that Bessie and your mom were giving one of them a sandwich and a drink."

"What markings?" I asked.

"During the depression a lot of folks were out of work, Fred," dad explained. "Some men began traveling around the country looking for jobs and they would ride the rails because hitching a freight was the easy way for them to travel. Those boys would check out all the local residences near the rail lines for a bite to eat, but some folks didn't take to that very well."

"Can't say as I blame them," I said. "Who would want to bother with a bunch of bums!"

"Hold on, little brother," Dick said. "These men weren't bums. They were hobos, knights of the open road."

"What's the difference?" I asked.

Dad explained. "A bum is someone who wants to live off the goodness of other folks. He's basically lazy in most ways, but hobos were men who weren't afraid to earn their keep anyway they could. They were willing to work for whatever you gave them. They would chop wood, haul water, run errands or patch up things that needed fixing around your property. Most were respectful of other folks and they had a sense of pride about themselves,"

"And most kept themselves as clean as being on the road would allow," Dick added.

"Were there any troublemakers?" I asked.

Dad looked at Dick in a serious way.

"Again, most weren't," he noted. "but occasionally there were a few bad apples… renegades they called them."

Dick prodded the fire, sending up a shower of bright sparks that mingled with the stars in the night sky.

(1941)

The rabbit showed signs of being uneasy as it munched its dinner of dandelion stems in the small meadow.

Petey remained dead still and soon the rabbit gave in to the temptation of the turnip bait. Slowly…cautiously…it moved toward the propped crate. Petey waited patiently, barely breathing. As the rabbit began to nibble the purple delicacy Petey jerked the trip line and the rabbit was his!

"Heh, Heh, Heh, Heh," he laughed through yellow teeth in his high-pitched gravelly voice.

"Wait till the boys see you," he mused. "I'll bet none'a the others gets one as good as me this time!"

The skinny little hobo quickly gutted and skinned out his prize. How many times had Petey come up short-handed in finding lumps for the mulligan stew? But not this time. Fresh meat for the pot was always the grand prize. This time he would be the honored one. After cleaning his catch the old hobo pulled his sweat-laden cap down over his brow and headed back to the jungle.

Evening shade was beginning to darken the forest as Petey entered the jungle. The familiar sights and smells of the cook fires and the men that gathered around them gave Petey a sense of family, a sense of belonging. Four fires lit up the camp which contained a dozen small tent-like structures and a few wooden domiciles made from crates found around the stations at Thompsontown and Millerstown.

This hobo jungle was well hidden down a small hollow in the forest two miles east of Thompsontown. It was close enough to the town to seek handouts and yet far enough not to be bothered by the local police or harassed by the town bullies.

Further east lay Millerstown, a small tank town where most trains stopped for coal and water. This proved to be an advantage to the transient men who were coming in or moving out of the area. A short siding located there usually provided an empty box car or two for temporary shelter from the elements.

This hobo jungle, as was true of so many jungles, was a melting pot for tramp-dom. All types, ages and personalities stayed here at one time or another. Most were ambitious and willing to work; they were just a little down on their luck. Some were vagabonds with itchy feet that were meant for traveling, but that didn't make them bad people. Proof of this was the amount of activity going on in this particular jungle and how most pitched in with what had to be done.

Four men were busy boiling clothes in an old metal drum and hanging them on a makeshift clothes line. Some of their clothing was washed and boiled so often they were bleached white. Another was sewing up a pair of bib overalls while yet another was showing off his skill as a barber. A group of six had just come in from the west. They were worn out from 'riding the rods' and were sacked out near one of the campfires.

These men came and left the camps with little fanfare and they rarely discussed family or personal relations for here was a place where every man's past was his own. They lived closed lives and granted others the same courtesy. The only real interest they took in each other was to hear about conditions in the towns they came through, the work available, good places for handouts, police harassment, and other significant details that one might need if they were a mind to travel in that direction.

Several younger men were gathered around one of the fires, listening to 'Poke Belly', an experienced knight of the road, spin one of his tales. All hobos had experiences while traveling the road, but only a few sages like old Poke could make them sound so damned interesting and watching the more experienced hobos and listening to what they had to say taught the fledglings how to act.

The huge scar-faced hobo lifted young John's bib overhauls out of the boiling vat with his wooden ladle and laid them across a board fastened between two trees.

"Thanks," John offered.

"Jes don speak to me," the big man grunted in a low, menacing voice.

"What?" John asked, a bit perturbed.

John's older friend, Willy, much wiser than his years, took John by the arm and led him over to another camp fire.

"I was just tryin to…"

"I know what your meanin was, Johnny," Willy said, "but some here are best left to themselves."

"I don't see why bein friendly should bother anyone," John argued.

"Listen, Johnny," Willy continued, "a few o' these ole boys got scars that go deeper'n what's on their faces and a few got wounds that ges don't heal too easy."

"So?"

Willy picked up some firewood from a pile and refueled the fire.

"So, life's dealt purty hard with some 'o these and some never get over it," Willy continued, noticing the confused look on John's face.

"Hell, he ain't got nothin against you, boy," he explained. "It's a hurt inside he's tryin to deal with,"

The confused look on John's face began to melt into understanding.

"You mean like me missin' my mom and sis back in Connecticut?"

"Willy slapped the young lad on the knee.

"Now yer gittin it!" he exclaimed with a high-pitched chuckle.

Petey entered the jungle and joined his buddies at one of the camp fires. His pal Dev was frying some sliced gut (pork sausage he had mooched from a local) on an old broken-handled coal shovel while the others were adding their gatherings to the mulligan stew that was starting to boil.

"What'd you get?" Dev asked Brownie as he joined the others.

"Only found some leeks," he replied.

"Damn, don't this bunch stink enough already without more leeks?" Dev noted with a shake of his head. "How about you, Max?"

"Managed to grab these taters and corn in some farmer's field over yonder," he replied, pointing in the direction of some farmer's field.

"Okay, Petey, you must a got somethin good or you wouldn't be grinnin like a Cheshire cat," Matt, the tall, husky, self-appointed leader of the group said. "What you got in those grubby paws behind your back?"

Petey exposed several turnips he had in his left hand.

"More rabbit food," Matt groaned. "Can't any of you fools catch some meat?"

"Well," Petey began, "I jes' happen to cetch the critter that was munchin on these greens," he said with a grin as he held out his prize.

"All right!" Dev exclaimed.

"Way to go, Petey," Max added.

"Bout time you got something good for a change," Matt declared.

"Yea, but even a blind squirrel gets a acorn once in a while," Brownie added with a chuckle.

Petey's glory was short lived as Brownie grabbed the rabbit, shoved a pointed stick through it lengthwise and thrust into the fire.

"Hey!" Petey protested, "I caught it and I get to cook it."

"You can get cookin by fetchin more firewood," Brownie growled as he pushed the hapless Petey toward the darkening forest.

As the others washed and cut up their offerings, Matt stirred and tasted the mixture as it boiled.

"Not bad," he said. "Needs a little more seasoning."

The others laughed at of the thought of 'more seasoning'.

"This"ll flavor it up some," Brownie said as he de-boned the cooked rabbit, tore it into pieces and added it to the stew.

"Now it's ready," Matt stated after a final tasting. He ladled the stew into the tin cans as each man came by for his share. The fire turned to a warm glow as the men finished their meager, but welcome meal.

"Man, a good cigar would taste great about now," Dev mused.

"Hell, even a lousy cigar would taste great about now," Matt quipped.

"I hear even those that got money are findin it hard to come by good smokes nowadays," Brownie added.

After dinner Bones Jones, Black Jack, and three others began washing the dinner ware. These five hadn't gathered firewood or rounded up anything up for the stew and by unwritten jungle law they knew this was their job. It was also common knowledge that dishes, pots, pans and the like were nobody's possessions except while being used and they had better be cleaned and stored upside down so the rain didn't rust them out. Any kindling or firewood that was used had to be replenished and all fires were doused at night so as not to attract any unwanted company.

At first, the commotion coming from the lower end of the camp sounded like a shouting match, but as the noise drew near it was evident that something more serious was taking place. Jake Rhodes and his buddies Sal and Mick were hustled to the middle of camp near the remaining fire.

"What's wrong?" Matt asked the men, but knowing Jake's reputation, he could have guessed.

"We caught these three jack rollin' a couple of boys while they was sleepin."

Matt frowned as he stared at the accused.

"We all know the penalty for that," he said with firmness in his voice.

The three showed no resistance as they were stripped to the waist, tied to a large oak and whipped.

"Let this be a lesson to all who would jack roll or otherwise take unfair advantage of their brothers of the road," Matt proclaimed.

The three were released to gather their bedrolls and the rest of their property. They grumbled and growled on their way out of the camp, but each knew they had broken one of the unwritten laws of the jungle.

Chapter 8
UNWELCOME VISITORS

True to Kit and Danny's nature, they arrived three weeks later than they had said.

"Where have you guys been?" Dave asked Danny as they emerged from the spring path.

"Better late than never," was Danny's grinning reply. His round, ruddy face and cherubic features gave hint of his Irish heritage. Before being laid off, Danny McIntire had worked as a machinist for the Pennsylvania Railroad, but his fondness for alcohol and gambling kept him and Kit in dire straits most of their lives. His jocular nature and sense of humor made him a hit with the youngsters, but most of the adults in the family tolerated him simply for Kit's sake.

Kit, Dave's older sister by two years, greeted them with her customary toothy grin. A slight built woman with protruding brown eyes and dark curly hair, she was Danny's second wife who bore him a son. Joey died of scarlet fever at the age of two and the loss devastated her. She vowed never to have any more children and, right or wrong, Danny became her whole life.

Dave's eyes went from Kit and Danny to the two figures behind … and his heart sank.

"Dave," Danny began, "you remember Buck and Joe Grubb from the roundhouse."

"Yeah, hello boys." he said sullenly, remembering the two as dodgers and complainers on the job but aggressive with language, fists and liquor outside of work.

"This is Dave's wife, Cass."

The brothers grunted a brusque hello.

"Come on," Danny urged, "I'll introduce you to the rest of the clan."

The three headed toward the cottage.

"Who are those two characters?" Cass questioned as she looked them over with a wary eye.

"Just two of Danny's drinking buddies," Dave replied.

"Well, they'd better not be drinking here, especially with the kids around," she stated coldly.

Inside Danny's boisterous mouth could be heard throughout the cottage.

"Yeah, I told these two so much about Glen Afton that they just had to come and see it for themselves," he stated.

Danny was always quick to give others access to what didn't belong to him, especially where he wasn't financially involved.

"What do you think, Buck?" Danny asked the older brother.

"Yeah, it's nice all right," Buck replied in a tone of one who sees such things with an air of envy rather than appreciation.

"What did you bring us, Danny?" Bessie asked, motioning toward the four large sacks they toted in.

"A real treat! he replied. "You know that old woman who bakes for Wagner's store at Millerstown?"

"Mrs. Shaffer," Cass noted.

"Yeah, that's her", he continued. "We just got off the train and went into the store when her and this other woman, I guess it's her daughter, walks in with their arms loaded with pies and cakes. They told us they were fresh baked just this morning so I said to Kit I'll bet the gang could use something good for a change, so we bought all four of her cakes and a couple of pies."

Dan pulled out one of the cakes and proudly displayed it for all to admire.

"Looks good, doesn't it, Dick?" he said, holding the cake under the youngster's nose.

"Sure does, Uncle Danny."

He could have bought eight bags of decent groceries for what he paid for that stuff, Cass thought, but her appreciation of any offering from Danny kept her silent.

"What's in the other two bags, Danny?" Bessie inquired.

"Oh, just some extra clothes and the rest of my fishing gear," he replied.

"Are the fish bitin, Georgie?" he asked.

Danny was the only one who called GW by that name and it always managed to set the old timer's teeth on edge.

"Sure," he lied. "There's loads of 'em under those snags up river about a half mile."

Dick & Jimmy's Adventures at Glen Afton

"Well what are we standin' here for?" he said to his buddies. "Let's go try our luck."

Cass looked at Kit, who grinned a toothful grin and shrugged her rounded shoulders as the three men headed for the river.

Dick and Jimmy watched from the end of the dock as the three men piled into GW's new Hoffman boat.

"Now we'll have us a little fun," Danny grinned as he gave Buck and Joe a glance at the large brown bottle he had hidden in his fishing creel. As they rowed out past the end of the dock, Danny noticed the boys.

"What are you two scalawags up to?" he inquired.

"Just loafin," Dick returned.

"Why there's a whole river full of fish out there just beggin to be caught," Danny claimed.

"We were fishing yesterday," Jimmy replied.

"Then how about froggin?" Danny suggested. "Nothin better than a mess of fried frog's legs."

The boys looked at each other.

"Could we do that?" Jimmy asked.

"I guess so," Dick returned. "I heard Gramps tell about how he used to do it."

"Let's go ask him how it's done," Jimmy returned with the thought of another adventure at hand.

"Good luck, boys." Danny shouted, flashing his big Irish grin.

At the cottage GW instructed the pair on the use of a pole, clear leader line, a hook and a small piece of red flannel cloth.

"Just slip up behind them real quiet-like so they don't see you and dangle the cloth about six inches in front of their nose," he instructed.

"If they don't grab it right away, make it jump a little," he advised as he twitched the pole a bit with a slight motion of his wrist.

"Just like that," he added as he watched the boy's eyes light up with enthusiasm.

"Thanks, Gramps," Dick said as the two apprentice froggers made for the dock with their bucket and newly made poles in hand. They boarded the small, wooden two-man pram and rowed across the river to a small opening in the woods that Dick's grandfather told them about. No sooner had they beached the pram and tied it off when Jimmy's sharp eyes spotted what appeared to be the object of their quest.

"There's one," he said in a hushed, but excited voce.

"Okay," Dick whispered. "Let's get him."

They moved slowly and quietly toward the bug-eyed amphibian as it sat dead still on the marshy shore. They were five feet from their quarry when it hopped and plopped into the muddy shallows.

"Dang!" Jimmy said disappointedly. "What spooked him?"

"Don't you remember?" Dick reminded him. "Gramps told us to come at them from behind."

More wary and experienced now, the two slowly moved along the shoreline and soon another hopper was sighted near the water's edge.

"Let's be careful this time," Dick cautioned.

They flanked their prey and then approached it from behind as Jimmy dangled the felt-covered hook in front of it's nose. It shifted slightly, but otherwise remained motionless.

"Twitch it," Dick whispered.

Jimmy did and the bait was snatched by a lightning-quick tongue.

"Got 'em!" Jimmy shouted.

"Bring him over here," Dick said.

He grabbed their catch by the body, removed the hook and taking it by its legs, he smacked it over a nearby rock.

"Number one for dinner tonight," he exclaimed as he tossed it in the bucket.

"He sure has rough-looking skin," Jimmy noted as he peered into the bucket for a closer look.

"Yeah," Dick agreed. "He must be an old-timer."

The hunt continued and soon another was sighted and Dick caught his first.

"Nice big one!" Jimmy said admiringly.

"You crack this one," Dick insisted.

Reluctantly Jimmy grasped the wiggling animal in hands unaccustomed to such fare. He managed to remove the hook and then, gripping its legs, dashed it on a rock with such force that it splattered both boys with its vile juices.

"You didn't have to pulverize it," Dick exclaimed, "just whack them enough to break their necks."

"I didn't want him to suffer," Jimmy replied.

A few hours later the bucket was filled with brown-skinned beasts and the two proudly headed back to the pram with their catch.

The bright afternoon sun had given way to dark, ominous clouds that had quietly slipped into the sky without the fanfare of wind or thunder. A distant solitary loon issued forth its mournful cry that carried far and full through the dead-still air that hung above the Juniata. The boys docked the pram and headed up the switch-back stairs with their bounty in hand. Clare Stackhouse met them as they crossed the lawn.

"What've you got in the bucket, boys?" he asked.

"A nice mess of frogs," Dick said proudly, holding them up for inspection.

"We're all gonna feast on frog's legs tonight," Jimmy added enthusiastically.

Clare smiled as he examined their catch.

"Well, you do have a nice mess there, but I doubt if you're going to feast on frog's legs tonight," he said with a chuckle as he continued toward the dock.

Puzzled by Clare's reaction, the boys looked at each other, shrugged their shoulders and headed toward the cottage.

"Hey, Gramps," Dick shouted when he spotted him working in his garden. "Is this how your supposed to catch frogs?"

GW stood up and walked over to the boys.

"Well now, it looks like you two had some good luck your first time out," he said with a smile as he saw the overflowing bucket at a distance. His smile soon faded as he examined their bounty close up. He shook his head and gave out with a chuckle, not unlike old Clare.

"I guess I should have gone with you, bein this was your first time at it," he said.

"Why?" Dick asked with a glance toward Jimmy.

"Then I could've shown you the difference between frogs and toads."

"Aw, man," Dick said.

"You mean we killed all these little guys and now we can't eat them?" Jimmy asked.

"Now, it's not a complete loss," GW assured. "Any creature makes good fertilizer so let's just tuck these little fellas under my tomato and pepper plants and see if that'll help them grow any better."

"Will you take us out tomorrow and show us how its done?" Dick asked.

"Sure," he replied, "besides, I had my mouth set for a nice mess of frog's legs anyhow."

Later that afternoon Clare returned from the dock where he had been fishing. He walked over to where Dave, Cass and Kit were standing.

"Danny's up to his old tricks," he whispered to Dave as he continued toward the path leading to his cottage.

The three watched as Danny and the Grubb brothers stumbled up the dock stairs. Kit's usual smile faded.

"Come on, Kit," Cass said, taking her by the arm. "We should be helping Hat and Bessie in the kitchen."

Dave started walking toward the garden.

"Hey Dave," Danny called out as the three approached him. "There's a short snort left here in my happy bottle," he said, his cherubic face glowing red from the sun and whiskey.

"No thanks, Dan," he replied, "it's a bit early for that."

"What's the matter, Coleman," Buck slurred, "ain't we good enough for you to drink with?"

"Yeah," Joe said. "I thought that lesson Buck taught you at the roundhouse would've learned you some manners."

(1937)

It had been four years earlier at the roundhouse in Altoona where they worked on the great steamers that Dave first met Buck. They were working on a K-4 engine, installing new coupling rod bearings on the engine's huge drive wheels. Working above, Dave had removed the locknut and was attempting to loosen the retaining nut.

"Come on, Coleman," Buck shouted, his lack of patience beginning to show.

Buck wasn't tall but his barrel-chested build gave him the look of a prize fighter. His physical strength and temper came from working as an apprentice stone cutter for his father in his younger days. His Father, a surly brute of limited skill, hated to school anyone in his trade…half because it slowed his pace and half because he was afraid the new-comer would eventually show him up. This attitude held true even more for his oldest son and after a year of abuse and putdowns, Buck left for a job on the railroad.

Buck's attitude toward his underlings was much like his Dad's. While others might have shown some compassion toward their fellow workers based on their own experience of abuse, Buck continued to mirror his Father's attitudes in the mistreatment of his fellow workers.

"I'm turning as fast as I can," Dave replied. "The darned thing wants to stick."

"Well put some oil on the damn thing," Buck retorted.

Dave jumped down and grabbed the oil can off the tool bench, not daring to ask Buck to hand it to him in his already incensed state. He applied some oil to the stubborn nut which splashed down on Buck.

"Watch what you're doing, you numbskull," he yelled.

Now Dave was beginning to become a bit irritated.

"Then don't stand under here where I'm working!"

"Just turn the damn thing," Buck replied. "We have to get this done."

Strange words, Dave thought, from a man who could talk a ten minute coffee break into a half-hour bull session.

"Okay, stand back a little," Dave warned.

Buck stood defiantly and as Dave applied more pressure to the stubborn nut. The wrench suddenly slipped off and caught Buck on the side of his head.

"Damn you!" Buck cursed as he bent over, clutching his head. His string of profanities could be heard across the round house as Dave climbed down to see how bad he was hurt.

"Get the hell away from me!" Buck yelled, pushing him against the side of the engine.

"Stupid, worthless jack-ass," he muttered, still holding his head.

"If you would've moved like I told you…"

"You don't tell me anything!"

Hearing the ruckus, their foreman, Bob Rouzer, came over.

"What's the problem, boys?" he asked.

"Aw, this stupid jack-ass dropped a wrench on my head," Buck replied.

"Hold still, Buck," Bob said, as he examined his head.

"Your ear's cut bad," he noted. "Look's like you'll be needing some stitches."

Bob took out his hanky and had Buck hold it against his blood-soaked head.

"This ain't over, Coleman," Buck growled as he and Bob headed to the medical station.

"Let it go, Buck," Bob warned. "You know accidents happen in here all the time."

He's right, Dave thought to himself. It was an accident and if Buck had moved when he told him this wouldn't have happened. But Dave knew no amount of explaining or apologizing would help. Buck was right…it wasn't over. Buck's only means of dealing with something like this would be eventual retaliation and he wasn't one to succumb to reason or compromise. Dave knew that…everyone in the roundhouse knew that.

A sickening feeling began to well up in Dave's stomach…that sense of impending doom we all come to know when confronted by the bully. We think of how easily the problem could have been talked out and explained away or how trivial the whole matter was, but there's that certain breed of cats that seems to look for any reason to vent their frustrations and anxieties on those around them.

But the 'problem' wasn't the problem at all. The problem was Buck's life-learned attitude, from his father's overly strict physical discipline to the beatings Buck received from the older boys in his neighborhood. It was the only way Buck knew, but Dave could also see a certain sadistic pleasure Buck got from bullying and belittling those around him.

Dave knew Buck was stronger and definitely more aggressive than he was but, by God, he wasn't going to back down! He had seen others back down and he sensed the feelings of cowardice those men felt that lasted much longer than any cuts or bruises a fight could produce.

"That's all right," the others would say, "you're smart for not fighting that maniac."

But inside, those men knew they were seen as a little less in the eyes of their peers. Call it a primal thing or a manly attitude, it was still there and you wore it like a badge in the order of affairs at the roundhouse.

Dave and his apprentice continued to work on the coupling rods when Buck appeared.

"How's the ear?" Dave asked, knowing what the response would be.

"It hurts like hell," Buck grunted, "but it don't hurt any worse than you're gonna hurt when I kick your ass after work!"

"What do you mean, Buck?" Dave returned. "It was an accident."

"Well then, we'll just consider the whippin' I'm gonna lay on you an accident," Buck returned.

"Don't wimp out or I'll get you later!" he grunted, poking a finger in Dave's chest.

He left, strutting that cocky swagger of a bully, believing he could easily take Dave. Buck was shrewd about who he would pick to fight. Larger, tougher men could reason with him and those who had kin working for the railroad, who might gang him, were passed over. But loners like Dave were the ones who most often suffered Buck's wrath.

Dave continued to work on the engine, trying to keep his mind off what was coming. His stomach tightened when the 3:20 whistle blew. He loaded his tools on the tool cart and began pushing it back to the supply room.

Dick & Jimmy's Adventures at Glen Afton

"Hear there's gonna be a fight," two laborers noted as they passed him.

Yeah, Buck had spread the word. This was what he enjoyed and he wanted an audience for his little production. Some would be there to see if Buck's new opponent would fight or back down and others came because they were glad it wasn't them Buck would be thumping.

Dave washed his hands and face in the bathroom and paused to look at himself in the cracked, water stained mirror.

Well, old buddy, you might look a bit different tomorrow, he nervously thought to himself. At the locker room he put on his cap, grabbed his lunch pail, and tossed his coat over his shoulder. No sense putting this on yet, he thought.

Passing through the North gate, he looked over at his '36 Ford sedan in the shop parking lot.

Wonder what shape I'll be in when I drive you home? he pondered.

He noticed a group of men standing next to the north wall just out of sight of the gate guards. He walked over to where they were, thinking of just getting this whole damned thing over with.

"Well, Coleman, you didn't wimp out like I thought you would."

Buck's gravelly voice struck renewed fear into Dave, but he didn't show it.

"Look, Buck, its like Rouzer said, it was an accident," he explained, trying once again to avert this childish battle.

"Time for talkin's over, Coleman," Buck said as he began to remove his coat.

Dave surprised them all by tackling Buck and dropping him hard to the pavement. Buck let out a grunt, but easily threw him off. Being the more agile of the two, Dave got to his feet first and caught Buck with a haymaker that brought a cheer from the other men.

Buck countered by trying to tackle Dave, but he side-stepped him and nailed Buck with clenched fists to the back of his neck. Dave danced away, fighter-style as Buck came at him. Buck's brother Joe came from behind and pushed Dave into Buck, who caught him with a hard left-right, sending Dave's cap sailing. As he turned back, Buck caught him in the stomach and followed with an uppercut to his chin. Dave staggered backwards as blood flowed from his nose and chin.

Buck grinned as he continued his attack and the fight held even until Buck's superior strength finally overcame Dave's valiant efforts. Buck hovered over him like a predator over it's kill as he turned toward the men, seeking approval of his apparent victory.

"All right, you two, break it up," the company policemen ordered as they separated the two brawlers. The on-lookers groaned in disappointment as the police dispersed them. Satisfied he had won the day, Buck yelled an obscenity at Dave as he and his brother left for the parking lot. Jerry Wendt, Dave's neighbor, came over and helped him to his feet.

"You okay?" Jerry asked.

"Yeah," Dave replied, checking his jaw and teeth. "Nothing broken or loose."

"You were damn lucky the police showed up when they did." Jerry exclaimed. "I think Buck had a notion to do you in."

"Yeah," Dave returned, wiping the blood and spit from his face.

Buck peeled rubber out of the parking lot as Jerry helped Dave to his car.

"All the mentality of a pair of morons," Jerry noted. "You sure you're okay?"

"I'm alright," he said as he got in his car. "Thanks, Jerry."

Dave started the engine as he checked himself in the mirror. His left eye and upper lip were already beginning to swell but a sense of pride welled up inside of him as he wiped the blood off his face. Dave didn't like to fight, but he knew that there are occasions in our lives when we must face the bully that we all encounter from time to time.

(1941)

"Okay," Dave said to Danny in order to keep the peace. "Maybe a little shot would taste good about now."

He took the almost empty bottle from Danny, wiped the top with his hand and downed what little was left.

"Not bad," he said, looking at the bottle, feigning satisfaction in Danny's choice of whiskey.

"Ah, knock it off, Coleman," Buck scoffed. "We all know old Danny-boy here would drink anything that came out of a bottle."

"Got any more up at the house?" Joe inquired, his need for alcohol apparently not satisfied.

"No," Dave replied. "We don't keep any here because of the kids."

"Sounds like you folks here are kinda stuffy," Buck returned, "afraid of havin a little fun once in a while."

Like most of his cronies, Buck equated "good times" with liquor, loud mouths and brawling. Any other way was foreign to him…a waste of time.

"Supper's on," Bessie shouted from the kitchen

To Dave, Bessie's summon came at a welcome moment.

"Let's go eat, boys," he offered, as he headed to the trough to wash up.

Inside, the smell of rabbit stew and freshly baked bread filled the kitchen and perked up everyone's appetite. The baking was done on cool days such as this one to help take the chill off the cottage.

"Come on," Cass beckoned. "there's room for everyone.

This was literally true because of another of GW's creations. The round oak table that was left with the cottage never had enough room to seat everyone. It didn't take the old boy long to solve the problem. By sawing the table top in half, fastening a system of sliding supports on the underside, and building a set of interlocking extension boards he was able to lengthen the table to an amazing twelve feet. This came in handy with the ever-changing number of folks at Glen Afton.

After Aunt Bessie's blessing, which made the Grubb brothers noticeably uncomfortable, all present began enjoying the meal. Conversation was somewhat subdued due to the presence of Danny's rather undesirable guests.

"So, Buck, what's the word at the roundhouse?" GW inquired in an attempt to loosen things up.

"Same as always," Buck returned. "Noisy, dirty, and more work than can ever get done."

"Doesn't sound like you enjoy it much," Hat noted.

"Only enjoyment is gettin paid and teachin some lessons," he replied, skinning an eye toward Dave.

"Oh, then you mean you get satisfaction out of teaching the newcomers about your trade," Hat continued.

Joe caught himself in mid-laugh as he thought of what 'teaching lessons' meant to brother Buck.

Conversation continued on a polite level and Danny's amusing stories of the railroad brought only moderate laughter. Outside the sky continued to fill with dark, menacing clouds. A chilling breeze swept up off the river and across the lawn running its fingers through GW's garden as it continued upward, rustling the oak and maple leaves in the trees high above Glen Afton.

After dinner, the women cleared the table and began their clean-up chores while the men retired to the screened-in rear porch facing the Juniata.

"Looks like we might be in for a little rain," GW noted as Danny handed out cigars to all present.

"It'll miss a good chance if it doesn't, Georgie," Danny quipped with his usual grin and chuckle.

"Hey Gramps, how about we take the rest of those worms we dug and go fishing down at the dock," Dick called as he and Jimmy rounded the corner of the cottage.

"Good idea," he replied, not really enjoying the present company. "The cool air should help persuade those large mouth bass to start feeding."

He and the boys gathered their gear from the shed and headed toward the dock.

"Gonna get their butts soaked," Buck noted as he watched them leave.

"Maybe, but dad's right," Dave replied. "Cool breezes and a little rain usually does make the fish bite."

"How would he know?" Buck returned. "He supposed to be some kind of expert?"

"Dad's been fishing these waters quite a few years and he knows…"

"Yeah, sure," Buck interrupted. "Hey Danny, who's the little dolly that was sittin by Bessie and you at dinner?"

"That's Olive Lee, Dave's sister," he said.

"Not bad lookin for a Coleman," Buck noted. "She seein anyone?"

"I think she's dating a fella at Gamble's department store," Danny replied. "She works there as a secretary."

Buck didn't feel exceptionally welcome at Glen Afton and in situations like this his reaction was to become offensive.

"Always seems like those wimpy stuffed shirts gets all the good lookin gals," he grumbled as he rubbed his neck. "Those guys with their suits and cologne, they look mighty sweet all dressed up but they ain't real men like us that works for a livin, right, Danny?"

"Well, those guys work in their own way, I guess," Danny answered nervously.

"I'll bet if Miss Olive got to know a man like me, she'd soon change her mind about guys like that," Buck noted.

Dave began to get those same feelings he felt when he and Buck first tangled.

Fay carried the vegetable peelings and table scraps out to the compost heap beside the garden while Olive Lee toted the dishwater out to the flowers around the springhouse. Buck spotted her and decided to make his move.

Olive Lee finished dumping the dishwater and noticed Buck approaching as she headed back to the cottage. Her stomach tightened as he came closer. His coarse manners and obvious stares at dinner didn't go unnoticed and she found nothing desirable in this rough-looking friend of her brother-in-law.

"Hey Olive," he called, flashing his crooked smile, "how about me and you going for a little walk after you're done?"

"I don't think so," she replied, "it looks like rain."

"Ah, a little rain won't hurt nothin," he said, "besides, little girls are made of sugar and spice, but you're a grown woman."

"I just don't want to get wet," she replied.

"Look, maybe it won't rain after all and even if it does, we could come runnin back," Buck argued.

"No thanks," she replied as she disappeared into the kitchen.

Just like a Coleman, Buck thought to himself, *thinks she's too damned good for the likes of me.*

Frustrated, Buck joined the other men who were standing on the edge of the lawn overlooking the river.

"What's a the matter with your little sister, Dave?" he complained. "She too good to take a walk with me?"

"It's like Danny said," he reminded him, "she's dating a fellow and…"

"Look, I just want to take a little walk, not marry her," he growled, becoming even more agitated.

Buck turned to Danny.

"You go talk to her, Danny," he insisted. "You could help her see I'm an okay guy."

"I'll try," he reluctantly agreed, "but you know how stubborn women can be."

"Just do it, Danny boy," Buck insisted, patting him on the back.

The sky grew darker and rain seemed assured as the wind continued to pick up.

Damn you, Danny, Dave thought as he watched him walk toward the cottage. *Why did you bring these trouble-makers down here?*

"You think Buck ain't good enough for your prissy little sister, don't you," Joe said smugly.

"I never said that, Joe," Dave replied, "but Olive Lee's allowed to decide who she wants to be with."

"Are you sayin she doesn't want to be with me?" Buck snarled. "She said it was because of the rain and not wantin to get wet."

"Yeah, that's probably it," Dave added, trying to cool the situation. "You know how girls are, they don't like getting their hair wet unless they're washing it."

"Cass says they're gonna be busy for a while, cleaning up and all, "Danny explained, half grinning.

"Well now, is that right?" Buck replied, becoming even more agitated.

"Yeah,' Danny stuttered, "and it is beginning to rain, so...."

"So if yer old man can fish in the rain it won't hurt your stuck-up little sister to take a stroll, now will it," Buck countered as he began walking toward the cottage.

Joe was all smiles, anticipating what was coming.

Damn, Dave thought, *here we go again.* He trotted ahead of the agitated Buck and stopped him.

"Let it alone, Buck," he tried to reason. "We don't want any trouble."

"Ain't gonna be no trouble if that stuck-up sister of yours just takes a little walk with me."

"She said she doesn't want to walk," Dave replied sternly, "now give it a rest!"

Buck squared himself with Dave, looking him in the eye.

"You gonna be your sister's protector, are you?" he growled.

"Seems I remember you got your ass kicked once before, so move before it happens again!" Buck shouted, shoving him away.

Realizing how volatile the situation was becoming, he grabbed Buck's arm in an attempt to reason with him but Buck reeled and backhanded him across the face.

"You want some more of this, do you?" he shouted as he shoved Dave aside and headed for the cottage.

Seeing they had reached the point of no return, Dave grabbed him by the shoulder and as he turned, he slammed his fist into Buck's stomach. He groaned as Dave caught him with a roundhouse that sent him staggering. *Finish him quick while you've got the chance,* he thought as he hammered him with one blow after another until Buck fell to the ground.

Dave prepared to finish him when he felt a sharp blow to the back of his head that put him on all fours. He looked around and saw Joe with a piece of firewood in his hand. Dazed, but furious, Dave jumped to his feet. As he faced him, Joe threatened again with the firewood, but his eyes revealed his cowardice and seeing the rage on Dave's face, he backed away.

"Hey, hey, come on, fellas, let's stop this," Danny pleaded, his hands raised and trembling.

The commotion drew the women to the porch. Fear and disbelief encompassed them as they watched in horror. As Dave turned away from Joe, Buck's punch to his jaw sent him reeling.

"Look, this is crazy!" Danny pleaded. "What are you doing?"

By now the women were on the lawn, yelling for them to stop. Dave looked at them and dropped his hands in compliance, but Buck took the opportunity and began hammering him.

"Sucker punch me, will you!" he yelled as he continued to pummel Dave.

GW and the boys looked at one another as the shouts and yells reached the dock. They dropped their rods and ran for the stairs and as they reached the top, Dick and Jimmy stopped dead in their tracks. The surreal scene of screaming women and fighting men burned into their minds. They had never witnessed anything like this, especially in their families.

While the boys stood frozen, GW ran past them and shouted for the men to stop as he continued toward the cottage. Dave and Buck were still toe to toe, slugging it out, both of their faces covered in blood and spit.

"Do something, Danny!" Kit cried to her immobilized husband. "Make them stop!"

Danny stood there, pleading.

Again Joe came from behind grabbing Dave around the neck and pulling him backwards to the ground. Buck seized the moment and jumped on him, driving his knees into his chest as Dave let out a painful yell.

"Damn it, Danny, help him!" Cass shouted.

Danny stepped closer to the fighting men and pleaded for them to stop. Unable to stand it any longer, Cass and Russell jumped in and tried to pull the men apart.

"Stop it," Cass cried, tears streaming down her face. "You're going to kill him!"

Dick, now realizing the seriousness of the situation, ran to his parents aide with Jimmy close behind.

"Let him alone!" Dick shouted as he jumped onto Buck's back.

Buck reached around to grab Dick when the twelve-gauge shotgun blast split the air, sending a shower of twigs, lead, and oak leaves down upon the fracas.

"Get off him!" GW shouted as he lowered his shotgun toward the men.

For a moment everything was dead still.

Buck got up and let out an oath.

"One more word out of you, Grubb, and you'll look like a watermelon with the seeds pulled out!" GW warned.

"Now, you and Joe get up that trail," he continued as he reloaded.

Slowly the brothers complied.

"As a matter of fact, I'll just escort you two to the railroad," he said.

Semi-conscious, Dave groaned and grabbed his chest, wincing in pain.

"Oh, Dave," Cass cried as she cradled her husband's head in her lap.

"Easy, boy," Bessie warned, "just lay there while we check the damage."

She took out her hanky and wiped the blood off his hands and face, revealing a few cuts.

"He doesn't look too bad," Cass noted.

"No, no he doesn't," Kit nervously agreed, wiping the tears from her face.

"We better check his head where that coward Joe whacked him," Hat noted, her voice full of concern and disgust.

"Hang on, dear, while we roll you over," Cass said softly.

Dave groaned as they slowly rolled him on to his stomach.

"Easy," Bessie cautioned. "you might have some broken ribs."

Eventually they got Dave to his feet and helped him to the cottage. Once there, Cass washed out the wound on the back of his head which was still bleeding.

"We're going to need Doc Peterson," she said, noticing the depth of the wound.

"I'll go get him," Danny offered.

"No!" Cass said with an icy stare, "you've done enough already!"

"Dick, you and Jimmy go fetch the Doctor," she instructed. "He lives in Thompsontown."

"It's okay, Mom," Dick cut in, eying his uncle, "we'll find him."

"Better take a lantern," Bessie advised.

The sky grew more foreboding as evening approached.

"Don't you two ever come around here again," GW instructed the brothers as they reached the railroad.

He moved closer with his shotgun raised.

"And if you've a mind to come back, this scattergun will do all the talkin' that's necessary," he added in a quieter, deeper voice

The brothers looked at each other and then back at GW. They paused for a moment, then turned and started for Millerstown. GW watched until the two were out of sight and as he turned to head back he noticed a flickering yellow light winding its way up the spring path.

"Where are you boys going?" he inquired.

"Going up to Thompsontown to fetch Doc Peterson," Dick replied in a quivering voice. "Aunt Bessie says Dad needs stitches and he might have some busted ribs."

The old timer sensed the pain in his grandson's voice.

"Come here, Dick," he said.

There was a note of seriousness in his grandfather's voice Dick had rarely heard.

"Those two I just sent packin are solely responsible for what happened today," he explained. "Now I know some here are going to want to blame your Uncle Danny…"

"He brought them here!" Dick said, half crying. "They're his friends! He didn't even try to help Dad. He's a damn coward!"

"Your Uncle didn't mean any harm to come to no one," his grandfather replied. "Sometimes he just does things without thinking."

"Those two are the ones you should be angry with," he said, pointing his gun down the tracks,

A cool drizzle began to fall as the night grew darker. It felt refreshing against Dick's hot face, but the anger he felt towards his uncle still showed.

"Your uncle learned a mighty harsh lesson tonight," his Grandfather assured, "and it's going to take him awhile to deal with it."

"It's going to take Dad awhile to get over his pain too," Dick said, choking back his tears. "I want to do to him what they did to my Dad."

"I know, but there's something you should know about your uncle," his Grandfather replied. "Believe it or not, Danny looks up to your father and he wouldn't have had this happen to him for the world."

"Then why didn't he help him?" Dick asked.

GW thought for a moment.

"I guess it's not in some folk's nature to fight, even when the time calls for it," he replied.

"I don't know," Dick said, not able to grasp all of what his grandfather meant.

"There's a lot of pain being felt here tonight," his Grandfather added, "you, your Dad, Danny…all of us."

The old man put his hand on his grandson's shoulder.

"We're family, son," he continued, "and we're going to have to pull together to get through this."

He looked deep into Dick's tear-stained face. "And that includes your Uncle Danny."

GW hesitated as he looked at the boys.

"You two go fetch the Doc now."

He turned and headed down the spring path. The drizzle turned into a soft, steady rain. The raindrops hissed and steamed on the hot, smoke-stained stack of the kerosene lantern as the boys trudged on toward Thompsontown.

"What are you thinking?" Jimmy asked.

Dick hesitated for a moment.

"I don't know what to think," he replied. "I still see Uncle Danny as a coward and I hate him for not helping Dad."

"But like your Grandpa said, he didn't start the trouble," Jimmy reminded him. "It was those two brothers, and your uncle did try to stop it…kinda."

Dick didn't reply.

The cold rain persisted causing the boys to shiver as they continued toward town.

GW returned to the cottage and helped move Dave upstairs to the men's bedroom.

"You sure those two are gone?" Cass inquired, with a hint of doubt in her voice.

"I watched them walking towards Millerstown until they were out of sight," GW assured.

"I wouldn't put it past those two birds to double-back here lookin for more trouble." Bessie insisted.

"Alright, alright," GW said, "if it'll make you feel any better I'll go to Millerstown in the morning and make sure they caught the train back to Altoona."

"We sure enough got our licks in on him this time," Joe claimed as the brothers trudged toward Millerstown. "Ain't likely he'll be wantin to fool with us any time soon."

"Sometimes you just have to teach a man a lesson," Buck acknowledged, with his crooked smile. "After all, I was just tryin to have a little fun with his stuck-up sister… didn't mean no harm."

"Not unless she was willin", Joe added with a smirk.

"Well, that might've changed things," Buck returned with a lusty chuckle.

They picked up their pace as the rain continued to fall.

Chapter 9
JUST DESSERTS

As Buck and Joe walked toward town the three hobo jack-rollers watched from the trees where they were holed up for the night. They were still licking their wounds from the beating they had received at the hobo jungle and were itching to take it out on anyone who might happen along.

Jake Rhodes, a large, tough, seasoned hobo was the self-appointed leader of the trio. Mick Brunette, was of medium build and the most educated of the three. Sal Peters was a tall lanky, raw-boned hobo who went along with whatever Jake and Mick agreed to do.

"Think those two morons got any money?" Mick asked in a hushed voice.

"Only one way to find out," Jake replied as they started across the tracks toward the Grubb brothers.

"Easy now, just a few more turns," Doc Peterson assured as he completed wrapping Dave's chest. "You'll want you to come to my office in about a week so I can remove those stitches. In the mean time dab a little alcohol on those cuts to ward off any infection."

"You sure he's going to be alright?" Cass asked.

"Yeah," he replied, "his ribs don't appear to be broken, just bruised. Take it easy for a while, Dave."

"The way I feel, that won't be hard to do," Dave returned while rubbing his chest.

"You consider pressing charges against those two, Dave?" the doctor inquired.

He though for a moment.

"No…no, it would only make things worse when I get back to the roundhouse," he noted, "and that would give Buck a reason to start another fight."

"Now don't go telling your dad any jokes," the doctor teased Dick. "He'll be feeling enough pain for a while without trying to laugh."

"Not much to laugh about around here," Dick said, as he glared at his uncle.

Danny's quick wit and smile were gone now. He turned and went down stairs to the living room with Kit following him.

"Danny," she said, "are you all right?"

He stood in the darkened room, staring out the window toward the spot where it had all taken place. It wasn't like Danny to stand so still and his gesturing hands were mute as he held on to the window sill.

"I guess I showed them what kind of man I am," he said as tears welled up in his eyes.

"You didn't know they would do something like that," Kit said, trying to console her husband, "and you did try to stop it…in your own way."

"No, no…I should have jumped in…I should have…"

"And then there would've been one more for the doctor to mend," Kit replied.

"Better than Dave taking it all." he said as he took out his handkerchief and wiped his eyes.

"I should've remembered about that scuffle Dave and Buck had a few years back," he contended. "Sure, Buck and Joe are characters, but I never thought they would cause any trouble down here."

He turned toward his wife, now gesturing with his hands.

"You see, Kit, those boys never had much of anything good in their lives," he explained. "I've always loved this place, with its beauty and its seclusion and I was hoping they would see it that way too. I was only trying to show them something good, something…"

"I know, I know," Kit assured, holding her husband as he wept.

Dick was beginning to understand what his grandfather meant about Danny's pain as he watched from the darkened hallway. But the image burned indelibly into his mind of that day wouldn't let him relinquish the animosity he felt toward his Uncle.

GW arrived at Wagner's store in Millerstown at 9:00 the next morning.

"Hey Stacky," he greeted his neighbor as he walked in the store.

"Hey, old timer," Clare returned as he continued polishing the big red delicious apple on his bib overhauls.

"What are you huntin with that scattergun this time of day?" he asked.

"Just keepin an eye out for varmints," he replied. "Is Jess around?"

"He's in the back checkin on some inventory," Clare answered as he bit into the crisp juicy fruit.

GW walked to the back of the store.

"Ain't no varmints in there," Clare added, noting GW didn't leave his shotgun outside. "You fixin on robbin ole Jesse?"

"Robbin' him of what?" he returned.

Clare laughed understandingly.

Jesse Wagner had a monopoly on the grocery trade in Millerstown before his wife, Martha passed away. That was when both the store and train station became too much for Jesse to manage by himself. The new super-market that opened up two years previous was more centrally located for most folks and that suited Jesse just fine, being that he now considered himself semi-retired. He still managed the train station which meant taking care of the mail service twice a day plus a few occasional passengers. He stocked some cans and dry goods and home-baked wares the widow Shaffer brought in from time to time. There was always a market for those items.

"What are you needing, George, some ammunition?" he asked.

Jesse was a tall, skinny drink of water, bent and stoop-shouldered from years of carrying groceries, baggage and mail sacks. He sported a thin border of gray hair that circumvented his bald head. A pair of wire-rimmed glasses perched on the end of his long bird-like nose afforded him the luxury of looking over them at you in a condescending manner whenever he felt the situation called for it. He was always dressed in the proper garb of a retailer with his green visor, crisp white apron, red vest and matching arm bands.

"No, I have all the ammo I need," GW replied, his tone becoming more somber.

"I wanted to find out if anyone boarded a train last night or this morning for Altoona."

"Yes, as a matter of fact, " Jesse replied, "and it was the strangest thing."

"How so?" GW asked.

"Well, I got here early this morning as usual to open the place up, you know, and here are these two characters, hobos I took'em for, sleepin on my benches. Well, I rousted them and was about to tell them to move along when I recognized them as the fellas that were with your daughter and her husband. Seems I remember them buying some of Mrs. Shaffer's baked goods before they left yesterday."

"Yeah, yeah, go on," GW urged.

"Anyhow the bigger one got a little hot, said they were railroad men and had train passes," Jesse continued. "That's when I noticed."

"Noticed what?"

"That they were in a bad way," he replied. "I mean they were cut and bruised something awful!"

"What did they say?" GW questioned.

"The smaller one couldn't talk at all, looked like someone smacked him in the face with baseball bat and his jaw and neck were covered with dried blood."

"What about the other one," GW asked.

"He did all the talkin' but I could tell that he was in some serious pain," Jesse continued. "He held his left arm like it was broken and his right eye was swollen clean shut."

"They say what happened?"

"Said they were jumped by some hobos and that they beat and robbed them," Jesse said. "He said it happened about a mile up the tracks last night around dusk."

"You see anything up there when you came by this morning?" Jesse asked.

"No," GW replied, "but I'll have a closer look when I go back."

"The big one sat there and had the other one removed his right shoe." Jesse continued. "He took out their railroad passes and handed them to me."

"Uh huh," GW replied, rubbing his chin.

"They got on the 7:40 run," Jesse noted. "I told them they should stop in Thompsontown and see Doc Peterson, but the big one insisted they could make it to Altoona."

"I'll be darned," GW said in a hushed voice.

"You know those two, George?" he asked.

"Yeah, I do," he replied. "They were friends of my son-in-law."

"Looked like a pair of bad apples to me," Jesse claimed.

"You got that right, Jesse," GW assured. "Yesterday they caused a ruckus down at the cottage, beat up on Dave for no good reason, and stirred up the whole family. That's when me and Betsy here sent them packin."

"Dave okay?" Jesse asked.

"Couple of bruised ribs and a nasty cut on the back of his head," he said. "other than that he seems alright."

The shrill whistle from the express out of Lewistown cut through the cool morning air. The distant, rhythmic sounds of the steam pistons and smoke stack of the K-4 engine prompted Jesse to head for the station platform.

"Time for the mail," he said as he grabbed the leather mail pouch and trotted up the steps to the postal pick-up stand. He hooked the upper yoke clamp to the top of the bag and the lower clamp to the bottom and with both hands he swung the pick-up arm out toward the mainline until it locked into place.

"There, all set," he declared as he returned to where Clare and GW were standing.

The engineer waved as the speeding train roared through the station. When the mail car came by, a postal worker on board pushed the V-shaped grab arm out and in a flash it snatched the waiting mail pouch from its yoke. In one smooth motion the postal worker swiveled the V-arm receiver into the car and with his free arm tossed the incoming mail sack onto the station platform. The three men looked at each other and smiled in admiration at the postman's unique ability. The seven trailing passenger cars were filled with vacationers from the Altoona, Johnstown and Pittsburgh area and were headed for the coast and the promise of a good time at the Atlantic beach resorts. Some smiled and waved as the sleek train clattered by on its eastward journey. The men stood and watched until it was out of sight.

"Well, I'd better be gettin' back," GW stated.

"Hold on," Clare called out, grabbing his crutches. "I'll walk along in case those renegades try to jump you."

"And what do you intend to do?" GW teased," beat them with your crutches?"

"You'd be surprised what I can do with these two hickories," Clare snapped, "and keep on gettin' lippy, you just might find out!"

The two men made their way back to their homes all the while eyeing the forest for signs of the hoboes. Upon entering the lawn at Glen Afton, GW noticed his eldest son was up and walking around.

"Feelin any better, Dave?" he asked.

"A little stiff and sore," he replied, "but I think I'll make it."

"Those two maggots leave?" Bessie inquired from the front porch,

"Jesse said they caught the 7:40 run this morning," he replied.

"Too bad a freight didn't catch them last night," she added cryptically as she turned and went back into the kitchen.

"Well," GW replied with a bit of a smile, "you might just say one did."

Chapter 10

RENEGADE HOBOS

The three renegade hoboes slunk back into the woods where they had slept that night.

"Well, at least we got forty dollars from them two losers last night," Mick remarked. "That'll stay us for a while."

"It ain't gonna stay us for too awful long," Jake replied. "We need to hit on somethin better than jack-rollin…something that'll set us up for a year or more."

"How about bustin into huntin camps where no one's at like we did a couple of years back?" Sal suggested.

Jake smacked him across the head with his hat.

"Cept if you remember, you lunk-head, when no one's around, there ain't much money around either," Jake reminded him.

The three walked back to the tracks and headed for Thompsontown.

"No boys, we need to get our hands on some cash," Jake declared, "some cash and maybe some jewelry. That's the ticket, cash and jewelry, easy to carry, easy to fence, easy to stash."

"Only way to do that is to rob folks in their homes," Mick noted.

"No, that's too risky," Jake surmised. "You might find nothin of value and find the folks grabbin for a gun and blastin us."

"Yeah and if they see us," Sal added, "they can tell the law who we was."

"Yeah, yeah, that's true enough," Jake replied as he lit one of Buck Grubb's cigars. Nearby a song sparrow lit in a maple tree and began singing out several variations of its lovely song. Annoyed, Jake picked up a rock and threw it at the tiny songster.

"Damn noisy thing," he growled.

The rock barely missed the hapless little creature, sending it winging off to share its music with others more appreciative. Jake continued to mull over their situation and soon a broad, yellow toothed grin spread across his stubbled face.

"But they can't finger you if they ain't seen you," he observed.

"Now how do you reckon on doing that?" Mick asked.

"Easy," Jake answered, "we stake out a place that looks like they got money, then we wait for our chance to grab one of them."

"You mean kidnapping?" Mick replied.

"Yeah, kidnapping," Jake said, "and it's best to snatch a kid cause nothin makes a person more willin to cough up some dough than to think their kid could get hurt."

"Yeah, and kids would be easy to handle," Sal replied.

"How do we keep the kid from seeing us?" Mick questioned.

"We grab them from behind and pull a sack over their head," Jake explained, "and even if they get a quick look at us they'd be too scared to remember anything."

"Right," Sal agreed, "and maybe we could disguise ourselves."

Jake and Mick look at each other in disbelief.

"No, Sally boy, that won't be necessary," Jake assured him.

"All right, we'll work it this way," Jake began. "Sal, you're the best at sneakin around. You'll do the nabbin. Mick, since you can write good, you make up the ransom note. We'll put it on the door or someplace where they'd be sure to find it."

"What do you want me to put on this note?" Mick inquired.

"Just tell them we got their kid and if they want to see them again to get all the money and jewels they got and bring it to a place we'll have picked out."

"That's no good," Mick replied. "What if they bring the law?"

"That's right," Jake replied, puffing his cigar.

"How bout this," Sal suggests. "We tell 'em not to bring the law or the kid gets it."

"No way!" Mick exclaimed. "I don't mind robbin' but I ain't takin no part in killing anyone, specially a kid."

"Relax, Mickey boy, we ain't gonna kill no one," Jake assured him. "Ole Jake here ain't in no need of a murder rap hangin over his head anymore'n you."

"What's your job gonna be, Jake?" Mick asked.

"Yeah," Sal said, "what're you gonna be doin while all this is goin on?"

"I was gettin to that, boys," he replied. "I'll keep a watch on the spot where we tell 'em to bring the money and when they drop it and clear out, I'll grab it for us."

"What about the kid?" Mick questioned.

"How about we just take the kid back later on and let him go?" Sal suggests.

"I guess we could do that," Jake surmises.

"Wait a minute," Mick replied, "what if the kid takes off runnin and screamin to the house and they come after us before we get a chance to hightail it out of there?"

"Good point, Mick," Jake agreed.

Again they puffed their cigars and pondered the problem.

"I know," Sal said excitedly, "we take them into the woods about a block or so from their home and then shove them up a tree with the sack still on their head. Then we tell 'em not to come down till they know it's daylight and that we'll be watchin and give them a good thrashin if they do."

Jake and Mick look at one another in surprise.

"Well, it appears there are some brains in that hat rack you call a head," Jake claimed as he slapped Sal on the back.

Jake put his arms around his two cohorts and pulled them close.

"If this plan of ours works out the way I'm thinkin it will," he mused, "we'll soon be livin the good life and havin us some high times, eh boys?"

They agreed and soon plans were made for their first venture into kidnapping.

Brighton Acres near Harrisburg is one of the finer neighborhoods near Pennsylvania's capital city. Its expansive hilltop location on the western shore of the Susquehanna River provides its privileged residents with a spectacular view of the river and city while the gently sloping wooded terraces gave it an air of detachment from the hustle and bustle of the metropolis below.

But unbeknown to its residents, this sense of quiet seclusion also afforded Brighton Acres a certain vulnerability that Jake and company would soon attempt to exploit. The renegades hunched down in the thick brush that surrounded the stately three-story Georgian home. The forested development provided plenty of cover for the trio to hide and plan their day's work.

"This looks like a good place to start our little venture," Jake declared.

"Yeah," Mick agreed. "It's off by itself and there's kid's toys all over the yard."

"And it sure smells of money, don't it?" Sal added.

Jake and Mick chuckled and nodded in agreement.

"Okay," Jake said, rubbing his hands together, "now we just sit back and wait for junior to come out and play and then we'll let the fun begin."

An hour later Janet Edwards came on to the patio to shake out her dust mop. Soon two six-year old boys burst through the patio door and ran down the stairs into the yard.

"You two be careful," she warned.

"We will, Mom," the blonde-haired boy said as the two mounted their red see-saw.

"That's the one we want," Jake stated, pointing to the blonde boy.

"Why that one?" Sal asked.

"Because that's the one that called her mom," Jake explained. "I figure the other one's just a neighbor's kid."

"But how do we nab him without the other one seeing us," Sal questioned.

"We'll just bide our time, Sallie," Jake replied. "It'll all work out."

The boys played for an hour.

"I have to go to the bathroom, Billy," the dark-haired boy said as he headed for the house.

"Here comes our chance," Jake whispered.

"I'm coming too," Billy announced.

"Damn," Mick said in a hushed voice.

"Now, now…just be a tad patient, boys," Jake advised. "Our chance will come."

The three renegades continued to wait and watch and soon the boys returned and resumed their play. Two hours later a car pulled up in front of the house and soon after Janet stepped out on the patio.

"Harry," she called, "your mother is here."

"All right," was his reluctant reply as he headed for the house.

"I'll see you tomorrow, Billy," he shouted as he bounded up the patio stairs.

"See you," Billy returned.

"This could be it," Jake said.

Once Harry and Mrs. Edwards were inside Sal took up his position outside the fence. He waited until the unsuspecting boy's back was turned and engrossed in his play.

Then, with the stealth of a cat, he quietly jumped the fence and moved in behind the unwary lad. With one quick move he slipped the sack over the boys head, covered his mouth and carried him to the fence where Jake and Mick were waiting. Billy kicked and struggled to no avail as Sal handed the bagged boy to Jake and took the ransom note from Mick. In a flash he crossed the yard, bounded up the patio stairs and tacked the note to the railing. He shot back across the yard, hopped the fence and in a moment the three were gone.

"You're home early, honey," Janet remarked as she kissed her husband.

"We managed to finish that pesky Vipond proposal a day ahead of schedule," Brent replied, "so I gave John and myself the rest of the day off."

"I couldn't help but notice how tense you've been these last few weeks, Janet said. "That must be a load off your mind to get that done."

"You're right about that, but we're lucky to have any clients the way the economy is these days," Brent returned. "Why don't we take Billy out to dinner and catch that new Disney movie he's been talking about."

"Sounds great," she said as she walked out to the patio.

"Billy!" she called. "Billy, where are you?"

Janet looked across the yard. All was quiet and ominously still. She began to feel uneasy and was about to call out again when her hand touched something on the patio railing. She picked up the note and began to read it.

"Oh...oh no!" she screamed. "Billy, where are you?"

"Looks like Mom found our little love note," Jake said with a grin as the three moved deeper into the woods with their prey.

"What's the matter?" Brent asked as he came running onto the patio.

"Billy's gone!" she cried. "I...I found this note."

Brent read it in disbelief.

WE GOT YOUR KID. DONT CALL POLICE OR YOULL NEVER SEE HIM AGAIN. GET MONEY AT BANK. TONITE AT TWELVE TAKE IT AND WIFES JEWELRY TO THAT POND BEHIND DUFFYS STORE. WALK PATH BEHIND THE POND TO THE FORK. LEFT TO THE BRIGE. PUT IT ALL UNDER BRIDGE AND LEAVE! BETTER COME ALONE OR THE KID GETS IT! WE'LL BE WATCHING!

"I...I can't believe this!" Brent said in a stunned voice. "Wasn't he out there playing?"

"Yes...yes," Janet returned, trying to remain calm. "I just checked on him a little while ago."

Brent went down the patio stairs, ran across the yard and began searching along the fence, his mind racing.

How could this happen? he thought to himself. *Billy and his friends always seemed so safe playing out here in their own back yard.*

Brent continued to search, looking for a sign, anything to give him a clue as to what happened.

"Here!" he shouted to Janet as he noticed trampled grass and a broken trail leading into the woods. "Here's where they took him!"

He hopped the fence and began his pursuit.

"No, Brent!" Janet yelled. "You don't know how many there are and they might be armed."

Brent pulled up short, knowing she was right. Frustration and helplessness welled up inside him…he clenched his fists in anger.

"Damn it!" he yelled as he crossed the yard and returned to the house.

"I'll call the police," he said as he went for the phone.

"No, Brent," she warned. "If we call the police the note says they would…they would…" Janet broke down in tears, sobbing uncontrollably as Brent took her in his arms.

"It's all right….it's going to be okay," he said soothingly.

"Oh Brent, let's just do what they want," she sobbed. "I couldn't bear it if anything happened to our little boy."

"All right," he said, looking at his watch. "There's still time to get to the bank."

Later that night Billy's Father did what the renegades wanted.

"Easy pickens, eh boys?" Jake whispered, as the three watched from their hiding place.

Brent came to the bridge and cautiously looked around. The crescent moon dimly lit the surrounding landscape, but not enough to expose the loathsome trio and their victim.

Brent placed the small sack under the bridge and after taking another hopeful look around, he reluctantly left.

Jake quickly retrieved their ill-gotten booty as soon as Brent was gone.

"How much, Jake?" Mick asked.

"Looks like about five hundred and some nice looking jewelry," he replied.

"Not bad for a snot-nosed kid," Mick stated.

Jake and Sal nodded in agreement.

"Now, to take care of junior," Jake remarked as they turned their attention to the helpless lad.

The moon in the clear, night sky lit the woods enough for them to find what they were looking for. The small Maple with a low hanging limb fit the bill to a tee. Jake shoved the gagged and blindfolded boy up on the limb.

"Grab hold there!" he instructed as he put Billy's hands around the small trunk.

"Now, you stay up there till you hear the mornin birds a singin," he ordered.

"We'll be watchin so don't move or we'll come back and give you a good thrashin!" Jake growled as he gave him a shake. "You hear me, Billy boy?"

Billy nodded in mute compliance. The three renegades disappeared into the night, quite pleased with themselves and their new found vocation.

Chapter 12

GARDEN INTRUDER

The tell-tell signs were there... tracks in the soft earth around the garden's borders, the neatly dug hole under the chicken wire fence, and the produce missing from several plants. This evidence let GW know something else was enjoying his prized garden.

A faint rustling noise at the garden's far end told him his adversary was in residence. Quickly he made for the cottage and returned with his trusty twelve-gauge double-barrel shotgun. Listening intently, he quietly entered through the garden gate as experienced hunter's eyes slowly swept across the rows of plants as he waited in silence. A fly buzzed around his head and locusts sang out as the sun grew hotter in the noon-day sky. Faint sounds of laughter floated across the lawn from the bathers at the dock. GW was alone with his adversary and that was just the way he preferred it.

The waiting continued for several minutes. Eventually he heard a noise over in the pole-bean patch and the old fellow carefully positioned himself for a better view.

Realizing he was being stalked, the large brown rodent made a move toward his escape hole. Two shots rang out causing green beans and leaves to fly! The ground-hog quickly changed direction and made for a denser part of the garden. GW reloaded and moved slowly to the right, giving the his adversary clear access to his escape route.

With gun ready he moved forward to flush out the intruder.

The hog made his move and two more shots rang out sending a spray of red tomato juice and vines into the air! Again, GW reloaded, took hasty aim and fired, mulching several cucumber plants and a partially ripe melon.

Reaching his escape hole, the groundhog wriggled under the fence and started across the lawn. At the fence GW's initial shot popped a large divot out of the yard, but a second well-placed round ended the furry rodent's produce-stealing days forever.

That evening, the family dined on succulent par-boiled, pan fried ground-hog.

"This is one tasty ground-hog, Dad," Russell declared.

"But tell us, now," he continued, with a smile, "when do you figure on replanting?"

"Aw, I didn't do that much damage," he insisted without looking up from his meal. "Besides, this has to be the best ground-hog I've eaten in a while."

All nodded in agreement as they continued to enjoy that evening's meal.

Chapter 12
TAYLORS ARRIVE

"Hello, anyone up over there? Hello!"

The voice, accompanied by an occasional shrill whistle, carried across the Juniata on the still morning air from the far shore. Cass awoke and got out of bed. Pulling on her robe she headed up stairs to the men's bedroom.

"Dave, get up," Cass urged in a hushed voice.

"Huh...wha...what is it?"

"Someone's calling from across the river."

"What time is it?" he said, rubbing the night's sleep from his eyes.

"It's 6:00," she replied as her eyes adjusted to the luminescent dials on the Baby Ben alarm clock.

"Okay, okay, I'll see who it is," he muttered as he slid his feet out from under the sheets and on to the bare pine floor.

Again, the voice echoed across the lock. "Hello, anyone up over there?"

Cass's face lit up.

"That sounds like Bud," she exclaimed.

Bud Taylor, Dave's best friend from his old Altoona neighborhood, was Cass's favorite of all her husband's acquaintances. He was a tall, handsome man of forty, slim and ramrod straight, the perfect model of a Navy Lieutenant.

Dave quickly pulled on his pants and shoes and headed for the river. His chest and head were healing well from the wounds from three weeks ago.

The cool morning air helped clear the sleep from his head but the morning fog which blanketed the area gave little evidence as to who was on the far shore.

"Well, hello there!" he shouted as he descended the switch-back stairs. The fog was off the river and Dave could see it was who Cass had presumed. He quickly untied the Hoffman and proceeded to row across the Juniata.

The surface of the early morning river was mirror smooth, disturbed only by the progress of the large wooden craft. The fog hung in still silence six feet above the waters, a silence broken only by the clicking of the oars in their oarlocks.

"When did you folks decide to come visit?" Dave asked as he neared the shore.

"I received an unexpected vacation when my ship blew one of its starboard boilers," Bud replied. "We were twenty miles out of San Diego and had to limp back into port."

The Taylor family boarded the boat as Bud and Dave shook hands and began stowing their gear. Bud insisted on rowing back. Dave sat at the stern with Bud's wife, Marie, while their children, Buddy and Hayla, sat on the bow seat.

Bud, a career Navy man, met Marie at the U.S.O. club while stationed in San Deigo. She was a strikingly attractive woman, tall and slender with long, wavy blonde hair and large blue eyes. Although somewhat reserved in character and conversation, she was always a welcome addition at Glen Afton.

"So, how long are you planning to stay?" Dave asked.

"About two weeks," he said, "but don't worry, we brought along extra cash. We didn't come to mooch,"

"Now you two know you're always welcome here regardless of any finances," Dave returned.

He meant what he said because, unlike some of the guests at Glen Afton, Bud and Marie always pulled their weight when they visited.

"How deep is this river?" Buddy asked. He was a stocky lad of fourteen, the kind that clothing salesmen refer to as husky. Dave noticed that he looked much like his Father did at that age.

"Oh, it varies from about a foot in the rapids to about four feet in the lock, but you have to be careful," he cautioned. "There are some holes and washouts that can go as deep as ten feet."

"Anything dangerous in there?" Hayla asked with a wary glance over the side. Her flowing blonde hair, long limbs and developing figure belied her age of thirteen years.

"Well, I'll tell you, Hayla,' Dave continued, "I've fished and swam in these waters for nigh on to ten years and I've yet to be bitten by anything bigger than a horse fly."

All present laughed politely .

Dick & Jimmy's Adventures at Glen Afton

Dick and Jimmy bounded across the sun-dappled lawn, their bare feet covered with morning dew and grass clippings from GW's yard work the day before. They were up early, preparing to enjoy the 'Morning Invigorates'. The first day at Glen Afton, Dick's grandfather had explained this ritual to them. It consisted of going into the Juniata while the air was still much cooler than the water. Upon coming out of the river your skin tingled and you shivered in the brisk morning air.

"Nothing better to get a man awake and ready for the day's activities," GW explained to them.

Indeed, the boys found it to be quite exhilarating and so they made it a regular part of their morning routine. Dave was leading Bud's family up the stairs as Dick and Jimmy started down. The boys were surprised to see new arrivals so early in the morning.

Dick and Hayla's eyes met briefly as they passed.

"Hi," Hayla greeted.

"Hello," Dick returned, without thinking.

All at once, for no apparent reason, Dick's descent slowed and he found himself turning to watch this new-comer ascend the stairs.

Almost instinctively, Hayla turned back and looked at him. She flashed a smile and continued up the stairs. Dick stood there for a moment, trying to understand the new feeling that had just swept over him.

"Come on," Jimmy shouted with a note of urgency, "the air's going to be too warm soon."

After their Morning Invigorates Dick slipped out of the water and began drying himself. Jimmy noticed him staring toward the cottage.

"Ain't you comin back in?" he inquired.

"No," Dick returned, "I've had enough for right now."

"Must be something you ain't had enough of, though," Jimmy noted with a smile.

"What's that supposed to mean?" he shot back.

"I saw you eying that girl when she was goin up the stairs."

"Aw, bull!" Dick snapped in his defense. "Ain't nothing for a guy to check out a new girl."

"Whoa!" Jimmy exclaimed. "I better come over there and check your head for fever... love fever that is."

"Aw, knock it off," Dick returned. "Just because a guy looks at a cute girl once in a while."

"Better yet, maybe I should borrow someone's glasses to see who I'm talking to," Jimmy continued. " Is this the famous woman-hater or have we had a change of heart about the fairer sex?"

"Cut it out, Jimmy," Dick warned, becoming more perturbed.

Grinning, Jimmy climbed on the dock and shaded his eyes as he scanned the woods.

"You in there, cupid?" he teased. "I know you must be in there because only your arrows of love could change this poor woman hater's heart sooooo fast!"

Dick had had enough and with one quick motion Jimmy was airborne and in the river. He soon surfaced, sputtering and laughing.

"Come on," Dick said, attempting to change the subject, "let's get our gear and go catch some bass."

"Now you're talkin," Jimmy replied.

The boys were in the process of gathering their gear from the shed when Jimmy looked up.

"Uh oh," he moaned.

"What?" Dick asked.

"Female approaching from three o'clock," he warned.

Dick skinned an eye in her direction, but pretended not to notice.

"Hi," Hayla greeted them with a smile. "You guys going fishing?"

"What's it look like?" Dick replied without looking at her.

"Is the fishing good around here?" the undaunted Hayla continued.

"It ain't too bad," Dick replied, trying to show a lack of interest. "Dad and Grampa do most of the catching. Me and Jimmy just drown worms."

"That's silly," she cooed. "Do you think I could go along and try…"

"Naw, Fishing's a man thing," Jimmy cut in. "You could probably help the women in the kitchen though."

"Were you properly introduced to these two yet, Hayla?" Dick's mom asked as she came on the scene.

"Not really," she replied.

"Well boys, this is Bud and Marie's daughter, Hayla and Hayla, this is my son Dick and his friend Jimmy."

"Nice to meet you," Hayla returned.

The boys nodded.

"Now, before you two fishermen catch any more fish, how about going to the spring and netting some cats and bass for tonight's supper."

Jimmy wasted no time at seizing the moment.

"You and Hayla go on, Dick," he insisted. "I think I'll just fish off the dock till you get back."

Before Dick could object, Jimmy grabbed his gear and headed across the lawn.

"I'll tell your mother where you're going, Hayla," Cass said as she walked toward the kitchen.

"But..." Dick started.

"Dick, you be sure to look after her," his mother reminded him, " and don't forget to take along some fish food."

Dick stood there in stunned silence, pondering the desertion of his so-called best friend and of his mother's brusque instructions.

"Is it very far from here?" Hayla asked.

Dick paused, trying to collect his thoughts.

"No...no," he finally replied, "it's just up that path and down the tracks."

"Tracks?"

"Railroad tracks," he snapped.

"Oh," she replied shyly. "I thought I heard a train earlier."

Dick rolled his eyes in mock disgust.

"Okay, let's go get the buckets and yoke," he said as he headed to the shed.

"A yoke, what's a ..."

She stopped short, thinking how stupid her questions must seem to her new mentor.

"Here, you carry these," he said, handing her the buckets and net. "I'll get the food."

Cass had just finished mixing up a batch of GW's fish food which consisted of a special mixture of ingredients guaranteed to make the fish taste better. With buckets, yoke, and food in hand, Dick went ahead of Hayla as they started across the front lawn. As they walked on in silence, Dick continued to ponder the strange new feelings he was beginning to experience.

"Did your Mom plant all these pretty flowers?" Hayla inquired.

"Nah, my Grampa does all that," he replied.

"He sure does a nice job," she commented. "Everything around here is so beautiful."

The glaring sunlight caused the pair to squint as they emerged from the shadowed spring path and into the open expanse of the main line railroad.

"Was your Grandfather a gardener before he retired?"

"Nah, he worked for the railroad," Dick replied. "He just likes to work in the dirt and make things look good."

"I'll bet that was interesting, working for the railroad I mean," she continued. "Does he ever tell you stories about it?"

"Oh sure," Dick replied as they began walking side by side. Hayla glanced at him with each new question, but Dick only replied with a forward stare.

"He told me stories about how many trains he would control at one time as a yard master."

"What's that?" she questioned.

"Well, the way he tells it," he continued, "a yard master is in charge of all the train traffic in the Altoona yard. Trains come into the yard from all over the country and are taken apart by the yardies and connected together into new trains that will go to the same place, like Chicago or Pittsburgh."

"Understand?" Dick questioned, trying to imagine how a girl could possibly grasp such a complex concept.

"I think so," Hayla replied with a serious look on her face. "It's kind of like mail coming into a post office from all over town and being sorted into different mail bags and then being loaded onto trucks and railroad cars that will take them to the right towns all over the country."

Dick stopped short. He thought for a moment and then, for the first time, looked at her.

"That's right," he said in amazement. "How do you know so much about mail?"

"My mother works at the San Diego Post Office," she replied, "and, like your grandfather, she tells me all kinds of stories about it."

"It's amazing how much their jobs are alike…in some ways, I mean," Dick said. He was astounded at how much he was allowing this stranger…this girl…to know about himself, but somehow he didn't care.

"Beautiful day," he said as they both glanced up at the clear blue sky with its white fluffy clouds that resembled huge snow covered mountains.

"Sure is," she replied with a glancing smile.

"Wow!" Hayla exclaimed as she looked into the old concrete trough. "I never saw so many fish in one place."

"How do you catch them?" she inquired as she watched them swim from one end of the trough to the other.

"You have to pick out one fish," he explained. "If you just start dipping you'll spook them and they'll scatter all over the place."

"How about that big one there," she said, pointing to a large mouth bass.

"All right," Dick replied, "watch carefully."

Hayla watched while Dick slowly dipped the net into the water. He maneuvered the net behind the unwary fish and then, in one smooth motion, scooped it out and into one of their buckets.

"Awsome!" she exclaimed. "Let me try."

"Okay, but go nice and slow so you don't spook them," he warned as he handed her the net.

"Now try to pick out one that's by itself," he instructed.

"There," she said softly, "that one."

The sweet sound of her hushed voice put Dick's heart in his throat, but he managed to swallow it back in place as they continued.

"All right, now easy does it," he advised.

Hayla gently lowered the net, but no sooner had it entered the water when the catfish swam out of range.

"What happened?" she asked.

"My fault," Dick admitted. "You have to make sure you don't lean over and cast a shadow on the water."

"I can do that," she assured.

They waited and soon the cat swam back into range. Hayla lowered the net from behind as Dick had instructed, but in her excitement she moved too quickly and again the cat swam away.

"Nuts!" she exclaimed, disgusted with herself.

"Here, let me help you," Dick offered as he reached around and steadied her hands. Together they lowered the net and gently the two of them scooped the chubby cat into the bucket.

"See?" Dick said.

"This is fun," Hayla exclaimed as she smiled into his eyes.

She's right, Dick thought to himself, *this is fun*. He smiled slightly, beginning to show his enjoyment of the time they were having together. Dick was never this close to a girl before, at least not intentionally and the way she moved and the expressions on her face soon began to affect him in ways he never believed possible.

Presently the two buckets were full of wriggling, flopping fish.

"Do we feed them now?" Hayla asked.

"Yep" Dick returned.

"Why didn't we feed these before we put them into the buckets?" she asked.

"You dummy," Dick teased, "those don't need to be fed because they're going to feed us tonight."

"Oh, that's true," she replied with a sheepish grin.

Dick handed her a large, clay-like chunk of his Grandpa's special mix.

"Now be sure to break it into small pieces…like this…and spread it over the top near the inlet," he explained as he demonstrated.

Hayla did the same and soon the whole trough boiled in a feeding frenzy as the hungry bass, cats and carp rallied to get their share. The pair watched until the last of GW's concoction was devoured.

"They sure like that stuff," she noted.

"Yeah," Dick agreed. "We'd better be gettin' back."

He attached the yoke to the two fish-laden buckets and swung it up on his shoulders.

"That's handy," Hayla said as she picked up the net and fish food box.

"Dad made it in the railroad shop where he works," he said.

"Is your dad a carpenter?"

"Yeah," Dick replied. "He makes all kinds of fancy wooden stuff for the passenger cars. He even made the special trim for the president's private car."

"You mean the president of the United States?"

"Naw, I think he meant the president of the railroad."

As they walked back to Glen Afton the initial tension between them eased as they became more familiar. Unlike his sister and the other girls at school, he could actually talk to this one and she seemed to understand and care about what he had to say.

"Oh, Dick," exclaimed Hayla. "Look at that!"

A cardinal flew across the small meadow to their right, its bright-red color contrasting sharply with the vivid green forest behind it.

"That was beautiful!" she exclaimed.

"There's a lot of neat things to see around here," Dick told her, "but most of it can only be seen in the morning."

"In the morning?" she questioned. "Like what?"

"That's when most of the animals come out to feed."

"Which ones?"

"The deer and squirrels and…"

"Deer? I've never seen deer in the wild," she admitted.

"Tell you what," Dick said, his mind racing, "how about you and me getting up early tomorrow morning and I'll show you."

Hayla thought for a moment.

"I don't know if mom and dad will let me," she replied.

"If we get up early enough, we can be back before anyone notices," he said.

"I don't know," she said.

"Come on," he coaxed, 'it would be like an adventure."

Dick couldn't believe how forward he was being with Hayla, but he knew he enjoyed being with her. Damn his own past prejudices and damn those who would tease him about it; he wanted to be with her and that was that!

"What've you got in the buckets?" Hayla's brother inquired.

"Look what we caught, Buddy," Debbie exclaimed.

"Where did you get all those?" he asked.

"They catch them out of the river and put them in the spring pond up by the railroad. They say it takes the muddy taste out of them," she replied. "Pretty neat, huh?"

"Yeah, I guess," he said as he looked at Dick.

"This is Dick," Hayla said cheerfully, "and Dick, this is my brother Buddy."

"We're goin' swimming in a little while," Dick said. "You want to go?"

"Maybe later," he replied. "I think I'll take a walk and see this fish pond of yours."

"It's up the trail," Dick began, " and across the tracks to the left …"

"I'll find it," he replied as he headed toward the trail.

"What's wrong with him?" Dick asked.

"Oh, he's always like that around strangers," she explained. "He'll be all right once he gets to know you."

"You up for a swim?" Dick asked.

"You bet!" she replied. "I'll go change and meet you at the dock."

She turned and ran toward the cottage.

Dick hesitated for a moment.

Hayla's long, golden hair glistened as it bounced around her shoulders in the bright afternoon sun, reminding him of the golden streaks across the evening river.

Her motion was smooth and flawless as she flowed across the lawn in her white and blue dress.

"Aren't you coming?" she said, glancing over her shoulder.

"Yeah…yeah, I'm coming," he said.

Composing himself he made for the cottage and his swim trunks.

As he descended the switch-back stairs he caught the eye of Jimmy who was fishing on the dock.

"Hey, lover-boy, how'd you make out with blondie," he teased, making kissing sounds.

"Knock it off, bone bag, or you'll be kissing the bottom of the river in a minute," Dick warned, "and her name's Hayla, not blondie."

"Touchy, touchy!" Jimmy responded as Dick closed the gap between them.

"Any luck with the fish?" Dick asked as he ran past and dove into the cool, refreshing water.

"No, and I guess I won't with a fat butt like you splashing around in my fishing hole."

"I won't be the only one splashing around," Dick said with a smile

"You mean blondie…I mean Hayla, is going to grace us with her presence?" Jimmy asked.

"Yep," Dick said.

"I hope she's wearing one of those hot new two piece suits," Jimmy said with a wiggle of his skinny hips. "Whoa! Hot stuff!"

"You meet her brother yet?" Dick inquired.

"You mean Mr. Personality?" Jimmy replied. "He came down earlier and looked around…didn't have too much to say."

"Yeah, he seems like a moody one all right," Dick replied.

"Hi, guys, how's the water?"

The boys' attention turned toward the voice coming from the top of the stairs. There, clad in her dark blue one-piece bathing suit, stood Hayla. Their eyes followed the slender, smiling blonde as she quickly descended the switch back stairs and just as quick Dick swallowed his heart back into place…again.

"Last one in is a rotten egg!" Jimmy shouted to her as he trotted back from the edge of the dock to get a running start.

"Let's do it!" Hayla said as she started across the dock.

Jimmy began his run toward the end of the dock with arms and legs in full motion but in an instant it was over. The sly girl dove into the shallow end near the shore.

"No fair, no fair!" Jimmy shouted as he threw himself off the end of the dock with a resounding splash.

Hayla swam out to them as Jimmy surfaced, only to be dunked by his waiting pal.

"Help me, oh help me! I'm drowning!" he wailed.

He continued his clowning, but noticed the brief glances and sly smiles exchanged by the other two.

"Supper's ready," Dick's mom called.

The three swimmers dried off and went up for a welcomed fish dinner served with a side of white patty-pan squash which had been rolled in an egg and flour batter, fried and served with homemade brown mustard.

"Did you enjoy your walk to the spring, Hayla?" Cass inquired.

"Oh, yes," she replied," and it's really neat how you keep all those fish in that pond."

After the meal the ladies began clearing off the table.

"Mom," Hayla began, "can I wear jeans like Fay and Katie do while we're down here?"

"No, you can't," her mother returned. "I still believe a young lady should wear a dress, even if we are in the wilderness."

"But mom," she argued, "no one's going to see me and it makes it easier to move like the others"

"I don't care!" her mother returned, "and besides, I doubt if they have anything here that would fit you anyhow."

"We have some of Dick's old bib overalls upstairs, Marie," Cass noted, "and I believe they would fit Debbie with a little hemming,".

"I don't know, Cass..."

"Please. mom, please!" Hayla begged.

Bessie returned from the men's room with a couple pairs of Dick's old bibs. Marie glared at her as Bessie held them up to Hayla

"Why, I can have these fittin you in no time, girl," she exclaimed. "How about it, Marie?"

"Oh, all right," Marie conceded, "but don't think for a minute you're going to take those horrible things home with you."

"Thank you, mom, thank you, thank you," Hayla replied.

As promised, Cass and Bessie had the bibs tailored to the young girl's form in no time.

"These are great," she exclaimed as she tried on the first pair.

Marie looked at her daughter with disapproval.

"Hayla, why don't you go do something interesting," Cass urged. "We can get the dishes cleaned up."

"Thanks, Aunt Cass," she replied with a hug and a smile.

Hayla headed out the kitchen door and across the lawn toward the river in her newly tailored cottage wear. She walked along the edge of the river bank thinking about the day's events and her feelings about it all as she watched the sun send silver streaks across the Juniata's wind-swept surface. Thoughts and feelings swept across her mind as she tried to fathom how she felt about this new intruder in her life…this boy who seemed so different than the others she had known. Before long she noticed a familiar form coming across the lawn toward her.

"Hello," Dick greeted.

"Well, hello yourself," she returned with a smile.

"Where'd you get the bibs?" he asked.

"Your Mother and Aunt Bessie found them and fixed them up for me," she replied as she repositioned the left strap that kept slipping off her shoulder.

Dick inspected them objectively.

"They look familiar," he claimed.

"That's because they used to be yours…when you were a bit smaller."

Dick blushed.

"Should've known," he remarked. "Mom never throws anything out she figures can be used again."

"Well, I like them," Hayla stated. "They're a lot more comfortable than those dumb dresses I have to wear all the time."

"You give any thought about what I said earlier?" he questioned.

"I don't know, Dick," she replied. "My mom…"

"OK, OK, but either way, I'm going," he said in a firm tone. "If you decide to go, I'll meet you on the stairs before daybreak."

Hayla looked at the ground, then into his eyes and shook her head.

"All right, Mister Coleman," she agreed. "I'm game."

They continued to walk together as the sun began to set in the western sky above the Alleghenies. Hayla took his hand in hers and again Dick's heart betrayed him as if it had a mind of its own. Each time their eyes met he felt new feelings…feelings he couldn't explain or understand, but that was just fine. He liked being with Hayla. It was like nothing he had ever experienced before…and that was just fine!

The evening air chilled the young couple and they reluctantly headed toward the cottage to join the others.

"What in the world is that!" she questioned, looking at the bull horn hanging on the porch wall.

"That's what we use to call the men for dinner when they go fishing down by the rocks," he explained.

Hayla took it down for closer examination.

"Does it really work?" she asked.

"Watch and learn, Madam," he said as they returned to the rear porch. Dick put it to his mouth and with a quick glance toward Hayla, he turned the horn directly at her and bellowed, "Dinner's ready!"

"You brat!" she exclaimed as she gently slapped him. "I'll get you for that."

"Dick, would you and Hayla go out to the water trough and wash off the kohlrabies and rhubarb your grandfather laid out there before it gets dark?" his mother asked, "then put them in the springhouse so the animals don't get them."

"Okay, mom," he returned, while grinning at Hayla.

The day's activities had taken their toll on the family and soon, one by one, they began to turn in for a welcome night's sleep.

Chapter 13
DICK AND HAYLA

The morning sun was preparing to chase the gloom from the night sky as a shadowy figure began moving about in the men's sleeping quarters. Quietly, Dick descended the stairs, being careful not to step on that one squeaky tread. Hesitating for a moment, he pondered on what he had experienced the day before. He never dreamed he would be doing this kind of thing with a girl! But no matter. He found this to be quite enjoyable and being with Hayla gave him feelings he wanted to continue to experience.

As he reached the bottom of the stairs he noticed something moving toward him down the hallway. He watched as he edged back up the stairs. A scant bit of light through the living room window revealed the slender silhouette of Hayla as she floated over to the stairs and knelt down beside him.

"I couldn't sleep a wink thinking about this," she whispered in a hushed, but excited voice.

"Neither could I," he replied. "We'd better get moving."

The two of them slipped out the living room door and into the quiet of the waning night. As they started across the lawn toward the spring path a low, menacing growl stopped them in their tracks. The large brown canine trotted up to inspect the couple.

"Quiet, Brownie," Dick scolded as he rubbed the old hound's head and ears.

"You stay here, boy," he instructed.

They continued toward the spring trail as Brownie happily bounded along.

"No!" Dick whispered harshly. Brownie stopped and cocked his head, not understanding.

"You can't come this time," Dick explained, "you'll spook the animals."

"Go on," he said, shooing him back.

The pair continued up the trail as Brownie sat and watched.

"Careful where you step," Dick cautioned.

Hayla caught his hand in hers and Dick smiled. The quiet stillness of the night began to give way to the morning sounds in the forest. Early birds were beginning to stir as they began searching for their proverbial worm.

"Look," Dick said as he pointed toward the top of a large white oak.

There, high above them a large nest of leaves began to shake and quiver. Suddenly two grey squirrels burst forth from their nest and began chasing one another across the limbs and then bounding from one tree to another. Soon the two scampered down a birch and scurried across the fern-covered ground leaving a trail of swaying ferns in their path. Dick and Hayla smiled as they watched.

The pair continued their trek, going across the tracks and following the main line toward Millerstown. The sun crept above the tree line and began illuminating the world around the young couple.

"What are those S-shaped pieces of metal in the ends of those boards?" she asked.

"They're not boards, they're ties and those are S-nails," Dick explained.

"They use them to keep the ties from splitting."

"Oh, I see," she replied.

"Here it is," Dick said, pointing to an old road that broke into the forest.

The morning dew glistened on the ankle-high weeds as it soaked their shoes.

"That's cold," Hayla complained as they started up the road.

"Keep in the ruts and you won't get so wet," Dick instructed.

"Is this an old farm road?" she questioned.

"Yes, but it was first used by loggers," he explained. "Gramps said they came here to cut down the white oaks and turn them into charcoal."

"What's charcoal used for?" she questioned.

"He said they used it as fuel to make steel in Johnstown," he answered.

"There," Dick said, pointing to a large, flat area cut out of the woods. "That's where they burned the wood and made the charcoal."

"That's all very interesting, but when are going to see some deer?" Hayla asked.

"The old farm is just up around that bend," Dick said as he grabbed her hand. "They like to graze in the grass and eat the apples in the old orchard."

The sun continued to climb higher in the morning sky, shortening the shadows and displaying everything in its true colors.

"We'll have to be quiet," Dick instructed. "Deer can't see very well, but they have a great sense of smell and hearing."

The old orchard contained several rows of spent apple trees. Only a few boasted any kind of a crop. A few gnarled yellow-transparent apple trees were the only ones producing fruit this early in the summer. The pair eased along the edge of the woods, moving up to a place that overlooked most of the orchard.

"This seems like a good spot," she whispered.

"Yeah, Dick agreed, "and it's down wind."

They sat together on a log beside a large maple.

"If we lean against the tree, it'll help hide us," Dick explained.

A slight breeze chilled the morning air and Hayla shivered.

"Here, put this on," Dick said, giving her his jacket.

"Thanks," she returned.

They sat together in silence, half trying to spot any signs of game and half trying to hide the affection that was growing between them.

"I really like being here," she said quietly.

They continued to search the forest for the elusive deer, but soon turned toward each other with a quiet fondling of the eyes. Together they began to open their hearts to an innocent love within that neither had known before.

As a young girl Hayla played house with her friends back in Southern California and, using her dolls, mimicked the love she saw that existed between her mother and father and dared to dream, as young girls do, of that special one who would come into her life, sweep her off her feet and take her to where they would live happily ever-after. Now, Dick wasn't quite what she had in mind, with his husky frame, ruddy face and rumpled shock of sandy brown hair, but until now no one had touched her the way Dick had with his clumsy politeness and innocent nonchalant ways. No, he wasn't exactly Prince Charming, but he had unlocked something new, something wonderful in her and she liked it.

The footfalls in the forest behind them startled Hayla and she squeezed Dick's hand.

"Be very still," he cautioned in a hushed voice.

Her heart was beating so hard she believed she could hear it. Dick had seen deer in the wild before, but never this close. The four doe and two spotted fawns trotted single-file ten feet from where the couple sat.

Hayla stiffened. Her eyes were as big as saucers and her mouth hung open in amazement as Dick returned her squeeze and gave her a reassuring look.

The whitetails were beautiful in their light-brown summer coats as they moved toward the orchard. The two watched as the deer began to graze on the soft meadow grass.

The largest doe went over to the nearest fruit-laden tree. She slowly walked around it and then stood on her hind legs and, with her slender snout, tore loose one of the apples. Shortly, the others joined her and soon all were enjoying the early summer harvest. The mother of the fawns pulled off several apples for her offspring and as the mother moved around, Hayla became aware of her noticeable limp. Closer examination revealed that her right front leg was missing.

"Dick, what happened that mother deer?" she asked.

"If you look close, you can see she has a withered leg," he said. "It's not uncommon for some to be born that way."

"It doesn't seem to slow her down much," she replied.

Suddenly the doe raised their heads in unison and faced in the same direction. They stood dead-still, only their tails twitching.

"Did they hear us?" Debbie asked.

"No," Dick replied. "It's something in the direction they're facing."

All remained quiet until the largest doe gave out a loud snort, causing Hayla to jump. The small herd ran to the opposite end of the meadow and quickly disappeared into the forest.

"What spooked them?" she asked nervously.

"Something over there," he replied as he slowly stood up to get a better view.

Now it was Dick's turn for wide eyes and open mouth.

"What is it?" she asked as she stood up to see.

Hayla couldn't readily identify the four dark shapes at the edge of the meadow until the mother black bear stood up on her hind legs to catch the smells of the meadow. "Oh my gosh!' she exclaimed.

She grabbed Dick's arm and the two eased around the other side of the maple.

"What'll we do?" she asked.

"Just…just be still and be quiet," Dick replied. "As long as we don't get between her and those cubs we should be all right."

They cautiously peered around the tree. The mother, who was quite large, was already under one of the apple trees. Again, she stood on her hind legs and with a mighty yank of her paw snapped off a branch loaded with apples. Her brood swiftly attacked the fallen bounty, grunting and crunching more loudly than the deer.

"Will...will they leave soon?" Hayla asked.

"I don't think so," Dick said. "They look hungry."

"Oh, God," she cried. Dick turned and saw tears welling in her eyes.

He remembered what his mother said to him the day before, "You be sure to look after her."

"It's alright," he assured as he put his arm around her.

"I'm really scared," she cried softly as she put her arms around him.

"It's going to be okay," he said as he eyed the bears.

" I'll take care of this," he assured her.

The black bears had now moved to a tree closer to the young couple and were busily stripping off its fruit.

"Let's move into the woods," he suggested. "We'll keep the tree between us and them."

"OK...OK," she agreed as they began to move away from the meadow and its predators.

Suddenly, the loud drumming of a startled ruffed grouse sent their hearts and voices soaring.

"Whoa!" Dick shouted in unison with Hayla's scream as the grouse soared out across the meadow. The two remained dead still, watching for the bears' reaction. Immediately the she-bear stood to investigate the commotion. She watched as the grouse passed overhead...then turned her attention to where the ruckus had started.

The pair froze!

A low, insidious growl came from deep within the large sow as she dropped on all fours and started a slow trot in their direction.

"Oh no!" Hayla exclaimed in a muffled voice with her hands covering her mouth.

It's now or never, Dick thought.

"Get behind that tree," he said.

He grabbed a large dead branch from the ground, took a deep breath and ran toward the edge of the meadow. I hope Gramps is right, he thought as he recalled his grandfather's words, 'If you cross paths with a black bear and it senses your presence, yell out and let it know what you are," he taught. "Once it knows you're a man it will high-tail it out of there because black bears fear man."

But does that apply to a mother with cubs, Dick thought.

"Hey, hey, hey!" he shouted as he frantically waved the branch in the bear's direction. The sow stopped and with a loud snort, raised up to her full height. She stood glaring and sniffing as did her cubs from under the apple tree.

Dick waved and yelled again…this time more frantically!

"Beat it…get out of here!"

The sow watched Dick for a while and then dropped down on all fours. She stood still…watching him with menacing eyes. After what seemed like an eternity, she gave out a grunt and walked back to her brood, occasionally looking back at the brave young lad. Dick watched as she gathered up her cubs. She eyed him once more and then trotted off across the meadow and into the woods. Dick let out a long sigh of relief, dropped the branch and returned to Hayla.

"Are they gone?" she stammered as she grabbed his hand and glanced across the meadow.

"Yeah," he replied.

"Let's be gone too!' she advised.

They started back to the old logging trail and jogged toward the main lines, occasionally glancing over their shoulders. The couple broke into the opening and began walking beside the tracks.

"That was the bravest thing I ever saw," she exclaimed.

"Aw, don't make a big deal out of it," he returned.

"No!" she said as she jumped in front of Dick, stopping him and putting her hands on his shoulders. Her face, now stained with tears and dirt, was as lovely as Dick had ever seen. She looked him in the eyes, slid her slender arms around his neck and hugged him tight.

"Thank you," she whispered as she kissed him on the cheek.

She grabbed his hand.

"Come on, they're probably wondering where we are," she said, pulling him along with her.

Dick, his mind now reeling over what had just taken place with both bear and girl, regained his composure, swept her up in his arms and began carrying her down the tracks.

"Stop it," she squealed.

"I promised you an adventure, didn't I?" he said.

"Yes, but next time, Mister Coleman, let's not do bears," she replied.

Hayla jumped down and ran off ahead of him, balancing herself on one of the shiny rails. Dick followed close behind, taking in all the loveliness, all the perky vitality that was Hayla Taylor.

As the pair started down the spring trail toward Glen Afton, they met Hayla's brother.

"Where were you?" he demanded. "Mom's been worried."

Hayla started, "We were just…"

"Where did you take her?" he questioned, noticing his sister's tear-stained face.

"I just wanted to…"

"Wanted to what?" he demanded, giving Dick a hard shove.

"Let him alone, Buddy!"

"You stay out of this, Hayla," he yelled. "This is between him and me."

"Don't yell at her, you big clown," Dick warned.

"And just what are you goin' to do about it, Romeo?"

"Stop it, Buddy!" she yelled.

Dick's stomach tightened.

"Okay, Romeo," he said, "let's just see what you've got!"

Buddy was bigger than Dick and he could see the same fire in Buddy's eyes that he saw in Buck's eyes when he fought his father. His first thought was to back down, to give in and let Buddy have his moment, but when he glanced past him to the spot where the other fight had taken place he remembered his Uncle Danny and how he felt toward him, of how Danny had done less than he could have. That put the fire back into Dick.

"Fine," he replied, "if that's the way you want it, Buddy boy!"

"Stop it," Hayla shouted as she ran toward the cottage. "You're both being ridiculous."

The two boys raised their fists and slowly circled each other.

"All right you two," Buddy's dad shouted, "knock it off."

"Let him alone, Buddy," Hayla implored. "He didn't hurt me."

"Aw, I wasn't going to do anything," Buddy insisted. "I just wanted to see if he had any guts."

"That's enough, Buddy," his father sternly replied.

Dick headed for the cottage.

"What were you two doing up so early?" Bud asked his daughter.

"Dick wanted to show me how beautiful it is around here in the morning and how the animals come out to feed," she replied.

"You should always tell your mother and me what you're planning to do," he scolded. "We were beginning to worry."

"I know,' she said , "but I was afraid you wouldn't let me go."

"Just be sure to tell us the next time or you'll be punished," he warned.

"Okay Dad," she answered. "You'll never guess what happened to us while we were out there!"

The kitchen was warm from the morning cooking and felt good to Dick as he entered.

"Where did you two go this morning, Dick?" his mother asked with a smile, somewhat amazed at her son's sudden interest in the fairer sex.

"Just took a walk, that's all," he replied.

"What's for breakfast?" he asked, attempting to change the subject.

"Just toast and white gravy," Aunt Bessie replied. "We need to make a run to the store today."

"Hey Dick, is it true what Hayla said…about the bears?" Buddy asked as he entered the kitchen.

"What bears?" Hayla's mother cut in.

"We saw a mother bear and her three cubs up at that old farm by the logging trail," he explained.

"Yeah, and they almost fed on us!" Hayla exclaimed as she entered the kitchen.

"What happened, Dick?" his father inquired.

"Well, we were watchin' four doe and their fawns feeding in the meadow when this old sow and her three cubs came along and chased them away," Dick explained. "The next thing you know the sow spotted us and decided to check us out. I just stood up and yelled to let her know what we were, like grandpa said, and she and her cubs took off."

"Good thinkin, boy," his grandfather said proudly.

"You should've seen him, Mom," Hayla said, smiling at Dick, "it was the bravest thing I ever…"

"Ah, cut it out," Dick said, becoming embarrassed. "It wasn't that big of a deal."

"You you faced down a grizzly and you say it wasn't that big of a deal?" Jimmy inquired.

"It wasn't a grizzly," Dick replied emphatically. "It was a just a black bear and yes, it wasn't that big of a deal."

"Not until I kissed you," Hayla added with a wink.

All enjoyed a laugh at Dick's expense.

Chapter 14

CABLE SWING

"I can't believe you're getting all exited about a kiddy swing, Andy," Fay said with a roll of her bright blue eyes.

"But dad said it wasn't just any swing," Andy explained. "He said this one is really high and…"

"Now let me get this straight, Andy Hahn," Fay quipped, "you're 15 years old and getting all excited about a swing ride?"

Katie smiled as she watched Fay work her brother.

"But, but Dad said its really, really high and…" he replied, looking at his sister for help.

"Maybe we should go, Fay," Katie added. "At least it will be something different."

"Yeah," Andy said enthusiastically, "and Dad said it swung out over…"

"OK, OK, "Fay said resignedly, "if it will shut you up, we'll go."

"Great!" he shouted. "Besides, there's nothing much to do around here."

"How far is it?" Fay questioned.

"Dad says it's about a mile down the tracks from Pap's place. He said to look for a trail near a big frog pond full of cat-tails to the right of the railroad," Andy replied. "He says to skirt around the pond and follow the trail."

"I'll tell Mom where we're going," Fay said as she headed toward the kitchen.

Cass, Marie and Bessie were busy snapping beans and shucking corn for the evening meal. During the depression they depended on GW's garden and the men's hunting and fishing skills for much of their food.

"Hey Mom, Andy and Katie and me are going to try to find that cable swing their dad told them about," Fay said.

Frederick Corbin

"All right, but be careful and be sure to be back here in time for supper," her mother replied.

"We will," Fay returned.

With that the three were off, not knowing other ears had overheard them.

"You ever hear of that cable swing, Dick?" Jimmy asked.

"Yeah, but I never knew where it was," he replied.

"But we're going to now, right Dick?" Buddy added.

"Got that right," Dick agreed.

And so the second trio was off in quest of another adventure.

Soon after, Hayla rushed into the kitchen. "Hey Mom, can I go with the boys to that cable swing I heard them talking about?"

"I don't know…"

"Please, Mom, please," she begged.

"Oh, all right, but you tell Buddy to watch after you," she instructed.

"Don't worry, Dick will look after me" she replied as she grabbed a freshly skinned carrot on the way out.

"Be careful," Cass added as Hayla bounded after the boys.

"Wait for me, guys," she shouted.

"Where do you think you're going?" her Brother asked with his hands on his hips.

"To the cable swing," she answered.

"Go back to the cottage, Hayla," he said firmly, "this is a guy thing."

"Yeah,' Jimmy said, "we don't need any girls holding us up."

"I won't hold you up," she insisted, "and besides Fay and Katie will be there too."

"Be where?" Buddy asked.

"At the cable swing," she returned as she finished her carrot.

The boys groaned as they continued on their way.

Dick was glad to see her come along, but he didn't let on.

As they emerged from the spring path, Jimmy nudged Buddy.

"She said she wouldn't hold us up, right?" Jimmy noted.

"Right!" he said, getting Jimmy's drift.

"Well, what say we stretch the old legs and see if we can catch Andy and the others ," Jimmy urged.

With that, he and Buddy took off down the tracks as fast as their legs would carry them. Dick followed suit to in order to save face and without saying a word, Hayla started her pursuit of the three boys. Dick tried his best to catch the others but he was no match for the older Buddy and the lighter, fleeter Jimmy.

As they continued their run Dick looked back and was shocked to see that Hayla had caught up to him. He sped up his pace but to no avail and to his mortification she smiled as she quickly sped out ahead of him. The other two were a quarter-mile up the track when Jimmy looked back.

"What the...?" he gasped.

Buddy glimpsed back, shook his head and laughed.

"What?" Jimmy questioned.

"I almost forgot," Buddy confessed.

"Forgot what?" Jimmy questioned.

"Hayla's on the junior-high track team," he stated as she wheeled past the two of them. "Best miler in San Diego county for her age."

"For her age?" Jimmy repeated blankly as he watched the golden haired girl widen the gap between them.

After waiting for Dick, they turned down the overgrown trail by the pond filled with cat-tails. Frogs and turtles splashed into the depths from their sunning and feeding spots as the four skirted around the water's edge. They were undoubtedly frustrated by this second interruption of their daily routine if indeed frogs and turtles can be frustrated.

Crickets and grasshoppers jumped and flew in every direction as the four waded through the waist-high weeds on the old trail. A pair of colorful pileated woodpeckers startled them as the birds machined-gunned an old dead hickory in search of some noonday nourishment. Fay and Katie's shrieks of laughter reached their ears as they continued along the path.

"Sounds like they found it," Dick noted.

The trail turned left and up a small bank to an opening that was once an old charcoal flat. It was now covered with knee-high weeds and surrounded by trees of various heights and species.

"My gosh!" Jimmy exclaimed. "Look how high that cable goes up that tree!"

The youngsters looked up in amazement. It extended up over 100 feet above them.

"Your Dad was right about this swing, Andy," Dick exclaimed.

All of the large oak tree's branches facing the flat had been removed except for the highest one which stretched out toward the center of the flat. A steel cable had been fastened to it and extended to the ground, was turned back on itself to form a loop two feet above the ground and was secured by two cable clamps.

There were two accounts of how this was done and who did it:

One story tells how Jim Yohn and his buddies from Thompsontown had stolen the cable from a railroad flat car. Jim, being the daring young buck that he was, climbed the oak with the aid of a rope sling and some large spikes. Upon reaching the highest limb he carefully shinnied out and lowered his mother's clothes line to the ground. He looped the remainder of the line around the limb and threw it down. The boys tied the steel cable to the rope and hoisted the lot up to Jim who secured the cable to the limb with two clamps. As he descended, he cut off the limbs facing the flat and removed the spikes to discourage anyone from stealing their stolen cable.

The other account tells how Digger Harrison and his two brothers from Millerstown had removed an old cable that stretched across the river as part of a defunct swinging bridge. They fastened a cable clamp to a light piece of rope and threw it skyward until it circumvented the highest limb. Then they tied the cable to the rope and hoisted it up around the limb and back down to the ground. They threaded the other end of the rope through the cable loop and pulled it skyward until the loop tightened around the limb like a noose. Next they formed a lower loop and secured it with two cable clamps, assuring a secure footing for any daring enough to ride the new swing. To this day the area's old timers argue as to which story is true. Nonetheless, it was there and the newcomers were about to put it to the test.

The four youngsters began exploring the area and at the far end of the flat they found a cliff that dropped into a canyon. The tops of the trees growing in the chasm were level with the floor of the flat giving anyone viewing it a feeling of great height.

"This must be the ravine your dad was talking about," Dick said.

"And it does look like the cable could swing out over it," Buddy noted.

Fay and Katie were already enjoying the swing as they pushed each other across the flat dragging the piece of clothes-line that was still tied to the cable. The sun was directly overhead, chasing all the shadows from the area and the air was dead still on that bright summer's day. Meadow larks and red breasted robins played and fed among the shrubs and bushes bordering the flat.

"Come on," Andy encouraged, "let's do some real swinging."

"Do you really want to swing out of one of those trees?" Katie asked Fay.

"Of course," was her eager reply. "but only from the lower ones."

"Hey Fay, watch this!" Andy shouted from a maple tree. He gave out with his best

Tarzan cry and with his foot in the cable loop he released himself. All heads turned in unison as they followed Andy's arching ride across the flat.

"Wow!" Buddy exclaimed. "I'm next."

"Not so fast, Buddy boy," Fay retorted. "We were here first, so we get dibs."

Andy, Fay and Katie began swinging out of higher and higher trees until they had conquered most of them.

"Come on, it's our turn now," Jimmy whined.

"OK, OK," Andy agreed. "Let's see what the wee-folks can do."

At first the boys pushed each other around on the flat to get used to the new toy.

"Let me try," Hayla coaxed

"Aw, go on back with the other women and wash some dishes!" Jimmy shot back.

"What's the matter?" Fay broke in, "afraid she might show you worms up?"

"Fat chance," Buddy replied. "Come on, Sis, we'll give you a ride."

He motioned for Dick and Jimmy to help.

"Okay, what do I do?" she inquired.

"What hand do you use?" Dick asked.

"Right," she replied.

"Then put your right foot in the loop," he instructed. "It'll feel more natural that way."

"Hold on tight, Sis," Buddy said as the three boys hauled her across the flat.

"Hang on!" Dick shouted as they released her with a hard shove. Hayla gave out with a squeal but soon her apprehension gave in to the delight of the ride. In no time the younger set were daring each other to new and higher challenges until, to the astonishment of the elder group, they had conquered the highest tree that they had done.

As they watched the younger ones swing across the flat, Fay's sharp eyes caught sight of something unusual in a high oak tree nearby.

She nudged Andy.

"What do you think that is up there?" she questioned.

"Up where?" he asked.

"Up there in that big oak."

"I don't see anything," Andy insisted, possibly in denial of what he thought it might be.

"Right near the top," she said, "sticking out of those branches."

"I see it," Katie said. "It looks like some boards or a, a..."

"A platform!" Andy remarked in awe of its great height. "You don't suppose…?"

"I do suppose!" Fay returned.

Katie saw that familiar gleam in her daring friend's eye.

"Oh no, Fay," she pleaded, "that's too high."

"Well, it wouldn't hurt to go have a look-see now would it?" Fay said with a taunting lilt in her voice as the twins continued to stare up at the half-hidden structure.

"What about it, Mister Andy Hahn, you up for a climb?' Fay asked.

"I don't know, Fay," he replied, "that's really up there…"

"Come on, Andy, it was your idea to come here in the first place." Fay reminded him as she trotted toward the base of the tree

Andy looked up at the small platform so high above the ground. He shook his head and followed after her.

"I guess it wouldn't hurt to have a look," he hesitantly agreed, "but it doesn't mean we have to go off of it."

"Of course not," Fay agreed with a wink in Katie's direction.

The two found that the lowest branches on the tree were too high to reach for a climb.

"Well, I guess that's that," Andy said with a sigh of relief.

"Not so fast, O timid one," Fay replied as she circled the oak.

"Ah, look here!" she said with an air of satisfaction. "Someone nailed these boards to the rear of the tree."

"Oh, Lord," Andy said as he and Fay began to scale this last bastion of derring-do.

"These boards seem strong enough," Andy noted as he cautiously pulled and tested each one as they continued their skyward trek. When they reached the upper limbs it became apparent that this take-off station hadn't been used in years. The new outgrowth of limbs and leaves made the climb a struggle.

"How's the view up there?" Katie called.

"It looks a lot higher than it did from down there," Fay shouted back.

Dick and the others looked into the trees when they heard Fay's voice coming from high above them.

"What do they think they're doing?" Jimmy questioned.

"Look above them," Buddy exclaimed, pointing to the platform.

The wooden structure was four feet square with a railing bordering one side. The front of it, facing the flat, was wide open. Andy carefully scanned across the wide expanse to the edge of the canyon where the cable would travel.

"What are you looking for?" Fay asked.

"I'm trying to see if there's anything in the way ," he answered nervously.

"Well apparently there isn't," she replied. "Others must have swung off here before."

"That's easy for you to say, since my body will be the first to go barreling across there!" he countered, as he continued to muster his courage.

"What makes you think you're going to be first?" she asked.

"Hey, if you want dibs, be my guest," he insisted.

"You want me to bring up the rope?" Buddy yelled.

Andy nervously rubbed the back of his neck as he looked at Fay.

"Yeah, bring it up."

With both hands on the railing, Andy began jumping and shaking the little platform.

"What are you doing?" Fay asked, surprised by his actions.

"Seems good and solid," he said with a touch of apprehension in his voice.

Buddy quickly scampered up the tree and handed the rope to Fay.

"Wow!" he exclaimed. "It does look a lot higher from up here."

Fay and Andy pulled up the cable as Buddy climbed back down.

"This isn't going to work," Andy said.

"Why not? she asked.

"Look at the angle of the cable," he noted. "There's no way I can get a grip on it and put my foot in the loop at the same time."

He shook his head, somewhat disappointed…somewhat relieved.

"There must be some way they did it," Fay said as she began to check out the platform. She noticed a large branch above the platform and then scanned the railing directly below the branch.

"I think I know how they did it, Andy," she declared.

"How?" he questioned.

"Look how wide the board is on the railing below this branch."

"Yeah, so?"

"See how the board is worn smooth here and here," she noted. "I'll bet they stood on it with one foot on the rail the other against the post."

"Yeah!" Andy exclaimed. "and they held on to that branch with one hand for support and, and…"

"And held the cable for the rider with the other!" Fay said excitedly.

Andy held the cable while Fay positioned herself on the railing.

"Be careful, Fay," he cautioned.

"I'm good," she replied. "Now, hand me the cable."

She was now able to hold the cable five feet above the loop allowing it to extend vertically down to the platform. This permitted a cautious Andy to put one foot in the loop and grab the vertical cable with apparent ease.

"Hold her steady," he said as he struggled to maintain his balance with one foot on the edge of the platform.

"Don't take too long," Fay warned. "This cable's getting heavy."

Andy quickly scanned his intended flight path one more time.

"It's now or never," he declared and with that he lifted his foot off the platform.

The cable snapped from Fay's grip and he was off! This time there was no Tarzan jungle cry. All was dead silent except for the whoosh of Andy's body cutting through the still afternoon air. All eyes followed in awe as he flew across the flat at a speed previously unattained! Andy flew out over the canyon and arched upward high above the chasm's trees. At the pinnacle of this human pendulum's swing Andy and the cable appeared to hang motionless above the canyon as if in a still photograph, but soon he swung down across the flat and back toward his point of origin.

"All right!" he shouted as he closed in on Fay at the platform.

"What a ride, what a ride!' he exclaimed triumphantly as he and the cable came to a stop. The others quickly gathered around.

"How did it feel?"

"Were you scared?"

"A little at first," he replied. "But after that, it was amazing!"

"Bring the cable up to me," Fay shouted. "I want to try it."

Now everyone was getting excited and even Katie seemed anxious to try. Andy held the cable for Fay as she had done for him.

"Did you come close to any of those trees," she inquired of the experienced flyer.

"I was going too fast to notice," he replied.

Then Fay was off!

Soon all were experiencing the thrill of the canyon flight…all except Hayla. Her fear of height was beginning to set in.

"Come on, Hayla," Fay encouraged. "You've already done the other trees."

"But that one's so high," she replied.

"Go on, Sis," her brother urged. "It's only scary at first."

"Leave her alone," Dick said. "She doesn't have to do it if she doesn't want to."

The older three soon tired of the new toy and left to cool off in the waters of the Juniata.

"Don't be too long, you guys," Fay advised. "Mom will have supper ready soon."

"We'll be there," Dick replied.

As the boys continued to ride the cable, Hayla mustered her courage.

"I'd like to try it now," she said.

"What?" Dick asked.

"I said I would like to try it now…off the platform."

"Oh my!" Jimmy wailed in a mocking tone. "It's much too high for little girls, especially little girls from California!"

"Don't forget, Jimmy, this little California girl skinned you in a foot race a while back," she reminded him.

Jimmy had no reply.

"Dick, will you help me?"

The other two boys joined in chorus. "Will you help me, Dickey, please?"

"Knock it off, guys," Dick shot back. "All right, let's go up."

Buddy and Jimmy took turns swinging while the two climbed up and positioned themselves on the platform.

"Be careful," Dick cautioned.

"I'm all right," she assured him.

"What do I do now?" she asked.

"Throw down the rope, dummy," Jimmy shouted.

"Oh, right," she said as she tossed it down.

Jimmy tied it to the cable and together Dick and Hayla pulled it up.

"I don't know," Hayla said apprehensively.

"It's great," Dick assured her. "You're gonna like it."

He mounted the railing and grabbed the overhead branch.

"Now, hand it up," he instructed.

"What do I do next?" she asked.

"Okay, now put your right foot in the loop and grab the cable with both hands," he coached. "I'll steady it until you get your balance."

She carefully did what Dick said.

Looking down at the ground, she remembered feeling this way the first time she topped the incline of her first ride on a full-size roller coaster at the San Deigo amusement park. Her mind raced! *Would the cable or limb break, hurtling her down to a certain death? No,* she thought. *It held the others, all of whom were heavier than her. Would she lose her grip with the same results or would her foot get caught in the loop and drag her helpless body across the ground?*

"You'll do fine." Dick said confidently. "It's a piece of cake. Just remember, Jimmy did it."

Her fears were somewhat relieved by Dick's continued reassurance.

"I'm going to do this," she sternly whispered to herself.

"You ready?" Dick asked.

"Yes!" she shouted as she lifted her foot off the platform. The cable snapped from Dick's hand and she was off!

For the initial part of the ride all appeared in slow motion to Hayla. At Dick's release her body lurched forward off the platform and was parallel to the ground below. As she and the cable fell, fear engulfed every fiber of her being! She closed her eyes and tightly gripped the cable. It was only when she felt the cable bear her weight that she opened her eyes.

As she sped across the ground the weeds slapped and scratched at her legs. At the far end of the flat the swiftly moving cable began to carry her skyward. The ground dropped from beneath her as she swung out over the canyon and the cable seemed to deliberately twist so that she was facing directly into that grand precipice at the pinnacle of her flight.

She gasped in fright upon seeing how high she was above the trees in the canyon. Slowly she began to descend toward the canyon's wall and again, fear gripped her with the feeling she would be dashed against that wall, but soon this fear was relived as the cable safely bore her across the canyon's edge. Again, the weeds and briars grabbed and stung her ankles as she was whisked across the flat and once again, the cable lifted her skyward. As she approached the platform she saw Dick's smiling face.

"You did it!" he shouted with clenched fists and out-stretched arms.

As she swung across the flat and back over the canyon she looked into it…this time with feelings of ecstasy and awe! Now she could see the sunlight playing on the little creek as it meandered through the canyon and the tops of the trees majestically reaching to the sky.

"Oh, yes," she whispered to herself.

Upon returning to the flat she hopped off the cable and turned to Dick.

"That was the most fantastic thing I've ever done in my life!" she exclaimed as she hugged him.

"You did great," he said, a little shocked by her hug.

Not to be out done by any of this, Buddy grabbed the cable.

"Come on, Jimmy," he said, "give me a hand."

"What are they up to?" Hayla asked.

"I think they're gonna try a new tree," he surmised.

Dick glanced at the tree they were climbing and with his mind's eye, he swung an arc across the flat and the path the cable would travel.

"Hey Buddy," he shouted. "don't you think you're gonna come a tad close to that big oak?"

"Naw," he replied confidently. "and if I do, I'll just kick myself away from it."

Jimmy handed him the rope and soon he was prepared for his ride. He grabbed the cable, gave out with a glorious yell and was off as all eyes followed him on his flight.

The three gasped as flesh and bark violently embraced!

"Oh my God!" Hayla yelled as Buddy crashed to the ground with a resounding thud. They ran to over to where he was. He lay motionless as blood ran from his nose and a cut above his right eye.

"He looks like he's dead," Jimmy observed as they knelt beside him.

"He's not dead," Dick assured. "He's still breathing."

"One of us should get help!" Hayla cried.

Buddy let out a groan and then tried to get up.

"Damn tree!" he cursed as he fell back down.

"Easy, Buddy," Dick cautioned. "Where does it hurt?"

" My head…mostly," he groaned.

"Anything broken?" Jimmy asked.

"I don't think so," he replied. "Help me up."

Dick and Jimmy managed to get him to his feet.

"A…little…dizzy," Buddy said.

"Easy," Dick warned. "Let's see if you can walk it off."

Buddy began to regain his bearings as they rambled around the flat.

"Damn!" he muttered as he felt the warm stream of blood coursing down his face. He pulled out his hanky and started wiping the cut.

"How bad is it?" he asked.

"Looks like you might need a few stitches." Dick said. "How's your nose?"

Buddy wiggled the bridge of his nose with his fingers.

"It hurts, but I don't think it's broken."

"You're lucky," his sister added. "the way you smacked that tree I thought you broke your fool neck!"

"Had you worried, huh sis?" he replied with half a grin.

"Look, I'm fine," Buddy said as he started toward the path. "Let's go back to the cottage and get something to eat."

Chapter 15
TAYLORS DEPART

GW was washing the dirt from his shovel and hoe by the water trough when he noticed the youngsters entering the yard.

"What happened to you, Buddy?" he asked upon seeing the blood on the boy's face and shirt.

"Aw, just a little run-in with a tree," he replied.

GW followed them as they entered the cottage.

"Oh my God!" exclaimed Marie.

"Olive Lee, get a towel and wet it down," Cass instructed as she began to examine Buddy's wounds.

"I…I feel woozy…" Marie sighed as she collapsed into her husband's arms.

"What's going on?" Dave asked as he entered the kitchen.

"Help Bud put Marie on the couch in the living room," Cass said as she continued to check on Buddy.

"You'd better have a seat yourself, young man," she insisted, noticing how the cut above Buddy's eye was still bleeding.

"Dick, go fetch Doc Peterson," she instructed.

"Jimmy's already on his way there," he replied.

With the aid of a cool damp cloth, Marie soon regained consciousness.

"We should've never let those kids off the property," she stammered as she tried to get up off the sofa. "First Hayla with the bears and now this!"

"Easy now," Bud said. "He's going to be just fine as soon as the doctor gets here."

"You best lie here for a spell, Marie" Bessie insisted.

"Okay, who is it this time?" Doc Peterson inquired as he entered the living room.

"Young Buddy here," Bessie informed him.

The Doctor sat down in the chair next to the couch and began to examine Buddy's injuries.

"How in the world did you do this?" he asked.

"We were ridin' on a cable swing and I guess I got a little too close to a tree," Buddy replied.

"That wouldn't be the cable swing down near where old man Duffett used to have his shack would it?" the Doctor inquired.

"Why yes," Dave returned. "I think it is."

The doctor laughed.

"I remember patching up John Harrison's boy, Digger I think they called him. He had the same kind of wound," he said as he began to stitch Buddy's cut. "Digger said the same thing, said he swung a little too close to a tree."

"Ouch!" Buddy wailed as the Doctor pulled the wound together.

"Easy son, we're almost done," he assured him.

"I thought that old cable would have rusted through by now," Dave noted.

"You knew about the cable, Dad?" Dick asked.

"I remember seeing it while I was hunting down that way a few years back," he said. "It slipped my mind until you mentioned it."

"Let me tell you, it works just fine," Jimmy added, "as long as you make way for the trees."

"Maybe I should give you folks a discount for all the business you've been giving me lately," the Doctor noted. "although, on second thought, maybe I should charge you more for having to row across that darned river each time."

"You probably had nothing better to do today anyhow," Bessie quipped.

Again the doctor laughed.

"Mom, you change that bandage every day and clean the wound with a little alcohol," he instructed. "Here's some extra gauze and a few bandages and if it gets infected, drop by my office. If not, come over in about a week and I'll take out those stitches."

"That won't be necessary," Marie stated. "We're leaving tomorrow and Doctor Anderson can take them out when we get back."

"All right, but make sure it doesn't get infected it the meantime," he replied.

Hayla glanced at Dick from across the room and walked out the kitchen door. Shortly after Dick followed.

"Where are you going?" Jimmy asked with a grin.

"Never mind," Dick replied.

From the rear porch, Dick could see her walking along the river bank. Once again her graceful motion stirred his heart as he walked across the lawn to join her. The setting sun began to tinge the undersides of the cotton-white clouds, igniting them in a glorious display of red and orange. A warm breeze drifted across the Juniata and up its banks, caressing the young couple as they walked together.

"I want to thank you, Dick," she began.

"For what?" he asked.

"For what?" she exclaimed, looking at him in disbelief.

"Yeah, for what?" he replied, a bit more reserved.

"For the walk in the morning, for the cable swing, for the deer and squirrels and…"

"And the bears?" he added.

"Now how could I ever forget those bears!" she exclaimed.

"Your Mom had you figured for bear food," he quipped.

"Yes, but it wasn't very funny at the time, Mr. Coleman," she replied.

Once again their eyes met and their hearts soared.

"I…a…" Dick stammered.

"What?" she coaxed.

Dick stopped and glanced across the river to the far shore.

"I guess I'll kinda miss you," he confessed.

"Really," she cooed as she took his hand. Again, their eyes met in a warm caress.

Hayla gently put her arms around his neck. Dick hesitated at first and then slid his arms around her tiny waist.

"I'm gong to miss you, too," she said in a halting voice as she cradled her head on his shoulder.

Dick searched for something to say, something to express what he was feeling, but it all seemed so inadequate. Hayla looked into his eyes and ever so softly, kissed his lips.

"Hayla!"

Her Mother's voice startled the couple.

"You best come in now and start packing," she said. "We're going to leave first thing tomorrow morning."

"Okay, Mom," the blushing girl replied.

Dick tried to catch his breath and make sense of it all, but the feelings overwhelmed his senses and he stood motionless…speechless. They stood together for a moment, looking at the sunset and each other. Hayla sighed quietly as they turned with hands entwined and began walking back to the cottage. The underside of the clouds had turned dusky gray leaving only a narrow strip of diminishing crimson along the crest of the Allegheny Mountains. The air felt cooler to the returning couple as the night closed in around them.

"Oh, I almost forgot," Hayla exclaimed. "Give me your address and I'll write to you."

"Oh, yeah, right," he returned.

Most of the ladies were sitting and chatting together on the front porch which was illuminated by the light coming through the living room window. The flame in the oil-filled hurricane lamp on the table sputtered and danced as the young couple entered the living room. The men were playing matchstick poker at one end of the large dining table while Kit was busy at the other end completing the border of the new jigsaw puzzle Bud and Marie had brought her from San Diego. It was the latest addition to Glen Afton's collection of such brain teasers, most of which actually contained all of their pieces.

"Hey Mom, do we have anything to write on?" Dick asked as he rummaged through the buffet drawers looking for a pencil.

"There should be a writing pad under my sewing basket," she replied.

"What's that for?" Jimmy inquired.

"Never mind, wise guy," Dick replied as he and Hayla went into the kitchen. Dick carefully folded the paper in two, creased it and tore it over the edge of the table.

"I'm not much on writing," Dick confessed. "I have trouble putting things down on paper."

"Just write about what you're up to," Hayla encouraged. "You know, what you're doing, how you're making out in school, things like that."

"Yeah, okay," he reluctantly agreed.

"I'll do the same," she added, "and don't forget to tell me how you feel."

"You mean…like if I'm sick?"

"No dummy," she teased. "How you feel about us…me."

"Oh yeah," he agreed.

The ladies on the porch began singing, as was often their nightly ritual. But instead of starting out with their usual strains of "In the good old summertime" they began with "I've been working on the railroad" with a lyric change to "someone's in the kitchen with Hayla."

Dick was somewhat annoyed by their melodious gesture, but he laughed it off, shaking his head.

Hayla smiled.

Early the next morning strains of "Oh how I hate to get up in the morning" emanated from the wind-up Victrola in the living room. It was the duty of the first one awake to rouse the others if they had to be up and about for something special.

Soon all were up and active as the ladies began to prepare a breakfast of scrapple and eggs while the men helped Bud and Marie lug their belongings out to the rear porch.

"We're gonna miss you two," Cass said.

"The next time we'll try to let you know ahead of time when we're coming so it won't be such a surprise," Bud promised.

"Don't be silly," Dave assured. "You folks are the kind of surprise we look forward to down here"

The family discussed the Taylor's long trip back to San Deigo over breakfast and how the travelers should be careful and travel safely. Goodbyes and farewells were exchanged as the families walked together across the lawn to the dock.

"I'll carry that for you," Jimmy offered, as he took Hayla's suitcase.

"Thanks, Jim," she said as they started down the switch-back stairs toward the dock.

Dick tried to focus on anything except Hayla, but his eyes and heart continued to betray him. Realizing nothing more would be expressed between them, he tried to maintain an attitude of nonchalance, but each time their eyes met the betrayal continued.

"What, no kiss goodbye?" Jimmy teased as they descended the stairs.

He waited for his friend's usual cryptic response…but none came. He noticed a slight sadness in Dick's expression. Jimmy ceased his teasing.

Hugs and kisses were exchanged and as Dave began to row the Taylor family across the Juniata Dick couldn't help feeling a small part of him was leaving as well. One last wave of farewell was shared from mid-stairs and mid-stream.

"Hey, old buddy," Jimmy began, "what say we go back to the flat and do some more flying?"

"Maybe later, Jim," he replied.

That was the first time Dick had ever addressed him as Jim and it took him aback.

"Why don't we grab our rods and go drown some worms down by the rocks?" Dick suggested.

"Sounds like a plan," he agreed.

The pair pushed off in the wooden pram as Jimmy manned the oars and started rowing toward the rocks downstream. The Taylor's Chevy sedan roared to life and slowly started down the dry, dirt road beside the river. The dual horns sounded and hands waved out the windows as they turned toward Beecham's barn and the highway to San Diego.

"She's a pretty neat chick," Jimmy noted as he cast his bobber toward the shoreline.

Dick smiled. "Yeah, I guess you could put it that way."

A large-mouth bass scooped up Jimmy's bait and quickly made for deeper water, causing his reel to sing.

"Whoa!" he shouted. "Guess it's time we start gettin serious about what we're doin here!"

"Right again, Jim boy," Dick agreed as he cast his bait downstream and his eyes toward the tan cloud of dust rising from across Beecham's farm.

Chapter 16
SKIPPED GENERATIONS

The sounds of hammering echoed throughout the otherwise tranquil dale where the Stackhouse cottage stood. A gentle breeze rustled the upper leaves of the great oaks that surrounded and shaded the small structure.

It was a tall, narrow cross plank dwelling of two stories with vertical, dark-stained siding and a small roofed porch facing the river. A tall stone chimney vented the large cast-iron stove which served as both oven and heating system for the little structure.

The steep-pitched roof that Clay was repairing was covered with corrugated steel sheeting that Clare had salvaged from a demolition site in Lewistown. Old Stacky declared that the galvanized, baked-on enamel finish would outlast any other roof in the county. GW declared the bright lime-green color of that particular roof could blind anyone within three counties!

Clare's cottage sat a good six feet lower and much closer to the river than Glen Afton, but its view of Yoder's Lock on the Juniata was every bit as lovely.

"What's for lunch, dad?" Andy called to his roof-repairing father.

"You'll have to check inside with the chief cook and bottle washer," he replied.

The three hungry teens entered the kitchen to find Clare busy working over a large kettle on the stove.

"What smells so good, pap-pap?" Katie asked.

Clare turned and greeted the three with his usual gentle smile. He was a tall man of medium build and only his legs appeared to suffer from his bout with Polio. Age had taken its toll on the old boy's gnarly face, but his ability to get around on his crutches amazed the folks who knew him.

"Well, your dad said he had a hankern for some of your mom's vegetable soup and since I just happen to have her recipe I told him to go bag a groundhog or rabbit and gather some vegetables from the garden and that I'd whip us up a batch," he said.

"Great!" Andy said as he lifted the lid to check it out. "I'm so hungry I could eat the whole mess myself."

"You pig!" Katie growled as she pushed him away to get a better look for herself.

"Katie, you and Fay set the table," Clare said, as he stirred the soup. "Andy, call in your father. This is just about ready."

After everyone had eaten their fill of the noon-day offering Katie and Fay cleared the table and did the dishes while Andy joined his roof-repairing father.

"Doin any painting, Pap-pap?" Fay asked.

"As a matter of fact, I am," he declared. "I set up this morning while Clay was out hunting."

"Where?" Katie inquired.

"Out on the lower path," he replied. "Why don't you two gals come out with me and maybe you can learn you a thing or two."

Clare retrieved his crutches and got up. Clare's crutches weren't just any ordinary lot. They were made of fine hickory by a local craftsman who, under Clare's guidance, fashioned them to fit his arms just right. Shapes of vines and grapes were carved into the legs from top to bottom and two small commemorative railroad coins that GW had given him were inlaid on each of the faces below the handles. Finally they were finished with sealer-primer and marine spar varnish to make them water tight.

"Now, you two fetch some hollyhocks out near the garden while I get a knitting needle," he instructed.

The girls eagerly did as Clare requested, knowing he would be teaching them something new as he had done so often in the past. The trio left and began walking the shaded river path between the two cottages. As they came to the spot where Clare had set up his easel the old timer stopped and carefully surveyed the view across and around the Juniata.

"Now then," he began, "notice how the breeze coming across the river creates a silvery sparkle on that stretch of water out there."

The girls nodded.

"Then see how it sweeps up the bank and turns the leaves on the trees to show their lighter underside," he continued.

"Yeah," the girls said in unison.

"How do you notice all these things, Pap?" Fay asked.

"Well, if you remain still anywhere on God's good earth, He'll take the time to show you some of the beauty He's created for us," Clare continued, "like that gray squirrel comin up the path."

The three remained silent and motionless as the squirrel continued its nut-hunting trek up the side of the river path. On and off the path he came, bustling through the leaves and shrubs, unaware of the eyes watching his every move. Upon finding a large acorn he stood up on his hind legs, popped off the cap of the nut and began munching his lunch not more than four feet from his observers. After completing his meal, he cleaned his face with his paws and headed back down the path toward Glen Afton.

"Wow!" Katie exclaimed.

"That was awesome." Fay remarked. "Are you going to put him in your painting, Pap?"

"Most likely," the old timer replied. "That's what makes painting so enjoyable for me, seeing the beauty of God's good earth and then trying my best to capture it on this canvas."

Clare eased himself down on the three-legged stool next to his easel. He took a brush in hand and with a few strokes and dabs created the same silvery patch on the river in his painting. Moving his brush to the trees he began to lighten the underside of the leaves just as the three of them had seen earlier. He continued to paint as he taught the enchanted girls, smiling to himself as he saw the wonderment in the eyes of his two young students. With his assistance they were now beginning to see past the obvious and into the sublime, into a deeper awareness of things beyond their physical senses.

At times there is something beautiful…something almost magical that takes place between those of skipped generations, something that rarely happens in a parent-child relationship. It was more…much more than teacher and student…much deeper than that. And it was happening now and Clare quietly reveled in its splendor.

"Pap, would you paint Glen Afton for me?" Fay asked as the two watched while Clare continued to work on his creation.

"Well, that would take a tad more paint than I've got on hand." he quipped.

Fay and Katie appeared confused until the old gentleman started his gentle laugh.

"Aw, Pap, you know what I mean," Fay said. "A picture."

"Okay, but it'll cost you," he replied.

"How much?" Fay questioned.

"Well, I've always wanted to know how your Aunt Bessie made her apple strudel, especially that crust," he replied. "Now, if you could wrangle that recipe from her, we could call it an even trade."

"Why don't you just ask her yourself, Pap?" Katie inquired.

"I would, but you see, Bessie and me ain't never seen eye to eye on much," he explained, "and I figure Fay could get it a tad easier than me."

"I'm sure Aunt Bessie would be glad to give it to you when she hears you're gonna paint a picture of Glen Afton," Fay assured him.

"Then it's a done deal," pap declared as he slapped his knee and shook Fay's hand.

"Now, hand me one of those Hollyhocks I had you pick," he said as he pulled out his knitting needle. Clare carefully separated the bud and the green stem from the blossom.

"I used to watch Grandma Hickey make these for my sisters," he continued. "She called them her Hollyhock dolls, but my sisters called them their little ballerinas."

Pap placed the blossom face down on a flat rock which formed the doll's skirt. Next, he pulled the green part away from the bud and made a small hole in the top of the skirt with his needle. Finally he inserted the bud and the stem into the hole which formed the dancer's head and body.

"Neat!" Fay exclaimed as Pap handed her his latest creation.

"Make one for me!" Katie insisted.

"Oh no," the old fellow replied. "I showed you how to do it and now you're on your own."

He handed the needle to Katie and soon the two were busy creating their own dolls under the watchful eye of their mentor. In a short time they had several little dancers set up in a chorus line along the river path. Loving smiles passed between instructor and students as they continued to practice their new-found skill.

Clare reached for his brush and added a length of path along the river's edge with two willowy figures playing on its course.

Chapter 17

DOG MEDICINE

The current lethargic condition of Freckles and Brownie led GW to check their stools for worms. His diagnosis correct, he paid a visit to Doc Peterson in Thompsontown and returned with an ample supply of worm capsules.

Now, GW is rarely given to swearing, but his temper was being worn paper-thin by his dog's refusal to ingest the capsules. About that time Dave entered the kitchen and watched the proceedings. After a while he began to chuckle at his father's fruitless efforts.

"And I suppose you think you could do better," his father snapped.

"Why don't I hold one of them and you force the pill down his throat?" Dave suggested.

"I guess it's worth a try," GW replied. "Let's start with Freckles."

Dave scooped up the wary canine and began calming him with soothing strokes and loving words.

"It's okay, boy," he encouraged. "We're not going to hurt you."

"You ready?" his father asked.

"Give it a shot," Dave replied.

GW carefully opened the reluctant canine's mouth and slid the capsule down as far as his fingers would reach. He held freckles' mouth closed and rubbed his throat. After a few of the dog's uneasy swallows they put him down on the floor.

"There," GW said triumphantly, "that wasn't so bad, was it, boy?"

The men began the same procedure with the larger Brownie. They had just begun when they heard Spot making sounds like a cat about to cough up a hairball.

Wrump, wrump, wrump, gag, spit and the capsule hit the floor, still intact!

The two men looked at the pooch and then at each other in frustration. With his tail wagging, Freckles seemed quite pleased with himself and Brownie's half smiling pant with his tongue hanging out didn't help matters much.

"Damn!" GW exclaimed.

"Why don't we try putting the capsules in some of that rabbit meat you have?" Dave suggested.

"Worth a try, I guess," his dad replied.

Excited by the smell of fresh meat, the dogs had the men believing victory was close at hand as the capsules were rolled into small meatballs.

"Watch this," Dave said as the dogs looked on intently.

"Here, Freckles," he called and, with a flick of his wrist, sent the medicine-laden meatball toward the unsuspecting dog. Freckles caught it in mid-flight.

"Ah ha!" GW shouted victoriously. "I think we found the secret."

Soon they had the same apparent success with Brownie.

"I believe that went rather well," Dave remarked just before they heard a familiar sound coming from Freckles.

"Wrump, wrump, wrump....." Brownie was just a few beats behind. The rabbit meat was gone but the capsules lay on the kitchen floor still quite intact.

"Damn it, again!" GW wailed in frustration as he slammed the pill box down on the table, sending some of the capsules skittering across the floor. Immediately the two dogs gave chase and quickly gobbled up the bounding pills.

Father and son stared at each other in stupefied amazement and then burst into peals of laughter.

"What's so funny?" Russell inquired upon entering the kitchen.

"You wouldn't believe us if we told you," Dave said as he wiped his eyes.

"Try me," Russell encouraged.

"These two dogs here aren't as dumb as they seem," Dave began.

" But they are a tad gullible," his father added as he and his son burst into another round of laughter.

Chapter 18
RUSSELL'S FUDGE

"Anything good to eat in here?" Russell inquired.

"Not much," Dave replied as he and GW got up and headed outside with the dogs.

"The women are over at the store picking up some things though," Dave added as he left.

Outside the sky, which for days had delivered nothing but hot sun, was beginning to fill with dark gray clouds.

"They'd better get back soon," Russell remarked. "It looks like we might be blessed with a little rain."

He began snooping around, searching for something to satisfy his craving.

A man could starve by the time those three get back, Russell mused as he continued rummaging around the kitchen. He pulled the brier bulldog pipe from his shirt pocket and, after changing the filter, packed the bowl with an ample fill of tobacco. Russ looked good clenching that pipe in his manly square jaw and he knew it. He snapped open and lit his Zippo lighter in one smooth motion and began puffing until the tobacco glowed an even red.

Now, what to make, what to make, he pondered as he continued to search for something to satisfy his appitite.

Something sweet... something sweet...

The Hershey's cocoa box on the top shelf of the cook stove gave him the answer.

Fudge, he thought. *Now where is Cass's recipe box?*

The recipe seemed simple enough, but were all the necessary ingredients available? He began searching all of the cupboards and then the newly constructed springhouse. All the items were there: milk and butter from the spring house, sugar, vanilla and that essential pinch of salt from the kitchen. Russell mixed and cooked the ingredients until the dark creamy concoction was well blended. Then, as he had seen Cass do so many times before, he sat down with the warm bowl in his lap and with a wooden spoon in hand, began beating the mixture into its proper consistency.

While contemplating on the soon to be gotten reward of his labors he was suddenly startled by a noise on the front porch. As he turned his head to see what it was, he lost the grip on his pipe and dropped it, bowl first, into the gooey mass! He quickly retrieved the sticky, sizzling pipe and took it over to the basin where he cleaned it off, but to his surprise, he saw that most of the tobacco in the bowl of the brier was gone! Looking up in wide-eyed amazement, he realized where it was.

Returning to the table he saw the tobacco was too well dispersed through the fudge to be effectively removed and believing the fudge might be ruined, he began to think of a solution his problem. He thought for a while and then, with a smile of confidence, sat the bowl on his lap, picked up the spoon and continued to stir the strangely altered concoction.

After supper that evening the family sat around the large dining room table, discussing the events of the day.

"I'm glad we made it back before those clouds let loose," Bessie announced.

"Yes and it doesn't look like it's going to let up anytime soon," Hat noted.

"Did you make fudge today, Cass?" Bessie inquired. "I swear I can smell chocolate."

"No," she replied, "but now that you mention it, I believe I can smell it too."

Fay got up and went into the kitchen as Russ began to feel a little uneasy.

"Here it is," Fay exclaimed as she reentered the dining room with the fudge pan.

"All right," Cass said, casting an eye around the table, "who made fudge and didn't tell anyone?"

They looked at one another.

"Russ, weren't you going to make something in the kitchen when dad and I left?" Dave questioned.

"Well, yes," he admitted, "I made it, but I don't know how good it turned out."

"Oh, go on Russell, it probably tastes just fine," Hat said as she took a piece and passed the pan around.

"Russell!" Cass exclaimed.

Russ glanced at her out of the corner of his eye, expecting a harsh reprisal.

"This really tastes good," she declared.

The others had to agree.

"What's your secret?" Cass continued. "It tastes a little different than mine. Did you use my recipe?"

"Uh, yeah, but I altered it a bit," he added sheepishly.

"What did you add to give it that special flavor?" she asked.

"Well I don't know if I want to reveal my secret," he replied, desperately trying to figure a way out of his dilemma.

"I know!" exclaimed Fay, holding up a small piece of tobacco.

Russell's face turned pale.

"It's coconut," she continued.

Russ breathed an internal sigh of relief.

"Yes," Hat added, "but it seems a bit stronger than coconut."

"That's because I toasted the coconut to give it a richer flavor," Russ replied, as he began to see light at the end of his problematic tunnel.

"Good job, Russ," Dave affirmed as the pan was quickly emptied.

"Maybe it's about time someone else takes over the job of fudge-making around here," Cass remarked with a smile in Russell's direction.

Later that evening, Russ stepped out on the front porch and lit up his pipe which now had a slight chocolate flavor. He grinned to himself as he viewed the rain-soaked scene of lawn and forest in the twilight of the evening.

"How 'bout a light?"

Russell was startled by the sudden appearance of Aunt Bessie.

"Sure," he replied, as he snapped open his Zippo and lit Bessie's corn-cob pipe. The two stood there, leaning against the railing, puffing their pipes, and quietly taking in the sights and sounds of the steadily falling rain.

"Fudge was alright," Bessie acknowledged, still looking out at the forest.

"Thanks," Russ offered, as he began to sense what was coming.

"But the next time you make it, remember to put down your smoke before you pick up your spoon." she said as she started to walk across the porch.

"It could have been coconut," he remarked.

"Ain't been a shred of coconut in this house for a some time, Russell," she returned as she put on her rain bonnet and headed for the outhouse.

Russell smiled as he watched her trot down the path with her funny limping gait, knowing his secret was safe with dear Aunt Bessie.

Chapter 19

FLOODS

- Camping 1954 -

The fourth day at camp proved to be hotter than the first three. We tied the tent's window and door flaps open as a large praying mantis hung on the side of the tent, devouring a grasshopper like an ear of corn.

"The sassafras roots are ready for brewing," Dick stated.

Dad carefully inspected them and agreed, explaining that the pink roots we found were a bonus over the common white.

"The pink root always has a richer, fuller flavor," he confided.

That evening's supper, consisting of grilled Spam, canned corn, freshly dug turnips and sassafras tea, tasted delicious after a full day of Indian arrowhead hunting and fishing. The Island fields, so named for their remote location on the eastern shore of the Juniata, rendered several unbroken spearheads and arrowheads that day. The gentle breeze that started before supper had picked up as dark, ominous clouds began to blot out the sun's hot rays.

"Man, that air sure feels good," Dick said as he wiped his brow with his large blue hanky.

"True, but those clouds look full and they're coming from the south," dad stated. "We better break camp and move up near the old foundation."

Dick and I looked at each other in disbelief, remembering the trouble we had clearing our campsite of weeds and debris let alone the time it took to set up the camp according to dad's specific instructions.

"You're kidding!" I said.

"No," he assured. "I've seen storms like this coming in from the south and they can bring the river up as much as five feet overnight."

He looked at us in a very serious manner.

"As much as I like to be near the water, night swimming in a tent is not exactly my cup of tea," he noted, holding up his mug of sassafras. "Besides, the flies and mosquitoes aren't near as bad up there and the air should be a little cooler."

We reluctantly agreed and started breaking camp. The switch-back stairs had washed away years ago, but the stair tread impressions were still there, which assisted our move. The wind began to pick up hindering our progress in reestablishing the new campsite, but we managed to complete the task just as the sun went behind the mountains on the western shore.

"We better stow everything in the tent that we don't want soaked ," dad said as we brought the last of our supplies up the bank. Our three wooden-canvas army cots inside the eight by eight umbrella tent left precious little room for much else, but Dick, with his knack for efficient packing, soon had our weather-susceptible goods stored out of harm's way.

"That should keep every thing dry," he assured.

As twilight began to wane and the clouds continued to roll in, we took one last look around and then retired for the night. Dad filled the brass lamp with fresh carbide and water and soon had it fizzing . After replacing the cap, he adjusted the lever on top and spun the built-in steel wheel against the newly installed flint. After a few flicks, the sparks ignited the slowly escaping gas as he adjusted the flame and soon our tent was filled with light.

We began discussing the next day's agenda, but the effort of moving our campsite and the day's search for arrow heads soon took their toll. Dick was the first to succumb as he nodded off. Dad snuffed out the lamp and the sound of the rain beginning to fall on our tent was soon joined by the raspy snoring of my father and brother.

The first flash of lightning woke me with a start! The wind intensified as our tent shook and quivered under its incessant gusts, but it held fast, a tribute to my dad and brother's expertise as experienced campers. I could hear the surrounding trees groaning as they heaved to and fro while the wind whipped through the brush around our camp site. I couldn't shake the feeling that our tent would be blown over or that a tree could come crashing down on us while we slept.

The next bolt of lightning was even closer than the last. Its thunder-clap was deafening, but the visual effects were amazing! The brilliance of the flash was so intense it appeared our tent had completely disappeared and for that one brief moment the trees and shrubs surrounding our tent could be seen as clear as if I was outside. The experience of that night, which I shall never forget, was both frightening and exhilarating. Dad and Dick continued to sleep, undaunted by the storm's fury as I lay on my cot, pulling the covers close around me.

Soon the lightning flashes became more separated from their claps of thunder as the storm made its way north. The wind began to recede, but the rain continued its steady drumming on our little shelter. My mind and body began to relax with the ebbing of the storm and it wasn't long till I was sleeping.

Next morning, I woke to the smell of warm canvas and paraffin as the late morning sun beat down on our little abode. All seemed calm outside and the only sound was that of a dog barking in the distance.

I stretched, yawned, scratched, and finally rolled out of my cot to check the results of last night's tempest. Unzipping the flap I saw the only remnants of the storm were a few charcoal clouds floating above the tops of the eastern mountains. As I rounded the tent and looked toward the river, I was astonished to see that dad's prediction had come true.

The usually calm Juniata had risen over five feet during the night which would have put our tent in two feet of flood water. I watched as the murky, brown river churned below our camp.

About then, I heard the two night sawers begin to stir from their sleep.

"Dad," I shouted, "come take a look at the river."

He came out, looked around, and smiled.

"I figured it would come up a bit, with the way that storm was gathering last night," he stated.

We continued to watch as the murky water sped along its course, cleaning its banks of all debris. Small and sometimes not so small trees, boards, tires, and an occasional boat drifted past our camp. I headed down the bank for a closer look at a phenomenon I had never before witnessed .

"Careful," dad warned. "that current is strong and can have a tricky undertow when its running this high."

"Did you ever see it this high before?" I questioned.

At that time, I didn't notice my father and brother looking at each other with solemn expressions, although I feel they must have.

"Yes, Fred…yes we have," Dad said in a somber voice with a faraway look.

-1941-

For five days the rain continued to pour down on Glen Afton and its surrounding hills and valleys. The ground was saturated and was like walking on a wet sponge. A musty dampness had settled in on everything including their spirits and cabin fever was beginning to set in on everyone.

"I believe the fish should be biting about now, boys," Dick's grandfather noted. "What say we go see if we can go out and snag a few?"

Anxious to do anything that would break the monotony of being penned up, the boys quickly donned their yellow slickers and headed for the dock. As they came to the edge of the bank they were amazed to see the dock was completely covered by water. Only the three boats tethered there gave hint of its existence.

"First things first, boys," the old-timer declared. "We best move the boats to higher ground so we don't lose them."

"What about the dock?" Jimmy asked.

"It's piers are well anchored to the river bottom," he replied. "It should be all right."

The three sloshed out onto the submerged dock to inspect the situation.

"Dick, go fetch that coil of rope on the top shelf in the shed," his grandfather said.

"Do you think the river will get much higher, Mr. Coleman?" Jimmy asked.

"By the looks of that sky, Jimmy, I wouldn't be a bit surprised if it did," he replied.

When Dick returned, GW tied the rope to the bow-eye of the pram.

"Take this line and go around that locust tree up there and when I give the signal you two pull it up the bank," he instructed.

Dick and Jimmy did as they were told and soon all three boats were sitting far up the bank and securely tied off to the trees above them.

"That should hold'em," GW claimed.

"How high did you ever see the river, Gramps?" Dick asked.

"Take a look here, boys," he said, pointing to a horizontal saw-cut on the side of one of the stair risers. "Five summers back we saw the water come up to this mark."

"Now that's high!" Dick remarked.

"Not the highest," he said as he pointed to another mark only two steps from the top.

"Are these marks really accurate?" Jimmy asked.

GW smiled as he put his arm around Jimmy.

"They may not be exact, Jim, but it's enough to let us know what's really in charge around here."

Jimmy shook his head in agreement.

"Think it will ever get that high again, gramps?" Dick asked.

The old-timer paused and thought for a moment.

"That highest mark happened over forty years ago and since then its never been close ," he noted. "I suppose that year was a bit of a fluke."

"What do you figure caused it to get that high back then?" Jimmy asked.

"I figure conditions had to be just right," he surmised. "A deep build-up of winter snow in the mountains and a lot of warm spring rain melting it off was probably the cause."

"No snow in the mountains now," Dick noted.

"I've a mind we won't have to fear that kind of thing happening again for a long time," he assured the boys.

The steadily increasing rain did little to dampen the spirits of the three fishermen and, as GW predicted, the fish were indeed biting. Soon their creels were full of large and small mouth bass along with a few cats and the three headed for the warmer, dryer sanctuary of the cottage.

In no time Cass and Bessie rendered that scaly, slimy catch into a succulent culinary delight and all present that evening dined on a savory batter-dipped fish dinner with a side of fresh garden vegetables and rhubarb pie while the sky continued its outpouring on the land.

The women were finishing up the last of the dinner dishes when there came a knocking at the kitchen door. Andy and Katie were the first to come bounding in with a cheerful hello and were soon followed by Clare and his son-in-law, Clayton Hahn.

"We were gettin tired of lookin at one another over there, so we figured we'd come over here and bother you good folks for a while," Clare stated as he raised a crutch in salutation.

"Good to have some company about now," Cass noted.

"Hey, old timer, what do you think of these tomatoes?" GW asked Clare as he exhibited two of the large fruits from his prized garden. The feud between these two old gentlemen over their gardens had been going on ever since anyone could remember.

Clare took one of the tomatoes, held it up to the light and inspected it quite thoroughly.

"Yup," he acknowledged as he handed it back. "My garden was a bit stunted this year too."

GW shook his head in disbelief and walked away as Clare winked at the others. "What's in the sack, Mr. Hahn?" Fay inquired, figuring Clay's love of music led him to bring along one of his stringed companions.

"Well, since there's not much to do until this rain lets up, I figured a tune or two would help lift our spirits," he replied.

Everyone agreed with the exception of the boys and soon all began to filter into the living room. Clay tuned up his six string and started the evening off with, 'In the good old summertime.' Soon all were harmonizing to the strains of 'Down by the old mill stream' and 'Mares eat oats and does eat oats.' Katie had a fit when her dad started to play the song she loathed, but even she was in a festive enough mood to sing along to the tune of 'K…K…K…Katie'. Favorite hymns and songs were called out and Clay played them all. The singing and merriment at Glen Afton continued well into the wee hours while outside the rain never missed a beat.

"One more tune should do it," Clay insisted." My fingers won't be worth a darn tomorrow if we go on much longer"

"How about 'Lord of the Dance'," Katie shouted. "That's Pap's favorite."

Clare nodded his head in agreement and soon everyone was singing the chorus strains, '**Dance, then, wherever you may be; I am the Lord of the Dance, said he. And I'll lead you all, wherever you may be, and I'll lead you all in the dance, said he.'** (1)

Sitting at Clare Stackhouse's feet, Fay noticed how joyously he sang this song. She looked up into his old hazel eyes.

"You going to dance someday, Pap?" she asked.

The old gentleman thought for a moment.

"The other day I saw a young robin with only one good wing," he began. "I suppose he was born that way, but, you know, that gutsy little guy tried with all his might to fly up with his kin, but all he could do was skidder across the ground until he hit something or got himself winded."

Clare paused as he sat back in the rocking chair.

"But that plucky little fellow kept on trying and trying until he was out of sight," he continued. "I saw him again next day down by the river, but that was the last. I suppose an owl or fox got him by now."

He noticed the sad expressions on Fay and Katie's faces.

"But you know," he said with a gleam in his eye, "I believe that gutsy little fellow is in heaven right now, circling the throne of God with two brand new wings and some day, mark my words, I'll be right up there with him dancing on my two new legs."

"No more crutches, huh Pap?" Katie added.

"Oh, yes, these crutches will be there too," he said to the amazement of the girls.

"Then I'll dance to the edge of the cloud and toss these hickories as far as they'll go!"

"You'll dance with me then, won't you, Pap?" Fay inquired.

"I'll dance with you and all the girls when we get to heaven," he replied with a smile.

"I guess we better pack it on home," Clay said as he stretched and yawned.

"You're welcome to stay the night," Cass offered. "That rain's still coming down hard and we can make room for the four of you."

"Thanks anyway, Cass," Clay said gratefully, "but I want to get an early start tomorrow. The main supports on the river side of the cottage need shoring up."

The four visitors donned their slickers and boots as Clay slid the glass chimney up on his hurricane lantern and lit the wick.

"Did you notice if the river was comin up much on your way over?" Dave asked.

"It's comin' up all right," Clare assured. "I suppose we'll have to go up to the railroad if the river path is flooded."

Dave walked out onto the back porch and aimed his flashlight toward the path.

"You're right," he noted. "It's covered."

The Glen Afton clan followed the visitors to the front porch to bid them farewell.

"Don't forget, Pap," Fay called, "you promised to start that painting for me."

"I'll be over just as soon as this darn rain lets up," he returned.

They watched them make their way across the front lawn and up the spring path until the yellow light from Clay's lantern faded in the distance.

"Never ceases to amaze me how that man gets around on those sticks of his," Bessie said with a shake of her head.

"He's had a lifetime of practice, Bess," Dave allowed.

Bessie nodded in agreement.

Soon the lights at Glen Afton made their way from the lower to the upper level as the weary, but gladdened souls laid their heads to rest on beckoning pillows. Before long the rain's continuing rhythm had lulled them all to sleep.

Jimmy was the first to rise the next morning to the sound of singing birds and the pressure of a full bladder. As he slid out of bed, he eyed the porcelain slop jar at the foot. *No way*, he thought to himself as he remembered his oath never to use such a disgusting contrivance. He briefly peered through the dorm window facing the front yard and noticed the rain had stopped and the clouds were breaking up.

Great! he thought, *now maybe we can get a little sun.*

The happy lad began descending the darkened stairs, humming one of the songs from last night's festivities.

Suddenly, he stopped dead as his feet entered the tepid water at the bottom of the stairs! As his eyes became accustomed to the dim light, he slowly looked down to find the whole first floor covered with several inches of the murky fluid.

"Oh, Lordy!" he gasped as he gazed around the flooded room. Magazines and kindling wood were floating around his feet. Dick's baseball mitt with the ball still inside floated against the leg of the dining room table as the smell of coal-oil filled his nostrils.

Outside he heard Freckles and Brownie begin to bark.

"Oh, Lordy, Lordy!" he exclaimed for all to hear as he bounded back up the stairs.

"Dick!" he yelled. "Flood…flood water…it's in the house!"

"What are you talking about?" Dick asked in sleepy frustration.

"Come down and see for yourself!" he beckoned as he pulled his half-awake buddy from his bed. The two bounded down the stairs as Dick rubbed his eyes and blinked, trying to comprehend what he was seeing. Hearing the ruckus, the other men woke and came down.

"What is it, boys?" Dick's father questioned.

"The river, dad… the river's in the house!" Dick replied.

They looked at each other for a moment and then sloshed out through the kitchen to the back porch. Russell gave out with a long, low whistle.

Outside, a large brown lake had replaced the once flourishing green lawn of Glen Afton. Beyond the lake, the Juniata was raging down its course, carrying everything from bottles and cans to trees and old tires. The morning sun was beginning to shine through the trees as the remnant of clouds moved northward out of the otherwise clear-blue sky. Spring water splashed from the pipeline into the vast body of murky water as if proclaiming what a fine job it had done filling up the surrounding area.

Further out toward the submerged riverbank two of the three boats were still tethered to their trees. The pram was gone.

"It appears that our old high water mark just got beat," GW noted.

"Dave!" Cass called from the ladies bedroom.

"We know, we know," he returned.

"Best see what we can salvage before it gets any worse," GW stated.

"Look," Dave said, pointing to the water along the porch wall. "The water reached its high-water mark here."

"You're right," his father acknowledged. "It's already starting to go down."

"Best thing to do is to get everything up and out of this mess until the water drains out of the house," Cass added.

All agreed and soon the whole clan was carrying rugs, furniture and everything that could be moved to the back porch. The water off the front porch was knee deep making it difficult to get to dry ground at the far end of the front lawn.

"Dave, why don't you and Russell see if you can retrieve those boats," GW suggested. "They'll make it a lot easier to move this stuff."

"Dick and I will help get them," Jimmy said.

"No, Jimmy, let the men do it," GW advised. "That current is strong and could sweep you away."

Dave and Russell agreed. They stripped down to their shorts and started swimming across the newly formed lake and out toward the two foundering vessels.

"Check those boats before you get in them," Bessie warned. "No tellin what might've crawled aboard to get out of the flood."

The brothers cautiously swam together toward the raging river. The tethered boats were pulling hard against the river's swift current.

"We'll start upstream and let the current take us to the boats," Dave suggested. Russ nodded in agreement and the two moved above the boats. As they began to float with the current, Dave looked up and saw something approaching his younger brother.

"Watch out, Russ!" he shouted as the large uprooted tree floated toward him. Russell tried to swim out of its way, only to have his leg snagged by one of its partially submerged limbs. He struggled, but couldn't manage to get free.

"Oh no, Look!" Olive Lee shouted as all on shore watched the drama unfold. Suddenly the current rolled the tree, causing it to pull the hapless Russ under. Dave dove down and followed the trunk to the limb that had entangled his brother. Following it out, he felt the limb's crotch where Russ's leg was trapped. He moved further out and tried to pull the branch away from the trunk, but it wouldn't budge! Letting go of the branch he surfaced for air.

"Where's Russ?" Cass shouted.

"I'll get him," Dave assured them as he dove again. This time he braced his legs against the trunk and pulled on the branch with all his strength. Finally Russ managed to pull free and the two men swam to the surface.

"There they are!" Bessie shouted.

A collective sigh of relief went up from all on shore as they continued to watch the two swimmers.

"You all right?" Dave asked.

"Yeah…yeah…I'm good," Russell returned.

Swimming more cautiously now, they came to the rowboat.

"All clear inside," Russell assured as he checked out the boat's bottom.

"I'll stay on this side while you work your way to the stern," Dave instructed. "I'll steady her while you get in."

Russ crawled over the stern board and pulled himself into the boat. Soon Dave joined him and positioned himself at the oars.

"Okay, untie her," Dave instructed.

They floated down to the larger flat-bottom Hoffman and grabbed it as they came along side, giving it a quick check for critters.

"You see him?" Russ inquired.

"Yup," Dave returned.

The large blacksnake lay coiled up under the center seat. While Russell steadied the two crafts Dave eased an oar under the seat and gently nudged the shiny reptile. It uncoiled and slithered to the rear of the boat. Dave repositioned himself and slid the oar under the reptile's mid-section and lifted it up. Having enough of this, the large reptile crawled into the river and swam toward the bank.

"You've got a visitor coming your way," Russell shouted to those on shore.

Dave inspected the craft once more and then slid into the Hoffman.

"We better tie them together," Dave directed as he steadied the two boats.

Russell hurriedly tied the bow of the rowboat to the stern of the Hoffman.

"All clear upstream," Dave noted as he untied the Hoffman from the tree.

The boats began to float downstream as the men took to their oars and together they rowed across the lake to the cottage. Soon the boats were filled with wet and dry belongings as load after load of goods were hauled to higher ground.

"This is going to be one lovely mess to clean up," Hat remarked, "and just how are we going to get that smell of mud and coal oil out of this place?"

"We'll just handle it like we do everything else around here," Bessie reminded her. "One calamity at a time."

"Besides," Cass added in an optimistic tone, "this place was due for a good cleaning anyhow."

The moving and cleaning continued until an ominous crashing sound was heard from upstream, causing them all to stop.

"What the devil was that?" GW said as he looked out across the Juniata.

"Might have been an uprooted tree falling into the river," Russ offered.

"No…it didn't sound like a tree to me," Dave stated.

"Look there!" Dick shouted as a mass of boards floated past the cottage. The water was continuing to recede across the lawn, allowing them to go out for a closer look.

"My God!" Dave exclaimed when he realized what he was seeing.

"What?" Cass questioned. "What is it?"

"I think it's the Stackhouse's cottage," he replied.

A familiar piece of bright lime-green roof floated by, confirming their worst fears.

Fay's eyes grew large as her mouth dropped open.

"Katie!" she gasped as she instinctively ran toward the flooded river path.

"No, Fay!" her father shouted. "We'll have to go up by the railroad."

She turned and sprinted past the others as they headed toward the spring path. Fay was far ahead of them as her long legs and deep concern for her friend carried her toward the Stackhouse homestead.

"Please…please, dear God," she pleaded, trying to hold back her tears, "not Katie."

She hurriedly covered the quarter-mile trek along the railroad and turned down the path toward the Stackhouse cottage. As Fay neared the homestead, she saw Andy coming up the path toward her. His face was sullen and rigid.

"Andy, where's Katie?" she asked in a breathless voice.

He didn't look at her as he passed. Fay grabbed his arm.

"Andy, where's your sister?"

He wrenched his arm from her grip and continued up the path without saying a word. Fay looked at him with feelings of amazement and fear.

"Oh no!" she cried as she continued down the path.

"Katie!' she yelled as she entered the property.

Fay stopped dead. The area was eerily quiet; she was horrified at what she saw. Only part of one wall was left on the fully submerged foundation where the Stackhouse cottage had stood.

"Oh, no…oh, no…" she uttered as she looked around the property for signs of life.

Eventually, she began to hear soft crying sounds off to her right. She looked across the lawn where she saw Clayton bending over something. Fay ran to him, trying hard not to believe what was happening. Coming closer Fay breathed a sigh of relief when she saw Katie sitting on a stump in front of her father. She was crying bitterly as Clay tried to console his daughter.

"Oh, Katie, thank goodness you're all right," Fay said as she touched her arm. "I was worried sick when I saw the roof of your cottage float by our place."

Katie continued crying as she looked at the ground. Fay knelt in front of her friend, taking her hands in her own.

"Katie," she said softly, "everything's going to be all right. It was just an old cabin and we can help you rebuild and…"

Fay fell silent…her eyes widened as she slowly stood up and looked around.

"Katie…Katie, where's Pap? Katie, where's your grand…"

"He's in the river!" she yelled. "The river took him just like it took my mother!"

She stood up, pushing Fay away from her.

"I hate this place!" she screamed through a distorted, tear-stained face as she began running toward the flooded river path.

"Katie, no!" Fay yelled as she stood up and chased after her friend.

Katie ran to the river path where it was flooded and continued into the murky brown water as Fay splashed in after her, catching her by the arm.

"Let me go!' she screamed. "I want to die!"

Fay desperately tried to pull her back to the path.

"No, Katie, no…please," she pleaded.

"Leave me alone!" she screamed.

Katie continued to struggle, tumbling both of them into the muddy, knee-deep water.

"I want to die…I want to…" She broke down, sobbing bitterly.

Fay cradled her hurting friend in her arms as she continued to weep. She looked at the sky through her own tears as she began to realize her friend's loss…and her own.

"It's all right…it's gonna be all right," Fay said, her voice breaking, as she tried to reassure her friend.

"Oh, Fay, I feel so bad….I hurt so bad…"

Tears streamed down the girls' faces.

"First mama…now pap-pap…I just want to die."

The forest and river seemed reverently quiet now. Holding Katie in her arms, Fay looked across the muddy waters in silent desperation as she sought to console her grieving friend. For the first time in her young life the proper words couldn't be found. Then…softly…quietly…she began to sing.

"Dance, then, wherever you may be; I am the Lord of the Dance, said he"…

Katie looked up at Fay.

Haltingly…she began to sing. "and I'll lead you all, wherever you may be and I'll lead you all in the dance, said he."

Both girls managed slight smiles through tear-streaked faces.

"Do you think pap-pap's dancing now…you know…like he said he would?"

"Of course I do," Fay assured. "He's probably dancing…dancing with your mother right now."

Katie hugged her.

"Thank you, Fay, thank you."

Fay helped her up and together, the two mud-soaked girls walked back to the remnants of the Stackhouse homestead.

"In all my days I never saw the Juniata come up as fast as it did last night." GW noted, shaking his head.

"I had no idea it would come up that high, or what damage it would do," Clay admitted.

"How did it happen?" Dave asked his friend.

"I was asleep when a grinding noise woke me up," he began. "Then I felt the whole cottage shake. I jumped up and looked out the window …the water was almost up to the second level!"

Choking back tears, he went on. "I woke the kids and called for Clare who was sleeping in the next room. I was still groggy from sleep, but realized it would be senseless to try to go down stairs. That's when I felt the house begin to move.

"I opened the window facing the woods and made Andy and Katie jump out and swim for the shore."

Clayton hesitated, trying to compose himself.

"I yelled for Clare again and was heading for his room when the whole house twisted, knocking me to the floor. I got back up and tried to open his bedroom door, but it was jammed. Pieces of ceiling were dropping all around me. That's when I heard Katie yelling for help."

He paused for a moment, wiping his eyes and looking around and then went on.

" I managed to dive through what was left of the window frame and when I surfaced I saw Andy pulling himself on to the bank. I looked downstream and there was Katie struggling against the current. I swam to her and was barely able to drag the both of us to shore. It was then I looked up in time to see it collapse into a pile of boards."

Dave and his father remained speechless as they listened.

"All that's left is that one piece of wall," he continued. "Andy dove in and tried to swim out to the wreckage but the current swept the whole mess farther out into the main stream. When he came back we followed it on shore for a ways, calling for Clare and searching for any sign of him."

He stopped and looked at Dave and GW.

"He's gone," he said.

Dave and his Father moved closer, consoling their friend as he wept.

Dick and Jimmy came running down toward the property.

"Oh God!" Dick exclaimed as he and Jimmy looked around at the devastated homestead.

They spotted Fay and Katie and went over to them.

"You alright, Katie?" Dick asked.

She shook her head.

Fay left Katie and took the boys over by the outhouse. She looked at them with the most serious face Dick had ever seen on his sister.

"Pap-pap's gone," Fay said.

"Oh, no!" the two said in unison. "How?"

"The cottage collapsed and swept him out into the river," she replied.

"Oh, man!" Jimmy exclaimed.

"Did you see Andy?" Fay inquired.

The boys looked at each other.

"No, we didn't," Dick answered.

"Well, you two had better go find him," she implored. "He needs somebody."

"Yeah, but what will we,,,"

"Just go find him, Dick!" she said with a stern look.

"Yeah…yeah, all right," he replied. "Come on, Jim."

The boys took one more look around at the destruction the river had caused and then headed back up the path toward the railroad.

"Where do you think he is?" Jimmy asked

"I'm not sure, but I have a hunch he'll be at the swing," he returned. "That's where I'd go if…you know."

A slow moving local freight ambled past the boys on its way toward Thompsontown.

"What are we going to say to him?" Jimmy asked.

"I don't know," Dick replied, a little annoyed. "I guess we'll just say we're sorry about losing his pap."

The two started down the path toward the oak swing.

"Yeah, but how do you know for sure that's the right thing to say?" Jimmy continued. "How do you know it's gonna do any good?"

"I'm not sure of anything," Dick confessed. "I only know Fay thinks we can help him somehow."

"Yeah, that's right," Jimmy agreed. "Trouble is I never knew anyone who, you know, who lost somebody this way."

They skirted the frog pond, climbed the hill and looked out across the flat. Andy was sitting on the cable loop of the swing, kicking the dirt beneath him. At first he pretended not to notice them. Dick and Jimmy looked at each other. They remained silent for a while.

"You okay?" Dick asked.

"Yeah," Andy replied without looking up as he continued to kick the dirt.

"Me and Jimmy here thought we'd come and see if you were alright," Dick added.

"I said I'm all right," he insisted as he began to swing around the flat, his back toward them.

Dick nudged Jimmy, looking for some help.

"We're real sorry about your pap and everything," he blurted.

He looked at Dick, shrugging his shoulders.

"If you and your dad need any help, you know, with the cottage and all, just let us know," Dick offered.

"Yeah," Jimmy added, "we'd be glad to help with anything."

Andy remained silent as he continued to swing around the flat.

"We'll be around, Andy," Dick said in a more serious tone.

The two went back down the hill and started toward the railroad.

"That was dumb," Jimmy observed.

"No, it wasn't."

"We sounded stupid."

"No we didn't!"

"I just wish we could've said your pap's all right," Jimmy continued. "They found him and he's all right or I wish I could clap my hands and their house would be…"

"Now that's stupid," Dick snapped..

"Yeah," Jimmy agreed, "but if we could've said something more or done something more."

Dick stopped and looked at Jimmy.

"Do you remember when Trix died?"

"Yeah, he sure was a good ole dog and …"

"And when you heard about it you came over to see me?"

"Yeah, so?" Jimmy replied.

"And you stood around, looking stupid?"

"I didn't think I looked that stupid."

"Well, you did," Dick recalled, "and you said a lot of dumb things, trying to cheer me up, but that's not the point."

"It's not?" Jimmy questioned.

"No," Dick explained. "Don't you see? The point is that you were there."

"You mean you were just glad I was there?" he asked.

"Of course," Dick assured, "and I think it's the same with Andy. Sure, we might have looked stupid and maybe we didn't say the right things, but he still knows we're there for him."

"Yeah," Jimmy agreed. "I guess you're right."

"Of course I'm right." Dick returned.

"I guess that's what friends are for," Jimmy added.

"Nah," Dick replied.

"Huh?" Jimmy said, cocking his head.

"Nah, friends are for grabbin and beatin on," Dick replied with a grin, as he grabbed the smaller boy and began to rough him up.

"Hey, let go! Cut it out!" Jimmy squealed.

"You see, Jimmy boy, smart fellas like me pick smaller guys like you for their buddies," Dick said as he continued his rough housing. "That way, if we get to arguing, I can always put a good whippin on you."

"Cut it out, Dick!" Jimmy wailed. "Some day I'll be bigger and then I'll…"

"Yeah, sure and someday bullfrogs will have wings and won't have to hop around. Hop, hop, hop, Jimmy boy," Dick teased as he picked up his hapless buddy and made him hop.

"Oof, damn you!" Dick bellowed as Jimmy sunk an elbow into his stomach.

Jimmy scrambled free from his tormentor and bolted down the tracks beside the mainline.

"You might be stronger, you big fat slob, but I can always outrun you!" Jimmy taunted as he continued down the tracks.

"I'll get you sooner or later, you skinny little runt!" Dick replied as he tore after him. The two were off again, putting aside, for a moment, the tragic loss and the awkward, but kind act they had performed for a hurting friend.

During the next few days the flood waters receded and the sun began to dry the land. The Coleman family continued to help the Hahns clean up and salvage what was left at Clare's cottage.

"You get straightened up from all this, Clay, and we'll help you rebuild," Dave said with a note of encouragement in his voice.

"I sure do appreciate that, Dave, but it might be a while seein how jobs are so few and far between," Clay said as he solemnly looked around at the emptiness that was once a cozy little homestead.

"And with Clare gone it just won't seem the same…won't seem the same at all."

"You know you're always welcome to come and stay with us," Dave added as they continued to search through the rubble.

"I know," Clay returned, "and I'm mighty grateful for all you folks have done for me and the kids."

"Mom says supper will be ready in about an hour," Fay said as she and Katie came on the scene.

"We'll be right along," her father answered.

"She wants to remind you and gramps about the living room rug that's still hanging on the line," Fay replied.

"Oh, that's right," Dave recalled.

"We'd better do it now," GW replied, "or we'll hear about it all through supper."

"You comin, Clay?" Dave asked as he and his father headed toward the river path.

"You fellas go ahead," he replied. "I'll be along directly."

As father and son walked the path, GW looked across the Juniata and then into the forest that separated the Stackhouse and Coleman properties.

"I guess it ain't too bad," he stated.

"What's that, Dad?" Dave questioned.

"I suppose this path Stacky laid out ain't as bad as I used to think," he replied.

"What do you mean?" Dave questioned, recalling to mind his father and Clare's feud about who designed the better section of the path connecting the two properties.

It started five years ago when the two agreed upon the need for a path connecting the two properties. Each man consented to construct and maintain his half of said path, but since both of them were proud, high-spirited men they were led to reprove and critique each others lackluster and unimaginative efforts during and after its construction.

"Well, I mean you do get quite a view of the Juniata from up here," GW admitted, "even though his section of the path is so damn straight."

"That's true," Dave agreed, noticing an expression of loss on his father's face.

But a smile of understanding crept across Dave's face as he realized how the badgering between the two old-timers was merely a cover for a friendship that went much deeper than words.

The shrill whistle of the approaching passenger train split the morning air as the Hahn and Coleman families stood together on the Thompsontown station platform.

Clare's body had been recovered a few miles below the rocks near Millerstown and the funeral at Thompsontown was held on a clear, warm, sunny day…a day that Clare himself would have relished.

"As soon as your dad finds a job, you have him bring you down here to spend the rest of the summer with me," Fay said to Katie as the seven-car passenger train screeched to a halt in front of them.

"I will," she replied as they hugged.

"I'm gonna miss you, Katie," Fay confessed as she wiped a tear.

"How about me?" Andy inquired.

Fay looked at him with smiling eyes.

"Now who could ever miss a red-headed clown like you?" she teased as she planted a kiss on his cheek.

The two families paused in silence as they watched the casket being loaded onto the baggage car. Clare was to be interred at his hometown of Granville next to his wife and daughter.

"We'd better get on board," Clay said to his children.

"Hold on!" a voice called out. "Don't leave yet!"

All heads turned to see Dick and Jimmy running up to the station platform.

"Look what we found down by the rocks," Dick said as he and Jimmy held it up for everyone to see.

"Now if that don't beat all," Bessie said in amazement.

Clare's hickory crutch was only slightly damaged.

"We found it floating on some boards near the shore," Jimmy noted.

They handed it to Katie.

"Thank you, boys," Katie said as she lovingly looked at the crutch and then at her friend.

"You keep this at Glen Afton, Fay," she said. "Pap lived here and this is where it should stay."

"Are you sure, Katie?" Fay asked.

"I'm sure," she insisted. "After all, I'll get to see it every time I visit."

"All right," Fay agreed. "I think pap would want it down here."

"It'll look mighty fine hangin on that bare wall in the living room," Bessie added.

Fay felt an emptiness inside as the train pulled away from the station and headed east toward Granville. It was a feeling friends have when parting, but knowing that someday they would be together again.

Neither of them realized, on the Thompsontown station platform, that it would be so final.

Chapter 20

RENEGADES AT GLEN AFTON

The renegade hoboes were becoming quite skilled at their loathsome livelihood. They had fine-tuned their nabbing techniques to near perfection and their random selection of locations left the local authorities in a state of confusion. However, their next to last job only netted them a trifling amount and their last stint almost ended in tragedy. It had to be aborted when a pair of German Shepherds gave chase just as Sal was about to bag their intended victim. He managed to clear the fence with only his pride and a large patch of his trousers missing as the trio hightailed it before they were noticed by the boy's parents.

"You see the size of those mutts," Sal said trying to catch his breath as the three headed toward the railroad mainline.

"All I saw was teeth when that first one had you by your rump," Jake replied with his guttural laugh.

"Good thing he didn't grab you any lower," Mick added, "or you could'a lost more'n your pants!"

"Wouldn't a been so damn funny if it was you gettin gnawed on," Sal shot back.

The three hopped a freight heading east out of Lewistown, the site of their last attempt at nabbing. It seemed the railroad police were becoming more aggressive in their dealings with hobos, sometimes to the point of cracking heads with bully clubs and throwing them from moving trains. With this in mind, Jake decided it would be best if they 'rode the rods'. This meant crawling under a box car, hoisting yourself up onto the lower supporting rods and laying face down directly behind the front wheels of the car.

Although this was somewhat uncomfortable, it provided a good place to hide and a great spot to see the legs of any railroad police in the vicinity. However, when traveling in this position, you had to keep your wits about you and your head tucked in most of the time. Any debris kicked up by the train's wind or wheels was likely to be hurled into your face. Many a hobo displayed scars or missing teeth to affirm this fact. Fortunately for this ride the wind and the weather were in the renegade's favor and even sporadic conversation was possible.

"Pickens were slim in that burg," Sal shouted above the roar of steel on steel as the engine labored and the train began to pick up speed.

"Yeah, but it's bound to be better back in Harrisburg and Philly," Jake noted. "I figure since we was workin our way west, the law will figure we'll be headin for Altoona or Johnstown next."

"At's right," Mick agreed. "By doublin back like this we'll fool 'em fer sure."

Only inches below, the wooden ties soon became a blur as the powerful freight topped sixty. Unaccustomed to such 'low travel' Mick nervously shifted around, opting for a more secure position. Jake noticed his companion's uneasiness.

"Don't be shiftin around like that," he warned. "I was ridin with Jackie Monroe and one-eyed Lukey Peters when Jackie took a mind to shift around just like you're doin. That's when he lost it and went under."

Jake paused and looked Mick in the eye.

"We walked back from the next water stop and found him…or what was left of him," he said dryly. "Crows and coons was already at him; could hardly tell it was a man we was lookin at."

Mick looked away, locking his position and closing his eyes. A half-hour later the freight began to slow as it neared the Durwood station near Millerstown. The young fireman swung off the M-1 engine and unto the water tower ladder while the engineer eased the steamer ahead. When the tower lined up with the M-1's tank inlet, the fireman lowered the spout and began to quench the mighty engine's thirst. Cautiously watching for railroad bulls, the trio got off to stretch for a while.

"Remember this place, boys?" Jake asked with a grin.

"Ain't too good a memories here," Sal replied, recalling the whipping they had received for jack rolling.

"Aw, them boys was only doin what they thought was right, Sal," Jake noted. "We was just too dumb and got ourselves caught, that's all."

"No sense headin back there where we ain't welcome," Mick said, "but I sure could eat a bite about now."

"There's a cottage I stopped at a few miles west of here," Sal recollected. "Maybe we could get a bite there."

"Most folks in these river cabins are about as bad off as we are," Jake noted.

"This one's different, Jake," Sal assured. "They keep it up real fancy and I always got a good handout there."

Jake rubbed his grizzled chin like he did when he was about to hatch a plot.

"You don't suppose they got a little cash and maybe some collectables lyin about in their fancy little cottage, do you?" he questioned.

"Could be," Sal replied, "but like I was sayin, they always treated us boys real good and…"

"Well," Jake cut in, "maybe them good folks of yours ain't never run into a breed of cats like us before, eh Mick."

The idea of a handout for which he might have to be grateful always stuck in Jake's craw. His aggressiveness and pride led him to take what he wanted rather than appreciate the goodness of others and be thankful for what they could give him.

The renegades covered the two miles and turned down the spring path toward the cottage. They slunk to the edge of the clearing by the lawn. The pristine beauty of Glen Afton impressed Mick as they cased the grounds.

It had been years since Mick last saw his Uncle Jed's summer place near Rhimer on the Allegheny River north of Kittanning. Glen Afton, which was much like Jed's place, brought back fond memories to Mick. He had spent many summers there with his favorite uncle and three cousins until Jed had to be institutionalized for 'loss of judgment in his doings'.

But no matter. They had more important things to tend to now than recalling old memories.

Their heads turned in unison when the outhouse door screeched opened. Olive Lee straightened her skirt by giving it a shake as she started toward the cottage. The renegades looked at each other with deviate smiles upon spying this natural beauty.

"Well, ain't this a made set-up," Jake said in a hushed voice, "and such a tasty young hostage to boot."

Mick and Sal agreed. They double checked the grounds to make sure no one else was in the vicinity and, as Olive Lee turned toward the cottage, they made their move. Quickly and quietly Mick and Sal bagged and carried the surprised and struggling girl up the spring path.

"Mighty frisky little wench, ain't you, darlin," Jake said as the three carried their victim further up the path.

Standing at the top of the dock stairs, as once before, Dick and Jimmy couldn't believe what they were seeing! They stood awe-struck for a moment and then ran toward the cottage where they burst in on Bessie and Fay in the kitchen.

"They took her!" Jimmy blurted.

"They've got Olive Lee!" Dick exclaimed.

"Who got her?" Bessie asked.

"Those three men," Jimmy said. "They put a sack over her head and are carrying her up the path!"

Dave, who was reading in the living room, came into the kitchen.

"What's all the fuss?" he questioned.

"The boys said three men grabbed Olive Lee and..."

Before Bessie could finish, Dave ran to the gun cabinet in the living room where they kept the shotgun and 32 caliber revolver. He opened the doors and found that they were both gone.

"Damn! he exclaimed. "Where the hell are the guns?"

"I think gramps has them," Dick replied. "He went hunting with Brownie and Freckles and..."

"That's just great," Dave said in frustration as he looked down at the remaining weapon...a home-made black-jack.

Jake's grin left his face.

"Sal, you jackass!" he shouted at the confused hobo.

"What?" Sal questioned.

"The note!" Jake replied.

Mick quickly penned the ransom note and Sal shot back down the path and stole across the yard toward the front porch.

"Dave," Bessie said in a hushed voice, "one of them is comin back; he's crossing the yard right now."

Dave raised up and thought for a moment, then he grabbed the black-jack and headed for the rear door.

"Follow me, boys and be quiet," he instructed.

They moved quietly off the back porch and around the right side of the cottage as Jake and Mick continued to move their struggling victim further up the spring trail.

"Let me go!" Olive Lee demanded.

"We will," Mick assured her.

"Just as soon as we get what we came for," Jake added.

"Hold on," Mick said as he pulled up short.

"What?" Jake questioned.

"Someone's comin down the path," he replied.

Jake turned to look and, through the trees and brush, he could see two men approaching from the upper end of the trail.

"Let's get her off the path," Jake instructed as they tried to move into the thicket.

"Ouch, damn it," Mick yelled as the thorn-covered vines entangled their legs.

"No good," Jake declared. "Let's get her back on the trail."

Hearing the commotion, Russ and Danny stopped talking and dropped their water buckets.

"What in the world...who is that?" Danny asked as they tried to discern what they were seeing. Upon recognizing his sister's skirt Russell's questioning expression turned to rage.

"Whoever they are, they've got Olive Lee," he said as they started down the path.

"What the hell do you think you're doing!" Russell shouted.

Jake and Mick feverishly looked for another escape route, but the brush on both sides of the path was too thick to penetrate.

"Keep your distance," Jake warned, "or I'll break her pretty little neck!"

The two continued to retreat down the path as Danny and Russ followed at a distance. Upon hearing Russ and Danny's voices Olive Lee became more aggressive in her struggle.

"Keep still you little..." Jake growled as he and Mick endeavored to subdue her.

Russ and Danny seized the opportunity to close the gap.

"I told you to keep your distance!" Jake shouted as they continued down the trail.

The renegades kept looking for an advantage when Jake's foot became entangled in the trip root and the three of them went down.

Realizing her chance, Olive Lee pulled off the sack and got to her feet before Jake and Mick could respond. Regaining her bearings, she started to run for all she was worth toward the cottage.

"Get her, Mick, she's our only way out of here!" Jake shouted as the two began chasing her.

Russ and Danny threw caution to the wind as they ran after the two hobos.

Sal was completing his task by quietly fixing the ransom note to the door, but as he turned to leave, he was met by Dave's black-jack. Semiconscious, he dropped to his knees as Dave brought the black jack down again.

"Wow," Jimmy exclaimed, "you sure nailed him."

"Just as hard as I could," Dave replied.

Their attention turned toward the spring path when they heard Olive Lee screaming. Dave quickly sized up the situation.

"Get some rope from the shed and tie this one up before he comes to, boys," he said as he started across the lawn.

Olive Lee broke into the yard, running as fast as her legs would carry her.

Dave grabbed his hysterical sister.

"You okay?" he asked.

"Yes, but they're right behind me!" she blurted.

Bessie and Cass came out of the cottage wielding a pair of butcher knives.

"Get in the house," Dave told them as the renegades broke onto the yard. He set his jaw and began a brisk walk toward the two intruders. Spotting him, the two veered around the spring house toward the garden as Russ and Danny joined Dave in the pursuit across the lawn.

Meanwhile, Dick and Jimmy finished hog-tying Sal.

"Let's see you get out of that," Jimmy exclaimed as he and Dick admired their work on the hapless hobo.

"Guard him, Jimmy," Dick said as he headed toward Bessie and his Mother.

He grabbed the knife from Bessie's hand and started toward the men.

"Dick, come back here!" his mother shouted. She turned toward Fay and Olive Lee with an anxious look on her usually calm face.

"You two get to Thompsontown and fetch the sheriff," she instructed.

Without a word, the girls quickly headed up the spring path .

With their retreat cut off, Mick rushed Dave and the two began the battle. Russ and Danny cut Jake off as he attempted to reach the river bank.

"You two don't want to mess with ole Jake, boys," he growled as he looked for a way out, but as he turned to try to reach the bank Russ tackled him, knocking him to the ground. Danny joined Russ and, at first the two had the upper hand, but the larger, more experienced brawler soon removed his two aggressors with a series of left-right punches.

As the three got to their feet, Danny's nature began to change. His light blue eyes flashed as he tasted blood in his mouth and for the first time, his usually calm demeanor vanished as he became enraged. Cursing, he slammed head long into Jake, bowling the fat hobo down on his back. He jumped on Jake's chest he began to pummel his grizzled face, but Jake managed to push the smaller man off and stood up only to have Russ jump on his back, grabbing him in a headlock.

"Want to grab my sister, huh,?" he yelled as he tightened his grip on Jake's neck.

Jake struggled and was able to strip Russ off as Danny attacked again wrapping his arms around Jake's legs. Russ slammed into Jake knocking him to the ground once again. The two had the upper hand until Jake spied Dick holding the butcher knife. Managing to break free, Jake grabbed the startled boy before he could react and wrestled the knife from him. Seeing Dick being assaulted, but not the knife, Danny attacked Jake with even more fury.

"You bastard, let him alone!" he yelled as he tried to subdue the big hobo.

The blade flashed and Danny's hot Irish blood flowed freely. He let out a scream and fell to the ground. The fighting halted as attentions focused on the fallen man. Bessie and Hat ran over to Danny.

"Where'd he get you?" Bessie asked.

"My arm," he cried.

Bessie ripped a swath of cloth from her dress and began to bandage the gash on his left arm. Sensing his chance, Jake grabbed Dick and held the bloody knife to his throat.

"Hold fast or I'll cut him good!" he growled.

Dave joined Russ as the two moved toward the renegades.

"I mean it," Jake shouted. "I've done worse in my time!"

"Now listen up," he continued, "we're gonna take this kid and a boat and don't none of you try to follow us or you'll never see him again!"

Jake and Mick started for the dock stairs while keeping an eye on Dave and Russ.

Dave's eyes widened at what he saw next.

"When are you going to let him go?" Dave asked, attempting to distract the renegades.

"Me and Mick will figure that out in our own good time," he replied.

"You harm that boy and we'll hunt you down, Jake," Dave warned as he and Russ cautiously moved toward them.

"Well, I think I'd kinda like that," the big hobo replied, "then I'd have the pleasure of doing you in."

"Why don't you let the boy go and give yourself up, Jake?" Dave implored, trying his best to maintain their attention. "You know you're going to be caught sooner or later."

"Hah," Jake laughed as he turned to Mick while backpedaling along the edge of the river bank.

"Listen to him babble now that we got him between a fryin pan and the fire," he continued, pointing the knife in Dave and Russell's direction.

The clang of Bessie's cast iron skillet on Jake's head echoed across the Juniata sending both Jake and Dick tumbling down the bank. Halfway down Dick grabbed onto a sapling as the semi-conscious hobo rolled and bounced to the river's edge.

"Nice going, Cass," Dave remarked.

Alone now, Mick turned toward Cass who raised her skillet again. He looked at her and then at the two approaching men and finally dropped his arms in surrender.

"Hit the ground, Mick," Dave commanded. "Bessie, get some rope from the shed."

Hat and Kit helped Danny back to the cottage while Cass joined Dave and Russell as they watched over the now docile Mick.

Jimmy ran to the edge of the bank to look for his fallen friend. Dick was busy pulling himself up the bank while keeping a wary eye on his aggressor.

Jake came to and began to assess the situation and then moved to the dock and began untying one of the boats. He winced at the crack of the rifle as a bullet ricocheted off a nearby rock.

"Hold it right there, mister!" Sheriff Jameson shouted.

"Is that one of them?" he asked Fay as his deputy rowed their boat toward the dock.

"Yes it is," she replied.

"What in the world is going on here?" GW inquired as he and the dogs came on the grounds.

"Nothing Cass and Aunt Bessie's skillet couldn't handle," Dave replied.

"Who are those characters and what are they doing here?" he asked.

"They tried to kidnap Olive Lee but Dick and Jim caught them in the act," Dave explained.

"I have a feeling these are the ones who have been doing the kidnappings we've heard so much about lately," Russell noted.

"And this proves it!" Jimmy announced as he handed the ransom note to GW.

"I would say it does," he agreed after reading it.

"Uncle Dan was the real hero," Dick added. "When the big one grabbed me Uncle Dan attacked him even though he had a knife."

"And he paid dearly for it," Bessie noted.

Dave explained to the Sheriff all that had taken place.

"These three fit the description of the kidnappers we've been looking for," the Sheriff agreed, "and I would say this ransom note puts a lock on it."

The deputies handcuffed the renegades and started walking them to the dock.

"Mind if we borrow one of your boats, Dave?" the Sheriff asked.

"Not at all," he replied. "You want some help getting these three across?"

"Thanks, Dave," he replied. "My deputies and I can handle them."

"The Judge will want you as witnesses at their trial," the Sheriff added.

"No problem," Dave replied as the three walked past him. "Just tell us when and where."

"This ain't over yet," the frustrated Jake snarled at Dave as he passed him.

"I'm afraid it is for you, boy," Sheriff Jameson assured as he shoved Jake toward the dock stairs.

Jake glared at Cass only to have her glare back and raise Bessie's skillet once more. Dave's eyes followed the big hobo as he descended the stairs. He couldn't help but think how much Jake was like Joe Grubb in attitude and aggressiveness. He had heard threats like that before and it never failed to make his blood run cold.

"Danny's going to need the Doctor," Cass noted.

"Yeah," Dave replied, as he watched the boats move upriver with their heinous cargo.

"You all right, sis?" he said, turning to Olive Lee.

"Still a little shook up, big brother," she replied while hugging him and her other protectors.

"Olive Lee, you sure have a way of attracting a bad class of suitors," Russ said as she hugged him.

She managed a faint smile.

"Dick, you and Jim go fetch Doc Peterson…again," Dave said, shaking his head in disbelief at what had just taken place.

"I think I can make it there, Dave," Danny said.

"Why don't you boys go with Dan just in case he takes a fainting spell,"

GW suggested.

"Sure thing," Dick replied as the three of them started off toward Thompsontown.

Dick gained a new respect for his uncle that day and he began to see that Danny wasn't much different than most folks. Sometimes we lack the needed courage for the moment…and sometimes, through experience, we find it.

Chapter 21

PRISON TIME

The three renegades were quiet during their ride to the Huntingdon State Prison. Their trial at the Juniata County courthouse was swift and the verdict clear: twenty years for kidnapping and robbery. One could see a trace of resentment on Jake's face, but strangely his expression began to change as they passed through the gates of the newly constructed section of the facility. Perhaps it was from the hopelessness of the situation in a state prison or maybe even a repentant, remorseful feeling in his heart for what he had done.

But no.

It was only Jake Rhode's cunning mind shifting from one slippery mode to another. He was imprisoned before and had learned the hard way that, in a setting such as this, one could catch more flies with honey than with vinegar. Jake would bide his time and play his cards right. He knew the time would come when the circumstances would turn in his favor and he planned to take full advantage of the opportunities when they came his way.

As the weeks rolled by Jake proved to be a model prisoner and he volunteered for any and all tasks that came along. He was good with his hands and his part-time vocation as a handyman in the past led him to be a valuable asset at the prison. Jake could be very convincing in his ways and he soon gained the trust and respect of his immediate overseers.

"Okay, Jake," Tim said, "grab a cart and let's move out."

It was one of those cold fall mornings when the gray overcast sky puts a fine mist in the air that penetrates both body and soul. Jake shivered as he and Tim Estep, a young guard who took a liking to Jake, made their way across the recreation yard toward the old section of the prison. The wheels of the office supply cart Jake was pushing click-clacked over the cracks of the grey slate walkway.

Although it was built over a hundred years ago, the ancient prison still remained an impressive structure. Fashioned mostly from large gray limestone blocks it rose three stories high with peaked guard towers at the four corners and one mid-way on each wall. It stood majestically in the early morning fog, looking much like a medieval castle.

The new prison facility had only been occupied for a year and it now housed and cared for most of the four hundred inmates. The original structure contained a few dozen old lifers and some mentally disturbed prisoners. An attempt to relocate them to the new facility proved to be traumatic and through the surprising kindness of the warden, they were permitted to remain in their familiar surroundings. These inmates were lodged on the second floor of the building. The kitchen on the first floor was still being used for these inmates but the balance of that floor, the third floor and the basement were used for storage.

"How many more trips is it going to take to finish this job?" Tim asked.

"I'd guess about a dozen should do it, Tim," Jake returned.

Jake had been here several times before and had helped move the old files to the archive room in the new building and remove furniture and such from the basement to the upper levels where it would be kept until it could be used or sold at auction. But this was his first trip with Tim to the old structure and Jake would be alert for any opportunity that might present itself while in the custody of this young innocent.

Tim keyed the old lock and pushed open the large rusted iron door. Jake entered and turned on the lights while Tim locked the door behind them.

"I hope you know where all this stuff is, Jake," Tim said as he eyed the stacks of files and cabinets that partially filled the old dining hall.

"Never fear, Tim," Jake replied. "We'll find it all."

Jake took the list from the young guard and scanned it.

"Now, the 1910 files are over there in that far corner," he noted. "Why don't you get those and I'll see if I can..."

"Halt!" a voice called out from the doorway of the second dining hall as a beam of light cut through the dust in their direction. "Who's in here?"

"It's just me and Tim gettin some more old files, Luke," Jake replied.

Luke Ferguson, the oldest guard at the prison, put down his light and walked over to them.

"Well, do try to be a bit more quiet about it, lads," he returned in his Scottish brogue. "How can a bloke get any shut-eye with all the racket you two are a makin?"

"How about helping us move these cabinets, Luke?" Jake asked jokingly.

"No thanks, Jake," he returned. "I just come in here for an occasional break from all those loonies upstairs."

"You mean the inmates or the supervisors?" Tim inquired. The old guard laughed.

"I suppose you could say tis a wee bit o' both, laddie."

"I can see that," Tim replied.

"By the way, lad, how's your father doin?" Luke asked. "I heard he had a bad spell right after he retired."

"He did have a mild stroke," Tim replied, "but it didn't slow him down much."

"Tell me, did he ever start farmin those acres he purchased over by Ardenheim?" Luke asked. "That was always a dream o' his."

"Yes he did and he's even thinking of transplanting those young apple trees you grafted for him."

"Oh Lord," Luke said with a serious look. "That's tricky business, that is."

He thought for a moment. "Why don't you and I go into the kitchen for a mug o' coffee and I'll draw you up a plan of how your dad should goin about that task."

"Well, I don't know..." Tim said, looking at Jake.

"Nonsense," Luke exclaimed. "Jake knows where everything is and the door is locked, right?"

"Yeah, but we have these files to load up and..."

"And I'll bet Jake will have them loaded and ready to go by the time we get done, right Jake?" Luke replied.

"You go on with Luke," Jake encouraged. "I can handle this little job."

The guards walked through the second dining hall and into the kitchen. As soon as the door was closed behind them Jake trotted over to a certain cabinet and pulled out an old battery lantern he had found earlier that week. In a flash he exchanged its dead battery with the one from Luke's light that he had left on the table.

"Good," he said to himself as his lantern threw a bright light across the room. He returned both lanterns and went about his assigned task and soon he had the cart loaded with the files he and Tim were to take back. Checking through the kitchen door, he could

see Luke and Tim were still in deep discussion about the transplanting of apple trees. This gave Jake his chance. Grabbing his lantern, he went to the far end of the room and moved the cabinets that were stacked in front of the basement door. He turned the large brass knob and opened the door. A strong smell of mildew met him as he fumbled for a light switch.

"Good!" he exclaimed almost too loud as the light bulbs flickered on, revealing a wide wooden stairway leading to the basement. Reaching the foot of the stairs Jake encountered a door on either side of the short hallway. Opening the one on his right he snapped on the light switch to no avail.

Damn, he thought to himself.

As his eyes adjusted to the dark he noticed a bare bulb in a ceiling socket. He gave it a twist and it came on, exposing a long, narrow corridor with a door at the far end.

Interesting, he mused as he peered down its length. Opening the door on his left he felt for a switch. This time the lights flooded the large windowless store room which was filled with old furniture. Jake began rummaging through the castoffs, searching for anything that would aid him in his quest for freedom and at the center of the room he spied what he thought might just do the trick.

"What are you doing down there, Jake?" Tim called out.

He could tell Tim was annoyed.

"Just exploring, Tim," he returned, "and I think I found something that might put a feather in both of our caps."

"What are you talking about?" Tim said as he descended the stairs and walked into the storage room.

"You know how the men are complaining about how those new wall mounted writing shelves in their cells that ain't worth a damn?" he asked.

"Yeah…so?"

"Well, look here," Jake continued. "These desks must be out of the old cells and see how solid they are," he said as he sat on one of them.

"If they'll hold your weight, they must be good," Tim agreed as he looked around.

"There's dozens of them down here," he noted. "I wonder why no one else thought of reusing them?"

"They more'n likely forgot they were even down here," Jake returned. "Now, if me and a couple of the boys was to set up a little shop, we could fix the lot of 'em in no time."

"Not a bad idea, Jake," he agreed as he eyed the big hobo. "But what would you be getting out of the deal?"

"Look, Tim," Jake said as he put his arm around the young guard's shoulder, "anytime I get a chance to get out of that stuffy little cell I now call home is payment enough."

"All right," Tim replied, "I'll see what I can do."

As they walked back across the old recreation yard, the wheels in Jake's mind began turning faster than the ones on the cart he was pushing.

"Hey, Tim," Jake began, "how come the other guards have to use one key to lock our cells and another to lock the outside doors in the new prison, but you only have to use one?"

Tim stopped, looked around, and then proudly held up his secret.

"That's because they don't have a master key," he answered.

"Well, I'll be," Jake said as he took a closer look. "I wonder how that works?"

"I'm not sure, but if the warden knew I had it I could be in big trouble," he confessed as the two examined the key even closer.

"Don't be gettin any ideas, Jake," Tim said sternly as he clipped the key back on his ring.

"Aw, come on, Tim," Jake teased, "I only want to borrow it for one night."

"Fat chance, big boy," Tim returned as the two continued toward the new prison.

Back in his cell, Jake hurriedly began sketching the shape and size of the key he had just seen.

"What're you drawin?" Sal asked as he peeked over Jake's shoulder.

"I just might be drawin our way out of here, Sallie boy," he replied.

Sure enough, a week later the warden gave his approval to let three inmates set up a shop in the old prison. A large work table, some screw drivers, a hammer, some varnish and a few brushes were delivered to the dining hall and it wasn't long before Jake, Sal and Mick were busily repairing and refinishing the old desks to like-new condition. After a few days of seeing how contented and industrious the three were at their task, Tim's visits to check on them became less and less frequent.

"You boys be all right by yourselves for a while?" Jake asked his companions after a visit from Tim.

"Why Jake, you thinkin of makin a break for it?" Mick asked with a grin.

"You never know, Mick," Jake replied. "Now you stay here and keep on workin just like you're doin and Sal, you come with me."

He led Sal over to the basement door.

"Now, you park yourself inside this door just out of sight," he instructed, "and if Tim or anyone comes in, you hightail it down these steps and get me."

"Okay, Jake," he replied.

"Mick, if someone comes in, you stall'em, and if they ask where we are, you tell'em we're fetchin up some more desks to fix."

"All right," Mick returned.

Jake retrieved his lantern from the file cabinet.

"Come on, Sal," he said as the two descended the stairs and went through the door to the long hallway. Jake snapped on the lights.

"Now, if someone comes, you sneak down the stairs and flash these lights on and off," he explained as he demonstrated. "I'll see 'em and hot foot it back here."

"Got it, Jake," Sal replied.

"I figure a little exploring might just produce some new openings in our lives," he added with a grin.

Both men chuckled.

Jake started down the long, dank corridor. At the far end was the door he had tried to open before with no luck, but with Mick and Sal on guard he could afford to apply a little more force and after a couple lunges of his weighty frame it finally swung open. The light from the corridor revealed yet another set of stairs descending into a sub-basement. These were made out of cut-stone and were steep and narrow and lay tight against the high, circular stone wall of the stairwell. Jake found a switch but it produced no light. He stared down the dark hole for a moment and was about to leave when he noticed an electric cord laced through the stair handrail. Tracing it back, he found the balance of it coiled up in the corner at the top of the stairs.

Puzzled as to where its power source was he started to investigate the area and after a while he looked up and noticed an outlet on the last light in the corridor. He plugged in the cord and five bulbs flooded the stairwell with light.

That's more like it, he thought to himself. Looking up, he noticed an inaccessible rusted hulk of a light fixture hanging from the center of the ceiling high above the stairs. Water dripped from its sagging end.

No wonder it don't work, he mused as he started down the worn stone stairs on his quest for freedom. The smell of stagnant water filled his nostrils as he descended the narrow circular steps. At the bottom was yet another door. It was a large, heavily rusted steel door with a small viewing window and a hand latch on the stair side. Like the others before, it finally gave in to Jake's lunges. This door opened to a much larger corridor bordered on both sides by old isolation cells, but the light switch proved unfruitful.

Jake unfastened the last light from the stair railing and extended it as far as it would reach into the newly found hallway. He slowly walked into the dark compound, playing his light on the rows of isolation cell doors on either side. A scant amount of light streamed into the area from a few small, dirty windows high up in the corridor.

His expression soon changed from interested curiosity to one of somber familiarity. This man was no stranger to solitary confinement or isolation cells and indeed, at a very early age, his rebellious nature led him into a series of incarcerations.

Born near Wolfsburg in Bedford County, his father was killed in a bar fight when Jacob Rhodes was fourteen years old and this rebellious, strong-willed, yet intelligent lad was more than his mother could handle. After several bouts with the law for B & E and robbery he was sent to live with an aunt and uncle in Bedford. His Uncle Bob worked as a handyman and he began taking young Jake with him on his jobs. Jake proved to be a quick study and learned much from his kind uncle, but his rebellious nature rendered the same results as when he was home with his mother. Jefferson reform school was his next stop and after several failed attempts at reform, Jake escaped.

At seventeen, he threw in with two of his old reform school buddies, Sal Ritchey and Mick Brunette who were living near Harrisburg. From here their careers as professional criminals began. At twenty-two, Jake was the unfortunate one of the three to be caught during a busted jewelry store robbery and his uncooperative and abrasive attitude in prison earned him three terrifying months in an isolation cell such as these he was now surveying. After release from isolation, Jake began to tame his rebellious ways and started using his natural cunning to get what he wanted. This method worked well for him at the other prisons and was showing much the same promise here at Huntingdon.

Jake swept the lantern's beam from side to side as he continued down the long corridor. The harsh light on the bare concrete walls and ceiling gave this place of past incarcerations a ghastly appearance. A dribble of foul smelling water seeping from a crack in the ceiling created a yellow-green mass of slime as it coursed down the wall and into a floor drain. A large black cockroach hung on the wall two feet above the floor near a vertical drain pipe.

"Damn ugly thing!" he muttered as he raised his foot and smashed it.

Jake jumped back as several more of the ugly creatures scurried from behind the pipe.

"God!" he exclaimed as he moved further down the hall. The smell of decay hung heavy in this dismal enclosure as his light fell on a cluster of small animal bones and fur that lay in a recess off to the right.

Strange, he thought to himself. *Something had to drag these animals in here to feast on and it sure wasn't those cockroaches.*

Jake straightened up with a start. The low growl he heard was coming from a cell on the left whose door was slightly ajar. He approached the door, but a scurrying sound made him stop. The old hobo's better judgment told him to retreat, to find some kind of weapon, but his curiosity finally got the best of him. He slowly moved up to the door and eased his head and lantern into the cell.

A loud hiss startled him as this unknown assailant grabbed his leg with sharp claws, gave out with a piercing screech and then bolted into the hallway!

"What the hell," Jake exclaimed as he turned his light toward what had attacked him.

The large tan feline crouched and growled as it watched him with green iridescent eyes. As Jake caught his breath, he began to hear other noises coming from the cell. This time his light exposed a nest of three kittens, one calico and the others the same light tan as their mother. Jake was surprisingly touched by their confused and frightened cries.

"Hey," he called, "ain't no one gonna hurt you little guys."

For a moment he recalled a drunken, enraged father ripping a stray kitten from his arms and yelling, "We don't need no mangy, flea-ridden cats stinkin up the place!"

Jake's thoughts were interrupted by the mother cat's continued growls.

"Relax, mum," Jake assured, "I ain't gonna hurt your brood."

He thought for a moment.

This explains the bones, he mused, *but how did she get them in here?*

He moved toward the mother cat as she gave out with a hiss and ran toward the blind end of the hallway. Jake followed her as she stopped and crouched at the right side of the corridor.

"Seems like you got yourself cornered, mum," he observed as he played his light on her, "and it looks like I've hit another dead end."

To his surprise, the feline hissed once more, bolted across the hall and appeared to jump through the concrete wall on the left. Amazed, Jake moved in for a closer look at what he had just witnessed.

"Well, I'll be!" he said as a smile crept across his face.

A closer inspection revealed the mother cat's little secret: a thirty inch square hole four feet above the floor.

"Well, mum, what do we have here?" he said to himself.

A small sliding wooden door partially blocked the opening, but with a few shoves Jake managed to push it up and out of his way. He peered into the opening as his light revealed a stone-lined shaft extending upward. He watched as the mother cat disappeared beside what appeared to be a small wooden structure twenty feet above him.

Jake thought for a moment, trying to comprehend what he was seeing. Two small guide rails extending up the shaft gave him his answer.

This is one of those dumbwaiters, he thought, *and this is how they got the food down from the kitchen to the prisoners.*

Again, he looked up the shaft, realizing the wooden structure above was the dumbwaiter car that was blocking his way into the old kitchen. By observing his surroundings at the prison Jake knew the old kitchen had access to a service road which wasn't secured, since all the high-risk inmates were lodged in the new facility.

Jake squeezed his ample body into the shaft and began to climb. The rough, uneven sides made it easy for the big man to gain a foothold. Water dripped down on him from above as he muscled his way up the shaft. Halfway up, a pair of black bats flew past him. Anxiety set in as Jake became a bit claustrophobic. He stopped for a moment to compose himself and then, with a sense of mission to gain his freedom, he continued his climb. He reached the small wooden car which appeared to be intact. Jake gave it a shove and it started to move, but then jammed.

Damn, he thought in frustration. Bracing himself in the shaft, he grabbed the lift by its corners and prepared to give it all he had…when he stopped dead.

"You hear something, Pete?" asked Luke.

"Yeah," Pete replied, "sounded like it came from the dumbwaiter."

Jake quickly positioned himself directly under the wooden car and froze. The two walked across the kitchen, opened the dumbwaiter door and peered in. Luke flashed his light around the sides of the car which was ten feet below.

"Don't appear to be anything there," he said as he closed the door.

"Maybe it's that big tan cat I see around here from time to time," Pete observed.

"Those darn things can get in almost anywhere."

Jake breathed a sigh of relief as he heard the men move to the far end of the kitchen and quietly, he began to make his way back down the shaft.

As he headed back and started up the circular stairs he noticed his warning lights flashing! Hurriedly he ran down the basement hall toward the storeroom. Upon hearing footsteps coming across the first floor the sly old fox darted across the hall and into the storeroom.

"Damn it, Sal, get down here," he shouted. "I can't carry all these desks up by myself."

"Forget the desks for now, Jake," Tim called. "It's time I get you guys back for supper."

"Be right there, Tim," Jake hollered as he retrieved a coiled-up coat hanger wire he had found earlier.

The next morning Jake, Sal and Mick continued their work on the desks.

As Tim was about to leave, Jake called to him.

"We're gonna need some more varnish to finish up these last desks."

"All right," Tim agreed. "I'll have supply send up another gallon."

"Thanks, Tim," Jake replied, "and Tim, how about letting the door open. These paint fumes are about to suffocate us in here."

Tim thought for a minute, then realized the door led into the recreation yard and the only exit was the door leading into the new prison which he always locked behind him.

"Okay, Jake," he said, "but don't try to make a run for it."

"Yeah, right," he returned with a laugh.

As Tim made his way across the recreation yard Sal took up his position at the stairway door. Mick continued his work on the desks while Jake headed for the basement to complete the tasks that could assure their bid for freedom. At the end of the hallway, he examined the latch on the hall door leading to the top of the circular stairway. After oiling it, he worked it back and forth until it swung free. He then set it in a vertical position and firmly shut the door. The latch fell into its locked position which would imprison anyone on the circular stairway side of the door.

"There," he said with a smile of satisfaction. "One down and two to go."

Next he went down the stone stairway and laid the last bulb in the light stringer on the floor at the bottom of the stairs. Finally, he freed the latch on the door to the isolation cell hallway and with the aid of the tools used to repair the desks, he removed its support bolts and refastened the latch lever on the cell side of the door. This would complete the entrapment of anyone inside the stone stairwell.

Yes sir, now that should do it, Jake thought.

"How's it goin, boys?" Jake inquired as he entered the workshop.

"Question is, how're you makin out?" Mick returned.

"It won't be long now," he said, slapping Sal on the back.

"Come on," he beckoned. The three moved to the recreation yard door.

"Sal, you stand in front of the door so no one can see what we're up to," Jake said as he quickly removed the heavy steel screws from the door's strike plate and replaced them with a couple of short brass furniture screws.

"There!" he exclaimed with an air of satisfaction. "One good tug on this handle tonight should rip those little screws out and send us on our way."

Later that night, Jake finalized his plan that would free him to get revenge on those he held responsible for his incarceration.

Yes sir, he thought, *I can't wait to see the look on their faces when they see old Jake back at their fine little cottage so soon.*

Inside their cell Jake took out the coiled coat hanger and carefully began to shape it to the image of the key on his paper. After several attempts and adjustments the wire key began to turn in the lock.

"Sal," he called out in a hushed voice, "get over here and give me a hand."

Sal carefully wrapped the end of a blanket around the latch while Jake wiggled and twisted the key.

Soon a muffled click was heard.

"That's the last of it, Sallie," he said quietly. "The guard will be makin his rounds in about a half-hour so let's get to bed and be ready."

The guard's light beam ambled across the three sleeping hoboes as he checked each cell in similar fashion. As he continued on his rounds, Jake, Mick, and Sal quietly slid from their bunks and after carefully arranging pillows, blankets and extra clothing to resemble sleeping inmates, they moved to the door. A muffled click assured them the first hurdle of their bid for freedom was cleared. The three moved through the darkened area of the cell block toward the recreation yard door and another muffled click gave them access to the recreation yard.

The guard tower searchlight washed across the yard twice a minute. As it passed, the trio scrambled onto the slopping bank between the walkway and the fence. This

181

gave them cover as they crawled to the far end of the yard toward the old building. As the light passed, Jake jumped up and grabbed the handle of the old prison door and after a few hard pulls the altered lock broke loose as he had planned. He closed the door and rolled down the bank just as the light swept across the area. The three bounded for the door and were inside in a flash.

"We're gonna make it!" Sal said triumphantly.

They quietly crossed the old dining hall and entered the upper stairs

"Mick, You stay here till we get the hall lights on," he instructed. "When you see them come on, turn these off and come a runnin."

The lights in the hall came on and Mick joined the two other men.

"This way to freedom, boys," Jake said as they headed down the long damp corridor.

Jake opened the upper door to the circular stone stairway that led to the isolation cells below. As Mick and Sal entered the stairway, Jake quietly set the latch lever and as he pulled the door shut he heard the latch fall into place, assuring him they were now locked in the stairwell.

"I've heard stories about this place," Mick related, "about how they chucked the bad ones down these stairs on their way to solitary."

Jake moved ahead of them and started down the stairs.

"Just watch your step or you'll have us all bouncin down here," he warned.

At the bottom of the stone stairway Jake deliberately stepped on the light bulb that he had laid on the floor. As planned, the crushed socket shorted out the circuit and blew the fuse.

"Damn!" he said in mock disgust as the stairs were engulfed in darkness.

"What happened?" Mick asked.

"Must have blown a fuse," Jake replied. "Wait here till I get my lantern."

He slipped through the isolation block door and quietly locked it from the inside.

"Jake, where you goin?" Mick asked.

No response.

Jake picked up his lantern and hustled down the hallway. He heard the muffled pleas from his two companions as he crawled into the dumbwaiter.

Much harder for the law to catch one than three, he mused as he started crawling up the shaft. *Besides, you two tellin the law where to find our stash to get your sentences reduced never set too well with old Jake...not too well at all!*

At the top, he braced himself and began to push the wooden car up the remaining portion of the shaft. It slowly moved up and out of his way. He carefully opened the dumbwaiter's door and cautiously peered out, looking around for any signs of life. Muted light from a crescent moon filtered through the windows and onto the kitchen floor. Jake smiled as he realized freedom was now within his grasp. He stole across the empty kitchen and out through the rear door. The faint moan of a distant train whistle turned his head as he started down the old service road in the misty fog.

Time to catch a train to Thompsontown, he thought to himself as he headed out into the night.

Chapter 22
JAKE RETURNS

The east bound freight began to move out of Huntingdon toward Thompsontown. Jake approached it like a cat sizing up its prey, taking note of the box car's under supports and frame. Its structure was a familiar one to the experienced hobo. He rolled between the slowly moving wheels, grabbed the front support rods and pulled himself up into the frame. The powerful M-1steamer picked up its cadence as the train's wheels began their familiar rhythmic click-clack, click-clack over the rail joints.

Jake relaxed.

Good to be on the move again, he thought to himself.

How many travelers passed over these rails throughout the years thinking of known destinations and familiar faces to which they would return? How many traveled with hopes and dreams to unfamiliar lands and the thought of new acquaintances they would encounter and the possibility of new adventures they would experience?

But how few traveled as Jake did, with only vengeance in his heart and a cruel vendetta against those he held responsible for his imprisonment. Jake couldn't see that he was the instigator of all that had transpired. He couldn't see that he was the initiator of the actions that led to his incarceration. He couldn't understand that they were only trying to protect themselves and their loved ones from the threat he and his cohorts had imposed.

No…in his narrow, subjective thinking he could only see that they were the cause of his dilemma, that they must pay the price in order for him to be vindicated. This was his mission, his goal…to extract revenge.

The hobo jungle outside of Millerstown was deserted. Fall was approaching and the other hobos were headed south to winter in warmer climates or west to Chicago's

Hobohemia with its city atmosphere and part-time work. Jake entered the abandoned jungle and began looking around for what he needed to get the job done. Using a broken fry pan handle, he dug into the soft earth beneath a cluster of mountain laurel.

Good, he thought as he struck the canvas bag he had hidden there a few years earlier. The clothes and shoes he had removed from that dead hobo were still intact. As he unrolled the trousers they revealed a rusted ten-inch butcher knife. A large gray squirrel chattered at him from above in one of the great white oaks.

"Well, old buddy," he said, "you're not the only one who knows how to squirrel things away."

After changing out of his prison togs, he looked around and found the flat, smooth stone used in the jungle to sharpen their cutting tools.

Wetting the stone with spit he began to sharpen his knife and soon its edge began to take on a razor sharpness.

That should do it, he thought, as he stood up and tucked the knife in his belt and started down the railroad lines toward the path that led to Glen Afton.

The late morning sun shone brightly on that warm fall day and the leaves on the open side of the trees bordering the rail lines were beginning to show the first signs of autumn's brilliant colors. Splashes of scarlet, orange and yellow appeared along the right-of-way and the pungent smell of moist earth hung strong in the air as a large flock of birds circled overhead in preparation for their southern journey.

All of this went unnoticed by Jake as his mind focused on the matter at hand: his desire to settle a score. A twinge of exhilaration filled him as he lumbered down the path and prepared himself for the confrontation.

He cautiously entered the clearing above the cottage and a quick glance around assured him that no one was on the property. A light breeze in the trees above and the gurgle of spring water in the trough were the only sounds to be heard.

So far, so good, he thought to himself.

The splashing water drew Jake's attention to the springhouse and he quickly moved toward it with hopes that any food stored there would satisfy his noonday appetite. The cool air inside the small enclosure bathed him in welcome relief. Rough cut stones covered the floor and formed a shallow pool in the center where food was stored in glass jars and crocks. He pulled a bottle of milk from the water and drank deep and long. Wiping his chin he dashed the empty container against the wall. A cloth-wrapped block of cheese was torn open and partially devoured. The hind-quarters of a recently butchered deer hung against the rear wall. Jake examined it briefly, and then returned to the yard.

I wonder where they are? he thought to himself as he scanned the property.

He cautiously approached the cottage, listening and watching for any signs of life as he moved up onto the rear porch and entered through the kitchen door. He stopped and listened, but nothing gave hint that anyone was home.

Well, ain't this just fine, he thought as he relaxed and began his search, rummaging through drawers and cupboards, looking for anything worth taking. A peek into the warming closet above the stove revealed a freshly baked pan of apple dumplings. Greedily, he wolfed down several of the delicious morsels and tossed the half-empty pan onto the table. Belching loudly, he moved into the dining room where the small gun cabinet beside the buffet caught his eye. The glass door revealed GW's old twelve-gauge double-barreled shotgun. Jake looked at it with dissatisfaction as he pulled open one of the lower drawers.

"Well, now, that's more to my liking" he said to himself..

He pulled it out and examined the nickel plated thirty-two caliber revolver. The ammunition drawer produced a half-full box of cartridges. Jake loaded the weapon and soon a feeling of invincibility swept over the old renegade as he aimed and mock-fired at several targets around the room.

Sounds coming from the front yard brought him up short. As he moved into the living room and looked out the window, a broad grin spread across his face.

"Well, look what we got here," he grunted as he observed the two on the front lawn. He slipped out the back through the kitchen door and headed toward them.

"I hope Katie's dad finds work soon so he can bring her back before school starts," Fay said to her aunt as they sat together on the lawn swing.

"I sure do miss her and pap-pap," she said with a sad look on her face.

Olive Lee looked at her young niece with feelings of compassion.

"Jobs are scarce, Fay," she said, " but Clayton Hahn has a lot of skills and he's a good worker."

"I know," Fay returned, "and if anyone could land a job these days it would be him."

"It was nice of Katie to give you Clare's crutch that the boys found," Olive Lee continued.

"Katie was right," Fay said. "That crutch belongs down here at Glen Afton."

The two spotted Jake coming around the side of the cottage. They stopped what they were doing and took a wary stance. Knowing they were aware of his presence, Jake moved toward them exposing the pistol. With their ears perked up they sniffed the air, searching for a familiar scent, then broke their stance and trotted toward the intruder as Jake leveled the pistol at them.

The two dogs stopped as Brownie began his low growl that ended in a questioning ruff. He and Freckles had seldom encountered unfriendly humans at Glen Afton. Jake cocked the hammer of the revolver and aimed at the larger Brownie.

Nothing hurts folks more as when a family dog gets killed, he thought to himself.

"We should be getting back over there," Olive Lee stated. "The women will be coming back from the station soon and will want a hand preparing supper."

She saw a tear in her niece's eye.

"I'm sure this place holds a lot of memories for you, Fay," she added.

"Yes…yes it does," she replied, wiping her eyes as she looked around the vacant Stackhouse property.

"I never thought I'd see the day that…that…"

Olive Lee took her in her arms.

Brownie cocked his head, wondering what the stranger's actions meant as Jake hesitated for a moment and then lowered the gun.

"Nah!" he growled. "I'm after bigger game than you two old mutts."

He turned and walked up on the front porch with Brownie and Freckles following him.

"Gawan, git out of here before I change my mind!" he yelled as the two started to bark.

"What are those dogs fussing about?" Olive Lee questioned as they looked toward the river path.

"Probably a squirrel or a groundhog in granddad's garden," Fay replied.

"I don't know," Olive Lee said with wary look in her eye. "I could've sworn I heard voices over there."

"Maybe Dad and Granddad are back from the store," Fay offered.

"I don't think so," Olive Lee returned. "They took the big boat with them and I didn't see it pass by yet."

The girls gave each other a concerned look as they got up from the swing and started toward the river path.

Jake reentered the cottage and continued his rummaging. The sight of Aunt Bessie's large cast iron skillet conjured painful memories for him. Angrily, he grabbed it and smashed it repeatedly against the edge of the stove until it finally cracked apart.

"There, woman," he snarled. "let's see you smack someone's head with it now!"

Outside the girls were greeted by the dogs as they came across the yard.

"What was that?" Fay asked as they listened to the noises coming from inside the cottage.

"I don't know, but we'd better be careful," Olive Lee cautioned.

Fay quietly slipped up onto the kitchen porch and peeked in. Her eyes widened at what she saw as she ran off the porch and back to her aunt.

"It's him!" she said with a fearful look. "It's him!"

"Who?" Olive Lee asked .

"It's him! That big hobo who tried to grab you!"

"What?" Olive said as they watched the cottage while moving toward the river. "He's supposed to be in prison!"

"He must have escaped," Fay said," and now he's come back to get us!"

"Oh, God!" Olive Lee gasped as they hid behind one of the oaks on the river bank.

"What'll we do?" Fay asked her frantic aunt.

Meanwhile Jake moved into the first floor bedroom. The scent of sweet jasmine powder hung lightly in the air as he looked at the frilly bedspreads and the jewelry boxes on the mirrored dresser.

"Must be the lady's quarters I'm in," he said with a chuckle as he sat down at the dresser and began looking through the jewelry.

"Any goodies for old Jake, ladies?" he mused as he slipped two silver and turquoise bracelets and a gold ring in his pocket. Upon finding a pearl necklace, he held it up to his neck while looking into the mirror.

"Now ain't you the pretty one, Jacob Rhodes," he remarked as he popped the necklace, sending a shower of pearls across the floor. He opened one of the drawers and pulled out a bra and a pair of lace panties.

I wonder if that lass we tried to grab fits into these? he thought as he held them up for a closer inspection.

The girls summoned up their courage and once again moved toward the cottage.

"I think he's in our bedroom now," Fay whispered.

"What are we going to do?" her Aunt said impatiently.

"We've got to stop him," Fay said sternly.

The sound of breaking glass came from the women's room.

"He's gonna destroy everything," Olive Lee said in frustration.

Soon Jake turned his attention to the upper bedroom. He searched the dressers and closet for anything useful and it was then he noticed the pair of tomahawks hanging on the wall above one of the beds. Taking the larger one down, he felt its heft.

Not bad, he noted as he examined the handle which was covered with Indian-like markings. Jake grabbed the other one and began dancing around the room, whooping in mock Indian-style as he held the tomahawks over his head. Upon seeing his reflection in the dresser mirror across the room he stopped, took aim and flung the smaller one at it. The tomahawk hit it dead center, sending chards of broken glass over the beds and floor.

"Gotcha, white man," he whooped.

Looking around, he smiled his twisted smile, satisfied with the destruction he had incurred. Tucking the remaining tomahawk in his belt he began to sort through the men's clothing for anything he could use.

"Maybe if we got some knives from the kitchen, we could surprise him and ..."

"No, Fay!" Olive Lee broke in. "He's much too big and he's probably found Dave's pistol by now."

"Listen," Fay said in a hushed voice, "he's coming down the stairs."

Now, where's that stash of cash you folks is hidin from old Jake? he pondered as he reentered the kitchen. Being familiar as to where people hid their money, Jake started emptying out all of the containers. Sugar, coffee, and flour were spilled out onto the floor. A small brown paper bag secured with a rubber band fell out of the oatmeal box.

"Bingo!" he shouted as he unwrapped the small amount of cash it contained.

"Looks like my luck is changin for the good while yours is changin for the bad, folks," he quipped.

Upon reentering the living room, he noticed a small wooden humidor sitting on the buffet. He opened it and removed the four remaining cigars. Stuffing three in his shirt pocket and the remaining one in his mouth, he began searching for a box of matches. After lighting the cigar and puffing it to life, he looked at the burning wooden match stick and again, revealed his twisted smile.

"We just can't stand by while he destroys everything," Fay lamented.

"You're right," Olive Lee agreed. "Let's take the boat to Shaffer's store and get the sheriff."

"Yeah," Fay agreed. "The sheriff can come down the railroad and send his deputies across the river because that's the only two ways out of here."

The two hurried toward the dock and as they started down the switch-back stairs they heard the rear door of the cottage slam shut.

"Oh no!" Olive Lee said in a trembling whisper," he must have seen us."

Fay slipped up to the top of the stairs and carefully peered over the edge of the bank.

"No, he didn't see us," she replied as she started across the lawn. "He's heading for the spring path."

"Fay, no," Olive Lee said. "He might come back!"

Hesitantly, she left the dock and followed her niece. Fay started toward the spring path as Olive Lee came around the side of the cottage.

"He's gone," Fay assured her aunt with a sigh of relief.

They turned to go back to the dock, but what they saw inside the cottage stopped them in their tracks! Quickly they ran up on the front porch and into the living room.

The fire had begun to consume the table and was starting up the drapes.

"Water!" Fay yelled as she ran out the door and into the shed. She frantically filled the two buckets from the trough and ran back into the cottage while Olive Lee tried to beat the fire out with the stove shovel.

"Here," Fay shouted as she sat one of the buckets down and doused the table with the other. Olive Lee dropped the shovel, grabbed the bucket and soaked one of the flaming drapes. The two ran out and refilled the buckets, but upon returning they were amazed to see how quickly the fire had spread. Part of the other burning drape had dropped onto the overstuffed sofa, causing it to catch fire. The rest of the drape had caught the wallpaper on fire, sending it up across the ceiling as smoke began filling the cottage.

"If only we had a hose," Fay said in frustration as she poured water on the sofa.

Olive Lee splashed out another flaming drape, not noticing its flaming twin had dropped behind her. It touched the edge of her dress, catching it on fire.

"Olive!" Fay shouted. "Your dress!"

Olive Lee turned as the flames started up her back.

"Put it out, put it out!" she screamed.

Fay tried to beat it out with her hands to no avail.

"Outside," Fay ordered as they ran for the trough.

Fay began splashing water on her aunt, but the flames continued to increase. Olive Lee let out a scream as the flames reached her hair and in a last ditch effort, Fay grabbed her and shoved her headlong into the trough.

"You okay?" Fay asked as her aunt emerged from the water.

"Yes…yes, I think so," she sputtered.

"Good, let's go!" Fay said.

They refilled the buckets and as they continued to fight the fire, they heard a shot ring out from up on the spring path.

"What's he shooting at?" Fay questioned.

"More like who's he shooting at," Olive Lee corrected, with a worried look.

Dick and Jimmy were returning from the oak swing and had started down the spring path.

"That last swing almost smashed you into that tree just like Buddy," Jimmy laughed.

"Almost doesn't count, Jim," Dick returned, "besides, I had it measured just right so I would miss it ."

"Yeah, right, big boy, just about right into your face."

Jimmy laughed as he looked at his buddy, who now, had stopped dead in his tracks. He saw a look of dread on Dick's face.

"What?" he questioned.

Jimmy looked down the path and saw what had paralyzed his friend.

"O my God, it's him!" Jimmy exclaimed.

Upon seeing the boys, Jake quickened his pace. The boys turned and began running back up the path as Jake stopped, took aim and fired two rounds at the boys, barely missing them. As Jake attempted to close the gap, the old trip root did its work once more as it snagged the hobo's foot, putting him on his face!

"Damn!" he shouted as he got up and began looking for the pistol. After finding it, he continued his pursuit.

As the boys emerged from the path, a slow moving freight that had just left the water tower blocked their path.

"What're we gonna do?" Jimmy yelled. "He's right behind us!"

Dick noticed the caboose coming into view.

"This way!" he shouted.

The two ran beside the train and ducked behind the caboose.

"We'll use the train for a shield." Dick said.

They crossed the tracks and ran beside the slow moving freight as Jake emerged from the path and began looking up and down the tracks. Seeing nothing he dropped on all fours and scanned under the freight. He smiled as he spotted the two on the far side of the tracks. Patiently he waited for the train to pass. Stepping from behind the caboose he positioned himself on the ties of the next set of rails. He took careful aim and fired, sending a round through Jimmy's pant leg. The boys dropped to the ground as the second round whistled over their heads.

"He's really trying to kill us!" Jimmy wailed as they tried to maneuver out of the renegade's sight.

Jake grunted in dissatisfaction and again he braced himself on the ties and took more careful aim.

Upon seeing Jake, the engineer sounded his whistle and slammed on the brakes while pulling back on the throttle. The express began to slow, but not soon enough.

The impact sent Jake hurtling down the tracks in front of the huge K-4 engine as it continued to slow. Still conscious, Jake landed facing the huge engine. Desperately he tried to scramble off the tracks … but it was too late. The second impact carried Jake under the engine where the great steel wheels and undercarriage ravaged his lifeless body.

Horrified at what they were witnessing, the boys moved in for a closer look as the express train slowed to a stop. It was then Dick noticed a familiar object next to the tracks.

"That's Dad's pistol," he remarked as he picked it up. "He was stealing stuff from the cottage."

"I wonder if anybody was there when he came in?" Jimmy questioned.

Dick looked at Jake's mangled body and then at Jimmy.

"We'd better get down there and find out," Dick replied with an air of urgency in his voice.

They were almost to the lawn when Jimmy stopped in mid-stride.

"Look!" he shouted as he pointed toward the cottage.

"Oh no!" Dick gasped as they ran down the remainder of the path as fast as their legs would carry them. They stopped at the edge of the lawn, horrified at what they were seeing. Smoke was now billowing out of the upstairs windows and the crackling sounds of burning wood became more distinct as they shot across the yard toward the flaming structure.

"Go down to the dock and get the minnow buckets out of the boat," Dick shouted.

Wasting no time, Jimmy sprinted toward the dock as Dick grabbed the bucket from Olive Lee and began helping Fay Soon all four were attempting to quench the blazing cottage.

Dave and Russell finished loading the lumber into the Hoffman as GW talked with Jesse.

"Okay, George," Jesse noted, "that's ten two by fours, three two by six's, two boxes each of number 8 and number 16 common nails, one 75 foot hose and a nozzle."

"That should do it," GW agreed, "and that hose will sure come in handy for watering my garden."

"I'll square with you next week when I get my check, Jesse," GW noted, "and by the way, did you get any more of those cigars I like?"

"Why yes I did," he replied. "I got a case of them in just yesterday."

"I'll take about a dozen along if you don't mind?"

"I'll go fetch em," Jesse said as he headed back into the store.

"Did you light a fire in the trash barrel before we left?" Dave inquired.

"No," his father returned. "Why?"

"Did you, Russ?" he asked.

"No," he replied as they looked up-river and watched the trail of black smoke rising skyward from the direction of Glen Afton.

"Something tells me we'd better hightail it back," Dave added with a note of urgency.

Jesse returned to the dock and was somewhat puzzled as to why the they were untying the Hoffman boat from their rowboat.

"Secure the Hoffman for us, Jesse," GW instructed, handing him the rope. "I think we might have a problem."

"Oh, no," he replied, noticing the smoke. "I'll sound the fire whistle."

"Thanks, Jesse," Dave said as the three pushed off from the dock.

"Dave, wait!" John shouted, "take your hose."

"Good thinking," GW said as he grabbed it out of the Hoffman.

Russell began rowing as hard as he could.

"Let me take her, Russ," Dave said.

His strong arms and back had them gliding swiftly across the Juniata and soon the grounds of Glen Afton came into view.

"Better hurry, Dave," his father urged as he and Russell watched as the smoke and flames from the windows washed up over the sides of their cottage.

"My Lord," Dave exclaimed as he turned to look.

The three hurriedly climbed onto the dock.

"You two get up there," GW said. "I'll tie the boat."

"Get the hose, Russ," Dave instructed as he charged up the dock stairs, bounding three at a time.

The sounds of the crackling fire were intermixed with shouts of the younger four who were desperately attempting to save their homestead. The intense heat struck Dave and Russ as they neared the burning structure.

"Here, Fay," Dave said as he took the bucket from her hand.

She looked up at him through a wide-eyed, tear-stained face.

Russ dashed to the water trough and attached the hose to the faucet. After uncoiling it he rushed back to the cottage and began playing a stream of water on the raging inferno.

The six continued to work feverishly as GW approached the scene.

He stopped and looked. His face became hardened by what he saw and the reflection of the flames in his eyes told the story.

It's fruitless, he thought to himself.

"It's fruitless!" he shouted. "Get back, it's going to collapse."

Returning from shopping in Thompsontown and seeing Danny and Kit off to Altoona, Cass, Hat and Bessie entered the clearing from the spring trail. They froze in their tracks, unable to believe what they were seeing. They dropped their groceries and ran to where the others were standing.

They all watched as the fully engulfed dwelling started to creak and groan.

"Stand back," GW warned.

Its structural timbers began to weaken and finally, the cottage buckled and collapsed upon itself. The fiery roar produced by its fall seemed like a shout of victory for Jake's attempt at revenge. Buckets dropped from helpless hands as Russell turned the nozzle of the new hose to its off position.

Cass gently took the hand of her sobbing daughter. Fay looked at her mother and turned, taking hold of her father's strong, calloused hand. GW and Dave looked briefly toward the Stackhouse property and then at each other. As the fire began to lose its rage, all moved in closer to the waist-high remains of their beloved sanctuary. Nothing was said…but the quiet shedding of tears spoke volumes as they endured this time of loss together.

Chapter 23
BREAKING CAMP

(1954)

As the flames turned to glowing embers dad stirred our campfire, sending a shower of orange and yellow sparks into the night sky.

"And that's how it ended," he remarked.

"What did you do after that?" I questioned.

"The women spent the next few nights with friends in Thompsontown," dad continued. "The rest of us stayed here and slept on the lawn and in the shed."

"We cleaned up the place somewhat and turned off the water up at the pond," Dick added. "and we gathered up everything that wasn't burned in the fire."

"Did you ever think of rebuilding?" I asked.

"Oh, sure," dad replied. "Everyone had high hopes of doing just that and after hearing of our loss the railroad sent your grandfather a letter granting us permission to rebuild on the site with a guaranteed lease agreement."

"Then why didn't you do it?" I pressed.

"Fred, there was much talk in the family for years about how we would rebuild, about making it bigger than the original, but times were changing," dad explained.

He stirred the dying embers as darkness surrounded our camp. Mourning doves gave out with their sad refrain in the trees above as the bullfrogs croaked their guttural chant at the river's edge.

"The country was beginning to dig its way out of the depression and a new feeling of prosperity began to sweep the land," he continued. "Men were returning to work and the threat of another war kept everyone's minds occupied."

"The families that had been at Glen Afton began to reestablish their homes back in Altoona," Dick added.

"That still doesn't explain why you didn't rebuild," I kept pressing. "This is such a beautiful location."

"The talk of rebuilding went on for years, but the remoteness of this place and the cost of rebuilding always seemed to be out of reach," dad continued with sadness in his voice.

"It served us well, little brother," Dick added. "It was a great place, almost…like a sanctuary. Those here shared whatever they had with all the rest."

"We did what we had to do to survive as a family," Dad remarked as he scanned moistened eyes around the now darkened grounds. "There was such beauty in the sharing…such beauty."

He straightened up, took the last sip of coffee from his cup and set his jaw.

"Yeah, Jake might have succeeded in taking away our cottage by the river, but nothing or no one can take away the love and the memories," he said as he looked at Dick and me.

Setting his cup down, he stood and stretched as the three of us looked up at the star-filled sky.

"I believe we're going to have good weather for packin out of here tomorrow." dad remarked.

We settled into our cots and slept well that night.

The morning sky was bright and clear, much as Dad had predicted.

As Dick and I packed our canvas boat for the last trip across the Juniata, I paused for a final look around. I had begun this trip with high hopes of adventure and fellowship and in that I wasn't disappointed. But I gained so much more in hearing the wondrous and at times frightening tales that the others had actually experienced. No, I hadn't lived the Glen Afton experience…but in a way I had.

I could almost see my brother Dick and Jimmy climbing the switch-back stairs with that ill-fated bucket of toads. I could almost hear Aunt Bessie bellowing through her bullhorn to call the men who were fishing down by the rocks to dinner. And I could all but taste those bitter, burnt pieces of 'coconut' in Russell's special fudge.

As we unloaded the last of our camping gear, dad looked across the river for a moment and then at our old canvas boat. With a shove of his foot, he pushed it back into the river.

"Dad, the boat," I exclaimed.

"It served us well over the years, son" he stated. "Now it's time for a new one."

We boarded our car and started across the deep rutted lanes of Beecham's farm. I noticed Dick looking in the rearview mirror as we continued across the fields. I glanced back and saw what he was observing…a thin cloud of tan dust rising from the road.

In my later years, I've now come to realize a deeper sense of the bond that existed between Dick and Jimmy…Fay and Katie…Granddad and Clare Stackhouse, of Dick and Hayla as first-time lovers and the gentle sharing of an gnarled, old cripple who loved and taught the young around him. But like Glen Afton, those relationships happened and then passed into history. Each was there, giving a portion of their hearts and lives to one another and then moving on… moving on…like the waters of the Juniata as they flow past those precious grounds of Glen Afton.

CREDITS

1. Lord of the Dance
Words: Sydney Carter, 1963
Music: 19th Century Shaker tune; adapted by Sydney Carter, 1963
Harm. by Gary Alan Smith, 1988
Copyright: 1963, 1989 Galliard, Ltd.

Made in the USA
Charleston, SC
23 November 2013